D0482130

DEAD MAN'S MISTRESS

ALSO BY DAVID HOUSEWRIGHT

Featuring Holland Taylor

Penance

Practice to Deceive

Dearly Departed

Darkness, Sing Me a Song

First, Kill the Lawyers

Featuring Rushmore McKenzie

A Hard Ticket Home

Tin City

Pretty Girl Gone

Dead Boyfriends

Madman on a Drum

Jelly's Gold

The Taking of Libbie, SD

Highway 61

Curse of the Jade Lily

The Last Kind Word

The Devil May Care

Unidentified Woman #15

Stealing the Countess

What the Dead Leave Behind

Like to Die

Other Novels

The Devil and the Diva

(with Renée Valois)

Finders Keepers

DEAD MAN'S MISTRESS

David Housewright

MINOTAUR BOOKS

NEW YORK

DEAD MAN'S MISTRESS. Copyright © 2019 by David Housewright. All rights reserved. Printed in the United States of America. For information, address St. Martin's Press, 175 Fifth Avenue, New York, N.Y. 10010.

www.minotaurbooks.com

Library of Congress Cataloging-in-Publication Data

Names: Housewright, David, 1955– author.
Title: Dead man's mistress : a McKenzie novel / David Housewright.
Description: First Edition. | New York : Minotaur Books, 2019.
Identifiers: LCCN 2019002281| ISBN 9781250212153 (hardcover) |
    ISBN 9781250212160 (ebook)
Subjects: | GSAFD: Mystery fiction.
Classification: LCC PS3558.O8668 D4 2019 | DDC 813/.54—dc23
LC record available at https://lccn.loc.gov/2019002281

Our books may be purchased in bulk for promotional, educational, or business use. Please contact your local bookseller or the Macmillan Corporate and Premium Sales Department at 1-800-221-7945, extension 5442, or by email at MacmillanSpecialMarkets@macmillan.com.

First Edition: May 2019

10 9 8 7 6 5 4 3 2 1

FOR RENÉE

ACKNOWLEDGMENTS

Specials thanks from the author to Tammi Fredrickson, Keith Kahla, Alice Pfeifer, Alison J. Picard, Sabrina Soares Roberts, Deputy Will Sandstrom of the Cook County MN Sheriff's Department, and Renée Valois for all their help in writing this book.

DEAD MAN'S MISTRESS

ONE

She was arguably the most recognizable woman living in Minnesota. Even children attending the more progressive kindergarten classes knew her face, as well as other parts of her anatomy. Yet few people knew her actual name and even fewer realized that she had been living in Grand Marais for the past thirty-five years, including some of her neighbors. I didn't know these things myself until a friend sent me up there.

I knocked on her door. And waited. And knocked again. The door was pulled open and there she stood, dressed in jeans and a sweater, both faded with time, and bare feet on the hardwood floor despite the chill in the September air. Seeing her face up close and in person jolted me to the point where I couldn't speak aloud although my inner voice was screaming, *It's her, it's her, it's her.*

"Are you McKenzie?" she asked.

"Hmm?"

"McKenzie."

"Yes. Yes, I am."

"Please come in."

Her home was a small converted church that had been built on a hill overlooking the city's downtown and Lake Superior beyond. There was an oh-so-artistically carved sign in her front yard that read WYKOFF ART ACADEMY. I soon discovered that she had reserved the ground floor for the art classes she taught and for her own paintings that she sold in a gallery on the main drag. Most of them seemed to have Native American themes. Ojibwa, I guessed, since that was the tribe that lived in the area before the white settlers took over.

She beckoned me to a chair even as she perched on a stool across from it. I found myself looking up at her. There were worse sights.

She stared at me as if she were trying to peek inside my head before she spoke. "It was kind of you to come."

"My pleasure."

"Perrin Stewart says nice things about you." ·

"She says nice things about you as well."

"Can I get you anything?"

"No, thank you. I'm fine."

"I'm going to pour some coffee. Are you sure I can't offer you anything?"

"No, no."

She slipped off her stool and moved to a corner where a coffeemaker was set on a counter next to a small refrigerator. I seized the opportunity to look around. There were several workbenches and a dozen easels scattered throughout the large room. Most of the easels held canvases, some of them unfinished and some that looked finished to me, but what did I know? Other canvases were resting against the wall between two large windows. I wondered if any of them were hers. There was a white van parked outside that I could see through the windows. I wondered if that was hers, too. Unmarked vans made me nervous.

She returned to the stool and sipped her coffee from a mug adorned with wildflowers. Once again I found myself looking up at her. In the back of my mind I could hear the words my old man often repeated to me while growing up after Mom died of cancer—life is not fair. It's true of course. Some people get more. More beauty than you see in anyone else in the world. More time with their mothers.

"What do you know about me?" she asked.

"Only what everybody else knows."

"What does everyone else know?"

"You're That Wykoff Woman."

"Yes, my name forever an adjective. Call me Louise. What else?"

"Your face launched a thousand canvases."

"One hundred and thirty-three. Don't exaggerate."

"I was told you're in trouble."

"Trouble. Yes. Yes, I'm in trouble and hearing that was apparently enough for you to drive nearly five hours from the Twin Cities to see a woman you've never met?"

"Closer to four hours, actually. I have a fast car."

"I'm wondering if I can trust you."

"I've already broken several traffic laws on your behalf, so . . . You trust Perrin Stewart at the City of Lakes Art Museum enough to tell her you need help. She trusts me. That's why I was sent. If you have a better option, I'll wish you luck, grab a couple of banana cream bismarks at World's Best Donuts, and be on my way. Later, I'll tell all of my friends that the Wykoff woman told me to call her Louise."

"Is that still a big deal after all these years?"

"The paintings don't age."

"No, I don't suppose they do. What exactly did you do for Perrin that she trusts you so much?"

Stewart must have already told her, my inner voice said. *If she hadn't . . .*

"Something went missing from her museum," I said aloud. "I found the something and brought it back."

"What?"

"You know, it was so long ago, I don't remember."

Louise leaned forward on the stool, her legs pressed firmly

together, both hands clasping the coffee mug and resting it on her lap. Her toes curled over the bottom rung like she was trying to hold on.

"Something I own has gone missing, too," she said. "I would like it returned—without anyone knowing about it."

"I can only promise to do my best."

"You haven't asked what was stolen."

"You'll tell me when you're ready."

"I need to tell you a story first."

"If it's about *Scenes from an Inland Sea,* I already know."

"No, you don't. Nobody knows. Not even Mary Ann McInnis. But I'll start with what you do know, McKenzie. With what everyone knows. I'll start with Randolph McInnis freezing to death in a ditch . . ."

Randolph McInnis was revered in Minnesota in the same way we revere Bob Dylan, Charles M. Schulz, Judy Garland, Herb Brooks, Hubert H. Humphrey, and F. Scott Fitzgerald. Not many Minnesotans reach international celebrity and when they do we build statutes to them. There's one of Mary Tyler Moore tossing her hat in the air on the Nicollet Mall even though she's from Brooklyn Heights, NY, solely because her fictional TV show was set in only slightly less fictional Minneapolis. Not that we have an inferiority complex about these things.

McInnis was our most famous artist, a so-called American Regionalist renowned worldwide for his paintings of small-town America and the Midwest—he's often mentioned in the same breath as Grant Wood, Thomas Hart Benton, John Steuart Curry, and Andrew Wyeth. What's more, he chose to live here even after hitting it big instead of moving to where the winters are more forgiving, unlike most of our famous and near famous relations. We loved him for that. We loved that he would hang out at the Minneapolis Institute of Art, visit high school art classes, and give seminars to the undergrads at the University of Minnesota. We loved that he once helped judge the art exhibit at the Minnesota State Fair, telling the entrants that his first painting when he was fifteen was rejected by the jury, so hang in there.

When he died in the early 1980s, most of us fell into a state of intense grief that just seemed to linger. We wouldn't feel a loss like that again until Prince died decades later.

What happened, McInnis was driving home alone from Duluth. It wasn't particularly late, only about 8:00 P.M. Only it was winter in Minnesota and on I-35 between Hinckley and Duluth there were long stretches of highway without a light to be seen except for those that flickered in the night sky. A patch of black ice and a deep ditch alongside the highway—McInnis skidded across one and plowed into the other. Along the way, he whacked his head against the steering wheel, knocking himself unconscious (a year later Minnesota would pass a mandatory seat belt law).

It wasn't the blow that killed him, though. It was the cold. Thirteen degrees below zero. His car was invisible from the highway and his lights quickly died along with his car battery. He wouldn't be found until the next morning.

"Over five thousand people attended his funeral at the St. Paul Cathedral," Louise said. "I was one of them. I sat way in the back. 'Course, no one knew who I was then. I wouldn't become famous until . . ."

A month later, Mary Ann McInnis, Randolph's wife and business partner, gave the public its first glimpse of a suite of paintings that her husband had been working on before he was killed—*Scenes from an Inland Sea.*

McInnis had wanted to branch out, Mary Ann said, wanted to try something new. So, whenever he could find the time, he would drive alone to a studio he kept outside of Duluth. From there he would travel around Lake Superior, painting whatever interested him: Palisade Head near Silver Bay; the Split Rock Lighthouse just north of Castle Danger; Isle Royale near Grand

Portage; the Sleeping Giant in Thunder Bay, Ontario; the Porcupine Mountains at Silver City, Michigan; the Sea Caves and Apostle Islands off Bayfield, Wisconsin.

"He was tired of painting rural postcards, that's what he told me," Louise said. "He wanted drama."

McInnis had worked at it for nearly five years. Some of his friends called it a prolonged midlife crisis. Yet there had been no secret about it; he had even given hints about his side project in interviews preceding his death. Yet when she went to close the studio and collect his work, Mary Ann discovered for the first time that two-thirds of the paintings and more than half of the drawings featured Louise Wykoff. McInnis had painted her during all four seasons. Sometimes she was outside and pictured against the background of the great lake and its environs. Sometimes she was inside sitting on a chair, looking out a window, leaning against a door frame, or lying across a bed. Sometimes she was clothed. More often she was not.

The reaction was sensational, to say the least. The art world was startled by McInnis's newfound visual and technical force. It described the Wykoff paintings in nineteenth-century terms, comparing them to *The Four Seasons* by Giuseppe Arcimboldo and *Voyage of Life* by Thomas Cole. It spoke of the remarkable collaboration of artist and model; Louise became one of the few people who was famous simply for being in a painting like *Mona Lisa* and Whistler's mother.

The rest of us—well, we wondered about the collaboration as well. *People*, the *National Enquirer,* even *Time* and *Newsweek*, openly questioned the nature of the relationship between the artist and That Wykoff Woman. It didn't help that McInnis was four decades older than his model. Mary Ann McInnis remained silent on the subject. At least in public. To her everlasting credit, so did Louise, who fled the paparazzi and refused to answer a single question about the paintings for thirty-five years.

"Randolph hired me as an assistant," Louise said. "This was

right after I graduated with a BFA from the University of Minnesota—Duluth. He wanted someone to take care of the studio while he was away, take care of the paintings. Stretch canvas when he was here. Buy his paints. And his lunch. You know, assist. He also paid me to circle Lake Superior when he was gone and take photographs of anything and everything that interested me. I did this several times. I would show him the photos and if any of them interested him, we'd drive to the location and he'd decide if he wanted to paint it. It wasn't until the second year that he thought of painting me into the scenes. For perspective, he said. After a while, he started painting me instead of the lake."

"Okay," I said.

"Now you want to know, like everyone else wants to know—how close were we? You want to know about our relationship. Was it sexual?"

"I'm curious, like everyone else. But it's none of my business."

"No, it isn't. It's no one's business. Not even Mary Ann's."

"What I really want to know, though, is why I was asked to come up here. What trouble are you in?"

"I'm not sure 'trouble' is the correct word."

"Why don't you tell me about it and we'll decide together."

"After Randolph died, Mary Ann contacted me. Actually, I called her and told her that I was working as Randolph's assistant. She knew my name, of course, even though we had never met, because she was the one who signed and mailed the checks. Mary Ann took care of the business end of things, every last detail, Randolph said, so he could devote all of his energy to his art. He said it was a very good partnership. Lucrative, he said.

"Anyway, I asked her what she wanted me to do with the paintings and drawings. She seemed stunned when I told her how many there were. She knew what Randolph was doing but she didn't realize the extent until—McKenzie, I lied to her. When Mary Ann came to the studio, she found one hundred and thirty-three paintings and drawings. There were actually one hundred and thirty-six. I kept three of them for myself. I didn't steal them, McKenzie. Randolph gave them to me. He said he was nearly finished with the project and I should pick three of the paintings to keep for myself. Who knows, he said, they might even be worth something some day. That was on Friday. He died driving back to the Cities two days later."

"Where does the trouble part come into it?"

"Mary Ann doesn't know that I kept the paintings. I was afraid she'd be angry about—she didn't know about me, you see. Me being in the paintings. Won't the world be surprised when it finds out, Randolph would say. Well, it was surprised. Up 'til then he had been best known for painting landscapes, not portraits. Mary Ann was furious. She said—she said things to me that . . . It doesn't matter. What matters is that I was afraid Mary Ann would demand that I return the paintings, so I didn't tell her I had them. I didn't tell anyone. I didn't show them to anyone. Not once in all these years."

"Again, where does the trouble—"

"They've been stolen."

"When?"

"I don't know for sure. I kept them hidden upstairs. The last time I looked at them was about a week ago. I looked again—what day is it, Thursday? I looked Tuesday evening and they were missing."

"Was there any sign of a break-in?"

"None that I saw."

"Your security system?"

"McKenzie, I'm what they call a struggling artist. Sometimes I forget to lock the door."

"Does anyone know you sometimes forget to lock the door?"

Louise shook her head, but I could tell she wasn't sure.

"What else was taken?" I asked.

"Nothing that I know of."

"Nothing?"

"Just the paintings."

"Did you ask your students about it?"

"Did I ask my students if they stole paintings of the Wykoff woman? Of course not."

"Did you ask if they've seen anyone hanging around who shouldn't be hanging around?"

"No, because then I'd have to explain—McKenzie, no one knew the paintings were there, that they even existed."

"Obviously someone did."

"What I was thinking—McKenzie, it could happen this way, couldn't it? What I was thinking is that someone broke into my house and went upstairs because that's where I live, that's where my belongings are, and he was looking for something worth stealing and he found the paintings and recognized them for what they were and . . . The *News-Herald*, the county newspaper, it reported just the other day that property crimes were way up, that burglaries had increased something like a hundred percent in the past few years."

"Yes, it could have happened that way."

"I want them back, McKenzie. I need them. They're all that I have of him. Of Randolph. That's why I can't call the police. I can't let anyone know that I have them. If Mary Ann knew she'd take them from me. I know she would and not just because they're worth—I don't know what they're worth. I don't know what a collector or a museum would pay for three undiscovered McInnis paintings. Mary Ann sold the entire collection for $34 million. Only that was in the eighties."

Back when a million bucks was real money, my inner voice reminded me.

"McKenzie, you need to know—it's not about the money. If I had wanted the money, I would have sold the paintings years ago. It's about—I don't know how to say it."

"That's okay. You don't have to."

"Will you help me?"

"I'd like to." I stood because I tend to think better on my feet and crossed the studio to one of the large windows. "I don't know if I can." The white van was still there. I thought I saw movement behind the driver's side window, but it could have been sunlight reflecting off the glass. "I'm going to need to get the answers to some questions and people will want to know why I'm asking them."

"What if—what if we pretended that they weren't Randolph's paintings? What if instead we told people that they were my paintings that were stolen?"

"Would someone steal your paintings?"

"I'm not completely unknown. I sell. I have paintings hanging in the City of Lakes, the Milwaukee Art Museum, and at the Duluth Art Institute. Plus galleries up and down the North Shore. The Cities, too. Critics have compared me to Eastman Johnson."

I said, "No, kidding," as if I was impressed and I might have been, too, if I had known who the hell Eastman Johnson was. At the same time, I nearly asked if she sold because of the quality of her work or because she was That Wykoff Woman, yet managed to catch the question between my teeth before it slipped off my tongue.

"How much would your paintings be worth?" I asked.

"Between five and ten thousand dollars."

"Each?"

"For the three."

"That gives it felony weight, anyway."

"I don't know what that means."

"According to the law, the difference between a felony and an infraction or a misdemeanor is the value of what is stolen. If your paintings were worth only five hundred dollars . . ."

"I've sold my work for as little as that and was happy to get it."

"Still, it would be hard to believe that you would contact a private investigator, even an unlicensed one like me, to help recover them. A theft crime, though, where the value is over a grand—that's a different story. It means as much as twenty-four months in prison for a first-time offender. It gives us leverage. I might even be able to get some help from the local cops . . ."

"No police."

"Off the books, of course."

"The police would do that? Help even if I didn't register a complaint?"

"Sometimes, if it's not too much work."

"Yes, but—you would lie to the police?"

"It's okay. They're used to it."

Louise stared into her mug as if instead of coffee it contained tea leaves that might reveal something momentous. She spoke softly, "I need to get those paintings back."

"Okay."

"Where do we start?"

"I need you to make a list of everyone who's been in this house in the past year. Family, friends, students, plumbers, electricians, Girl Scouts selling cookies if they got past the front door. Everyone."

"All right."

"Tell me, who owns the white van parked outside?"

"My neighbor across the street."

"What do you know about him?"

"Her."

"Her. Does she know who you are?"

"Of course. She works part-time in a gallery downtown that sells some of my work."

"Has she been in your house?"

"Yes."

"You're friends then?"

"Acquaintances."

"Put her on the list."

"Any particular reason?"

"She owns an unmarked white van."

"What does that have to do with anything?"

"You have to start somewhere."

TWO

I told Louise that I needed to drive home, but that I would pack a bag and return the next day and we'd go over her list. She said okay. While heading back down I-35 between Duluth and Hinckley, I looked for a plaque or a sign that would indicate where Randolph McInnis had died. Of course, there wasn't one.

My Mustang had all the latest electronics so it was a simple matter to use the onboard communications system to make a hands-free phone call.

"Bonalay and Associates, attorneys at law," a woman said.

"Hi, Caroline. It's McKenzie."

"Well, hello. We haven't heard from you since—when was the last time you were arrested?"

"You're killing me, Caroline." By the way she laughed apparently she thought that was funny—her killing me. "Is the boss in?"

"She is. Just a moment, please."

A couple of moments later another woman said, "G. K. Bonalay," which is the way my lawyer always answered her phone.

"Hey, Gen."

"McKenzie, it's good to hear from you. Are you in trouble?"

"Why do you always assume that?"

"Given the nature of our relationship . . ."

"Yeah, yeah, yeah. Listen, I have a hypothetical question for you."

"You are in trouble."

"I'm not, Genevieve, c'mon. I'm asking for a friend."

"You realize, of course, that you're protected by attorney-client privilege, right? Instead of hypotheticals, tell me exactly what you need to know and why."

I did.

"Wow," G. K. said. "Louise Wykoff. That is so cool."

"You think so?"

"Has there ever been an art class taught in Minnesota that didn't include Randolph McInnis and That Wykoff Woman? I have the book, McKenzie, the whopping big coffee table book that includes all the paintings and pictures. Tell me—does she still look like she did in the paintings?"

"Pretty much. Her hair is the same color; her eyes are just as riveting. From what I could see she hasn't gained an ounce of weight. 'Course, she was wearing clothes so . . ."

"Very, very cool."

"So much for legal detachment."

"To answer your question, no. Wykoff won't be arrested for theft. Not a chance. She wouldn't have been arrested back when McInnis died, either. From what you've told me, there's no physical evidence that proves McInnis gave Wykoff the paintings, that they were a gift. Yet, by the same token, there's nothing to prove that he didn't do exactly what she claimed, give them to her. Considering the circumstances and the length of their relationship it would be very easy to rule that Wykoff was telling the truth and very difficult to rule that she was lying. No cop would arrest her. No judge would allow it to stand."

"So, she gets to keep the paintings?"

"Absolutely."

"You'd think that after all this time she would know her position."

"Not necessarily. Most people are pretty dumb when it comes to the law, aren't they? They only know what they see on TV and that's almost always wrong. On the other hand . . ."

"Yeah?"

"This is where the lawsuit comes in."

"What lawsuit?"

"I've seen it many, many times. 'I get to keep the china because Aunt Sue promised it to me.' 'That's a lie. She promised it to me.' 'I get to keep the lake home because I'm the eldest.' 'There's nothing in the will that says that.' And so on and so forth. The higher the value of the object in question, the more contentious these things get."

"Who is most likely to win if Mary Ann McInnis sued?" I asked.

"Whichever party has the most money to invest in the case."

"That would probably be Mary Ann."

"She could beat Wykoff into submission, wear her out, bankrupt her. Beyond that, though—you've heard the expression 'possession is nine-tenths of the law'?"

"Sure."

"It doesn't have any real standing in court; it doesn't carry legal weight. However, it is generally held that it is much easier to hang on to something than it is to take it away. An obvious example—the car you're driving is assumed to be yours unless someone can prove by a preponderance of evidence that it's not. Also, most of these kinds of cases are about the money, probably ninety-nine percent I'd say. The fact that Wykoff hadn't attempted to sell the paintings in all these years suggests that they hold greater value for her than just the monetary. That would also give her an edge with a judge."

"Good for her, then."

"Except . . ."

"Except what?"

"It works both ways. The person who now has possession of the paintings could say he bought them at a garage sale, discovered them in an attic, found them resting against a Dumpster along the side of the road. That they rightfully belong to him. My point is Wykoff would have to prove—in court, mind you—that the paintings actually belong to her, that whoever has them now broke into her house and stole them. Can she do that?"

I gave it a long hard think before replying although the answer was obvious the moment G. K. asked the question.

"No," I said. "She claimed no one knew she had the paintings and there was no sign of forced entry when she was robbed. She doesn't even know when she was robbed."

"Which means if you do find the paintings and took steps to—shall we say, recover them? You could be the one charged with felony theft. We're speaking hypothetically, though. Right? You would never knowingly break the law, would you, McKenzie?"

I glanced down at my speedometer. I was currently doing eighty-three on a seventy-miles-per-hour stretch of freeway.

"Never," I said.

I once told Perrin Stewart that she was a babe. She laughed at me and said I was just being polite. I meant it, though. She was one of those curvy women who weighed about eighty pounds more than what the body mass index labeled "ideal." Yet she carried herself so lightly and dressed so stylishly and spoke so smartly that meeting her convinced me that I had missed out by only dating women whose dress sizes (and sometimes IQs) were in single digits.

We were walking the corridors of the City of Lakes Art Museum. The museum had been closed for nearly an hour and the only sound we heard was the clicking of Perrin's heels on the marble floor. There was something magical about it. Not the clicking, the privacy.

"This is my favorite time to be here," Perrin said. "When I'm alone." She reached out and brushed my hand yet did not take it. "Or with a good friend. It's as if all this great art belongs to me, myself, and I."

"Since you're the executive director of the joint, technically it does, doesn't it? Belong to you and the trustees?"

"Ha."

"Where does all this stuff come from, anyway?"

"Some of it is on loan from collectors who want the work to be seen and not just gather dust in their basements. Some is the result of gifts or bequests from private collectors who are seeking financial and tax benefits. The rest we purchase outright, about half I'd say. Why? Do you want to make a contribution to our acquisition fund?"

"I like to think of myself as a patron of the arts."

"Donate a half million dollars or more and I'll make you a trustee."

"What do I get for fifty bucks?"

"I'll send you a CLAM button and a copy of our newsletter."

We took the stairs to the third floor. You'd think Perrin would have preferred the elevator, yet she didn't. When we reached the top step I was the one who was out of breath, not her. We walked some more. I told her that I thought it might be too quiet.

"Most people find it unnerving," I said. "It's like when you're in the woods and the birds are singing and crickets are chirping and then they stop. It means there's danger lurking somewhere. When it's too quiet your mind begins to wonder if something's going to happen. That's why if you go to a grocery store, go to Cub Foods—they pipe in music. Something to think about."

Perrin stopped and gave me a hard look.

"You're kidding, right?" she asked.

"Of course I am."

You are? my inner voice asked.

We continued walking.

"Although," I said. "A little Duke Ellington, some Wynton Marsalis . . ."

"You're a philistine, McKenzie. Besides, music would drown out the voices."

"You hear voices?"

"I do, especially when it's quiet like this. Sometimes it's like the paintings are speaking to me. Or perhaps the artist. I don't know which."

"Really?"

"Actually, I don't hear voices so much as sound effects. I'll stop in front of the Delacroix and I'll hear the clatter of the crowd in the bazaar or I'll stare at the Monet and the noise of the stormy sea crashing against the rocks becomes so real. We have a Rousseau—*Autumn at St. Jean de Paris, Forest of Fontainebleau.* Sometimes I can hear the birds singing in the trees. You probably think I'm crazy."

"I would never say that. Eccentric, maybe."

"That's so much better."

"Some people say that I'm eccentric."

"No, they say you're crazy."

We reached a section of the museum that was designated Contemporary American. There we found a room dedicated solely to the works of Randolph McInnis. It contained some of his earlier paintings, the postcards Louise Wykoff had called them, although a critic quoted on the placard claimed they were icons of American art. One in particular—*Olson's Barn*—was hailed for its bleak realism "so distinct from the abstraction and avant-gardism of the time."

"He had a very frugal, bare-bones style," Perrin said. "Muted colors. Precise brushstrokes."

There were two paintings that were part of the *Scenes from the Inland Sea* series that did not feature Louise, both donated to the museum by Mary Ann McInnis according to another placard. I asked about them.

"We were all shocked when she made the donation after our second year," Perrin said. "Mary Ann said it was essential that a Minnesota art museum feature Minnesota's greatest artist. Who were we to argue? Since then our curatorial staff has had only one standing directive—all the McInnis you can lay your hands on. Now we have nine including"—she gestured at the two paintings on the far wall, both of them featuring That Wykoff Woman.

"I was told that Mary Ann sold the entire collection in the 1980s," I said.

"Most of the collection, yes, including all of the drawings and paintings of Louise. She kept some pieces for herself, though, and gave a few away to family and friends. These . . ." She gestured at the Wykoffs again. "These we acquired from various collectors over the years. The man Mary Ann had originally sold the collection to—what was his name? A big-time real estate investor. They say he suffered some financial setbacks a short time after he bought the suite because of Black Monday in October of 1987. Stock markets all around the world collapsed. The Dow Jones lost something like twenty-five percent of its value overnight. Apparently—why can't I remember his name? Apparently, he began selling off the paintings a few at a time after that. Who knows? Maybe he had intended to do it all along. Buy low and sell high, isn't that what they say? I need to look him up when I get back to the office."

I examined all four walls of the exhibit space and couldn't find it so I asked, "Don't you also have a painting by Louise Wykoff?"

Perrin crooked a finger and led me out of the exhibit. She pointed at a canvas of brightly dressed Native American women on the wall next to the entrance with the title, *Daughters of the Ojibwa.*

"Not in the same room?" I said.

"Mary Ann McInnis wouldn't care for it and there's no way I'm going to piss her off."

"Yeah, I get that. Tell me, Perrin, did Louise tell you what she wants from me?"

"Yes."

"What do you think?"

"I think I'd love to get my hands on those paintings and put them on exhibit. Three missing McInnis canvases recovered after thirty-five years, my God that would be huge. The attention this museum would get. Locally. Nationally. Internationally. The boost in fund-raising. It would be wonderful."

"Except Louise wants to keep them all to herself. She doesn't want the world to know that the paintings even exist."

"I'm sure word would leak out somehow and when it does having Louise donate them to City of Lakes or even just loaning them to us might dissuade Mary Ann from suing her ass off."

"You have it all figured out then."

"No. Well, I didn't at first. At first—Louise called yesterday. She was very upset. We had met at a gallery in Duluth a few years ago and kept in touch. I like her very much. I like that she never tried to capitalize on her relationship with Randolph McInnis. She told me what had happened and I immediately thought of you, my knight in shining armor. Afterward, I thought—McKenzie, those paintings need to be seen. If not here then somewhere else. I don't know what Louise was thinking keeping them hidden all these years. This is some of the greatest art ever produced by an American. It doesn't belong to her. It belongs to—okay, okay. You don't need to hear my fund-raising speech."

"Still . . ."

"Yeah."

We drifted back into the exhibit hall, surrounding ourselves with the work of Randolph McInnis.

"You wouldn't be the one to leak that news, would you?" I asked. "Drop a dime to Mary Ann McInnis?"

"Drop a dime?"

"Make a call."

"I won't lie, McKenzie. I'd be awfully tempted, especially if it meant I would get the paintings. I mean the museum. You know what I mean."

"You still owe me a favor," I said. "From before."

"Yes, I do."

"Promise you won't say a word to anyone about the paintings without talking to me first."

Perrin didn't answer. Instead, she stared at me while she wrestled with my request. It was because she hesitated so long that I believed her when she said, "I promise."

"It's all moot, anyway," I said. "I haven't found the paintings. I don't even know where to start looking for them."

"I have a great deal of faith in you. After what you did last time . . ."

"I nearly got killed last time, remember?"

Perrin's eyes clouded over for as moment and she nodded. I gave her shoulder a squeeze.

If I remember correctly, she was more concerned about the Jade Lily than your health and well-being, my inner voice said. *'Course, at the time, she thought you might be the one trying to steal it.*

"All's well that ends well," I said.

"I have bourbon in my office."

"I knew there was a reason I liked you, sweetie."

"Sweetie you call me and we haven't even started drinking yet."

"Tell me something. Just out of curiosity—do you hear anything when you look at *Scenes from an Inland Sea*?"

"Not when it's the Wykoff woman, no. I do when I study the other paintings, the ones featuring the Apostle Islands and the lighthouse."

"What do you hear?"

"Wind. A low, mournful wind. I never met the man, of course, but if you study his work like I have, you have to conclude that despite his fame and fortune, Randolph McInnis was a dark and moody fellow, prone to melancholy."

"I don't see any of that in the Wykoff paintings," I said.

"Neither do I."

Perrin poured Knob Creek Smoked Maple Bourbon, a little sweet by my standards but tasty nonetheless. While we drank she pulled a large volume with the title *Randolph McInnis: Scenes from an Inland Sea* off the shelf behind her desk. She opened it to a page near the front.

"Flonta," Perrin said. "The man who bought the collection was named Bruce Flonta. He contributed an essay to the book. In fact, he published the book."

I made a gimme gesture and Perrin slid the tome across her desk. I picked it up. The damn thing weighed five pounds if an ounce. I started paging through it. Paintings and drawings of Louise Wykoff sitting by a window, standing next to a tree, staring at Lake Superior, walking along a rocky path, kneeling next to a fire, shielding her eyes from the sun, stretching on a bed . . .

"I remember the first time I met Louise," Perrin said. "I looked into her eyes, studied her face, tried to find the qualities of character and mood that McInnis had put into the paintings of her, only I couldn't. I've seen her a few times since, we've even Skyped. Obviously, she's an attractive woman. There's a kind of a glow about her. Yet I've never seen the woman in the paintings. I wonder—the warmth, the humor, the courage, the resilience, the strength—did McInnis actually see those things in Louise and find a way to render them to canvas or were all those qualities inside of him and Louise was merely the mechanism for how he chose to express them?"

"That's a question you're asking a guy who has a bachelor's degree in criminology?"

Perrin thought that was funny.

"It's the kind of thing that art majors talk about all the time," she said.

"You guys must be fun at parties."

"We have our moments. McKenzie, what happens now?"

"First thing tomorrow morning, I'm going back up to Grand Marais and see if I can find those damn paintings. Just don't ask me how I'm going to do it. Questioning Wykoff's students, friends, acquaintances ah, man."

"You can't tell when people are lying?"

"I can when they're not very good at it, only the people who aren't very good at it are the least likely to break into someone's house and steal their stuff. If the thief had stolen other things as well I could check out the pawn shops and antiques stores to see if he had attempted to unload them, get a line on him that way. 'Course, if the thief is a professional—very little stolen merchandise actually ends up in pawn shops these days. Besides, I can't picture the guy carrying three canvases into Pawn America and announcing, 'make me an offer.' I can't see him listing three priceless McInnis paintings on eBay, either. At least it's a place to start."

"Whoever stole the paintings will try to sell them to someone, though. Right?"

"Eventually, yes."

"How about the man who had tried to buy the Jade Lily, the one you told me about? Should we talk to him?"

"El Cid?"

"Yes."

"For the time being at least, we're trying to keep this a secret. Cid—tell a big-time fence like him that there are three priceless paintings in the wind and by tomorrow morning every grifter in the country will be trying to lay their hands on them.

By the day after, you'll have a substantial criminal element from Europe joining in."

Perrin sipped her bourbon thoughtfully before she spoke.

"I don't want you to get hurt," she said.

"Thank you, Perrin. I appreciate it. I'm not sure That Wykoff Woman cares one way or the other."

"Like I said, I don't know if she's the same person as the one in the paintings."

"We'll see."

Perrin lent me her book. She said there were plenty more copies available in the museum's gift shop. I took it to the high-rise condominium in downtown Minneapolis that I shared with Nina Truhler. She wasn't home, though. She owned a jazz joint on Cathedral Hill in St. Paul and spent more time there than she did here.

I sat behind the desk in the office area. The condo was wide open. We didn't have rooms so much as areas—dining area, kitchen area, TV area, music area where both my stereo system and Nina's Steinway stood. The entire north wall was made of tinted floor-to-ceiling glass with a dramatic view of the Mississippi River where it tumbled down St. Anthony Falls. You'd think one would never grow tired of it. After eighteen months, though, I find that I don't look as often. Instead, I started paging through *Scenes from an Inland Sea* again.

It read almost like a primer on how to make art. There were thirty-four sections and each one featured a series of drawings and sketches of a specific subject from different perspectives concluding with the painting that eventually came from them. They were accompanied by notes written by Randolph McInnis explaining what he was going for.

The first section was labeled *Sea Monster* and depicted the bow of a huge freighter escaping from a fog bank as it bore down on the narrow canal that led from Lake Superior to the Duluth Harbor Basin.

"When I first saw the freighter emerge from the fog I found its size both majestic and frightening at the same time," McInnis wrote. "I wanted to capture that. I also wanted to express what I was feeling at the moment the ship appeared to me. I felt inadequate."

Louise Wykoff didn't appear in the book until the seventh section, the one labeled *Lonely Heart*. She was fully clothed and sitting on a rock while gazing out at the great lake, the iconic Split Rock Lighthouse prominent over her shoulder. McInnis wrote "People are not very good at being alone. It makes us feel sad. It makes us search the horizon especially in our darkest hours for the flickering light that will lead us home."

Louise wasn't in sections eight through ten, appeared again in number eleven, and reappeared in section fourteen. She was in all of them after that. My favorite was section eighteen, which featured a nude Louise sitting in a chair, her elbow propped on a windowsill as she looked outward. The painting was titled *In Her Eyes*, even though you couldn't actually see her eyes, and about it McInnis wrote, "Sometimes you can gaze at one thing and see the world entire."

My inner voice asked, *Exactly what were you gazing at, Louise*—I glanced at the bottom-right corner of the page and read the number—*when McInnis painted number seventy-two?*

"Wait," I said aloud.

It hadn't occurred to me until that moment that all of the sketches, drawings, and paintings in the book were numbered one through one hundred and thirty-three and presented in chronological order. Plus, the notes from McInnis—*How is that possible? He was long dead when the volume was published.*

I returned to the front of the book. There was a preface, a foreword, and an introduction followed by twenty pages of text that waxed fondly on the artist and his work and where each stood in the canons of American art. Near the end of the text I found a paragraph explaining that "the meticulous McInnis, as was his habit going back to his days as an art student, had carefully documented the drawings and paintings that comprised the *Scenes from an Inland Sea* as well as what he was thinking when he drew and painted them."

Apparently, McInnis had decided early in his career not to allow his work to be defined "by the fevers of imagination" found in art criticism, so he and his wife Mary Ann worked diligently to control his legacy. That included "expressing his artistic style, personal preoccupations, and work habits in his own terms."

"I think businesspeople call that branding," I said aloud.

The sound of a door handle caused my head to turn. I looked up just as Nina came through the door.

"Hey, you," she said. "How was Grand Marais? Did you bring me donuts?"

"In the refrigerator."

Nina dropped her bag and coat on a chair, went to the kitchen area, found a couple of chocolate-frosted cake donuts in a bag, and heated them briefly in the microwave.

"Don't I even get a hug?" I asked. "It was like a nine-hour drive round-trip."

"Ah, poor baby."

Nina not only hugged me, she kissed me in a way that made me think of our master bedroom. She let me go, however, the moment the microwave pinged.

"God, I love these," she said, her mouth full of donut. "World's Best Donuts might actually make the world's best donuts."

"So, how's business?" I asked.

"Not bad, could be better," which was Nina's standard reply to the question during all of the nearly seven years that I'd known her. In an unguarded moment she might confess that Rickie's, the jazz joint and restaurant that she named after her daughter Erica, was doing very well indeed, although she nearly always added a qualifier—"for now." Despite her success, Nina nursed a nagging concern that the next new restaurant or club that caught the public's imagination would be the one that put her out of business. It was why getting her to take a vacation for longer than a week at a time was like signing up for elective dentistry.

"Did you meet her?" Nina asked. "That Wykoff Woman?"

"I did. She told me to call her Louise."

"How was she?"

"Very pleasant."

"Is she still gorgeous?"

"Yes, although not as gorgeous as you."

"Who is? Don't answer that. What did she want?"

I had promised Louise that I would keep her secret. On the other hand, I had promised Nina that I would never keep secrets from her and that promise came first. I told Nina everything.

"You're off on another treasure hunt then," she said.

"First thing in the morning. Want to come with?"

"I don't think so."

"You love Grand Marais."

"I love it when we're hanging out, enjoying the lake, the rivers, the woods, the bars, the restaurants. Are we going to be doing any of that?"

"Probably not."

"Well, then . . ."

"I don't know how long I'll be gone."

"Just as long as you come back in one piece, that's the main thing." Nina held up the paper bag. "Oh, and bring more donuts."

THREE

Most people know Grand Marais as a tourist town with a sheltered harbor guarded by a small lighthouse and iconic bars and restaurants with names like the Angry Trout, Crooked Spoon Café, and Sven and Ole's Pizza. It also hosts a vibrant and renowned art colony that attracts visitors from around the US and Canada. Yet it has a residential and community life as well. There are grocery stores, pharmacies, hospital and clinics, several churches, a high school with the nickname Vikings, a weekly newspaper, a public library, a bookstore, a playhouse, a historical society, a county courthouse, a sheriff's department with a dozen active deputies, volunteer firefighters and first responders, a dog pound, a nine-hole golf course, and a municipal liquor store.

The traffic was heavy driving Highway 61 into town at 1:00 P.M., which didn't surprise me a bit. In autumn, tourists mob the North Shore of Lake Superior in search of spectacular colors. Yet I was surprised when I couldn't find an empty parking space in front of the Wykoff Art Academy. Instead, the spots were filled with various vehicles including a white van that was not the same as the white van I had seen the day before. Its doors were open and after I parked down the street and walked back

I could see lights, grip stands, small sandbags to keep the stands from falling over, tripods, rags and frames, reflectors, generators, electric cords, microphones, and a lot of other equipment I couldn't identify both inside the van and lining the boulevard between the street and the sidewalk. My first thought, TV news. Only there were no garish call letters painted on the van's sides.

People carried equipment in and out of the converted church. I dodged a couple of them until I reached the entrance. I peeked inside. Louise Wykoff was dressed in a long dark blue skirt and light blue sweater. She was sitting on the same stool as the day before, directly across from a man who sat in a canvas chair. Lights and a handful of cameras were pointed at Louise from a variety of angles, yet none were filming him. Another man, about twenty-five and in good shape, held a boom mic above Louise's head.

She said, "Often he would have me paint the same scene as he was painting and critique it. I thought I understood composition, perspective, how to lead the viewer's eye, color, the value of light and dark. I knew nothing. I didn't even know how to hold a brush properly until he taught me. Four years I studied art at UMD. Randolph taught me twice as much in four months. He paid me while he did it, too. I almost felt guilty taking the money. Only then he would have one of his tantrums and I'd think I'm not getting enough for this."

"These tantrums," the man said. "Were they about his work?"

"Almost never. At least not about the *Scenes*. Instead, they were nearly always about the life he was living outside of Duluth, about the images the public, the critics, and his wife expected him to churn out on a regular basis."

Someone pulled my arm, a young woman. If she had told me she was selling Girl Scout cookies I might have believed her except for the tattoo of flower petals that seemed to reach out from beneath the collar of her shirt and grasp her throat.

"Mister, you can't be here," she said.

"Why not?"

I let her take my arm and lead me down the steps away from the church entrance to the sidewalk.

"Why not?" I repeated.

"We're filming."

"Filming what?"

"A documentary."

"On Louise?"

"On the *Scenes from an Inland Sea*. Do you know what that is?"

"I'm familiar."

"It's the thirty-fifth anniversary."

"Of the paintings or Randolph McInnis's death?"

She didn't answer.

I offered my hand.

"My name is McKenzie. I'm an acquaintance of Louise. In fact, I have an appointment to see her."

"I'm Jennica. I'm an assistant to Mr. Mehren."

"Jennica?"

"My parents couldn't decide between Jennifer and Jessica, so they compromised. Someone told me once that it was a real name, that it meant 'white wave,' but I didn't believe him. I'm sorry about your appointment. Ms. Wykoff knew we would be filming most of the day. I don't know why she didn't tell you."

"Artists, am I right?"

"Huh? Yeah, artists."

"Mind if I hang around? I promise I won't get in your way, I won't make a sound."

"I guess it'll be okay. Just don't let Dad see you."

"Dad?"

"Mr. Mehren."

"I'll keep out of his line of sight."

"He won an Oscar, you know. For *We Gotta Get Out of This Place* about the Vietnam War."

"I seem to remember that. When was it? Ten years ago?"

"Nearly twenty. I was an infant at the time. I didn't even

know about it until years later so I'm never surprised when other people don't know about it. My mom said the awards ceremony was very la-di-da. She met Clint Eastwood and Steven Spielberg."

"Cool."

"So, just—okay . . . If I get a chance I'll tell Ms. Wykoff that you're here. McKenzie, right?"

"Yes. Thank you."

Jennica scrambled up the steps to the church and cautiously peered inside before entering. I moved to a tree on the boulevard and leaned against it while I accessed my smartphone. Coverage in Cook County was iffy at best. Stay within Grand Marais and you were fine. Drive five minutes in any direction and suddenly you were cut off from the rest of the world. There was a time when that wouldn't have bothered me. Like most people I would have preferred it. Now we're so thoroughly connected that when we lose connection even temporarily we feel anxious. Go figure.

I Googled Mehren. There were a couple hundred thousand results including a Wikipedia page:

Jeffery James Mehren is an American director, producer, screenwriter, and editor. He is best known for directing documentary films. He received an Academy Award for Best Documentary Feature for directing *We Gotta Get Out of This Place (If It's the Last Thing We Ever Do)* (1999). He has also received numerous awards from film festivals, including the Sundance Film Festival and Los Angeles Film Festival.

It turned out Mehren had shot a couple of dozen documentaries since *We Gotta Get Out of This Place*, named for the 1965 song by the Animals that was featured throughout. Yet none of them had achieved the status of his award-winner, although the films he made immediately afterward were well received. Much of his later work was poorly reviewed, however, with at least one critic lambasting him for his self-indulgence while another lamented that he had squandered his gifts as a filmmaker. His most recent documentary was called *The Poison in Our Water* and dealt with the poisoning of groundwater due to fracking. Someone had written that "Mehren's tedious pacing made the audience yearn to drink the water."

"I need this," I said aloud. "I really do."

At the same time my inner voice asked, *Why didn't Louise tell you that a documentary filmmaker was lurking about? What's next? Reporters from* The Washington Post?

I had been hanging around for nearly a half hour when another white van approached, moving slowly. A garage door opened across the street from where I was standing. The van slid inside the garage and the door closed behind it. Less than five minutes later, a woman left the house. She moved easily as she walked toward me like someone who got plenty of exercise. She wore tight shorts and a tight T-shirt and I thought it was a pretty skimpy outfit given the temperature.

On the other hand, my inner voice said. *If you lived in a place that averaged 39.8 degrees Fahrenheit, 64 might feel downright balmy.*

"I take it you're not with the film crew," she said.

"Just a curious onlooker. How 'bout yourself?"

"I live over there." She pointed at her house. "I saw you here yesterday."

"You did?"

"It's a small town. You tend to notice strangers."

"Grand Marais is a tourist town. It's loaded with strangers."

"Very few of them wander away from the lake and almost none this deep into the residential areas."

"Okay."

"I know what you're thinking. I'm either a conscientious community watcher or a notorious busybody. You can take your pick."

"Since I'm not from around here, I'll let you decide."

"I'm Peg Younghans."

"McKenzie."

I shook her hand. Her grip was firm. I guessed she was fifteen years older than me which made her about sixty, Louise Wykoff's age.

"Younghans," I said. "There's a St. Paul boy named Tom Younghans who played pro hockey for the Minnesota North Stars back in the day."

"Never heard of him."

"Okay." I gestured at the church. "Do you know what's going on?"

"These people?" She made it sound as if they were rowdy fans of a visiting sports franchise. "They rolled in at about seven o'clock this morning. Loudly. I don't know what you're used to but seven o'clock in Grand Marais is supposed to be quiet. The little girl you were talking to before, when I came out to complain she told me they were filming a documentary about the paintings that guy did of Louise years ago. Other than that . . ."

"I take it Louise didn't tell you they were coming, either."

"She's very secretive that one. I don't blame her. Back when the paintings were done the media hounded her relentlessly. It was one of the reasons she escaped to Grand Marais, I guess. Personally, I don't see what the big deal is. Nude paintings. I have some nude photographs I could show you that are a lot more enticing."

I couldn't tell you why I thought that was funny, yet I laughed anyway.

"Maybe later," I said. "Tell me—have you seen any other strangers lurking about besides me?"

"No. Why do you ask?"

"Someone broke into the art academy and stole a few things."

"When?"

"Louise isn't sure."

Peg stared at me for a few beats.

"Kids," she said.

"What makes you say that?"

"If you were a teenager growing up in Grand Marais wouldn't you want something that belonged to That Wykoff Woman? Her panties, maybe."

Oh my God.

"They stole a couple of her paintings," I said aloud.

"Oh. Never mind, then."

Geez, lady, my inner voice added. *Get out much?*

"Why would someone steal her paintings?" Peg asked. "What could they be worth?"

"Depends on who you talk to. Louise thinks they're worth a lot."

"She would, wouldn't she?"

"Don't you work for an art gallery that sells her paintings?"

"You'd be amazed what tourists buy while on vacation that they would never buy when they're at home. Are you a policeman?"

"I used to be back when I was young and impressionable."

"What are you now?"

"A friend of a friend."

"Are you trying to get them back, the paintings? Is that why you're hanging around?"

"Something like that."

"Makes sense then, you being here. I was wondering before. Louise doesn't get many visitors, you see, at least not male visitors. For a while I thought she might be gay only she doesn't have many female visitors, either."

"Who does visit her?"

"Wannabe painters I guess."

"Is she a good teacher?"

"I've never taken a class so I couldn't say. The courses she teaches—she conducts daylong, weekend-long, and even full weeklong seminars and they always seem to fill up. She gets students from all over, too. Even Duluth and Thunder Bay up in Canada. If someone broke into Louise's place, why didn't she call the sheriff's department?"

"My understanding is that she's afraid of bad publicity. 'Course, now that you know . . ."

"I'm not a gossip, McKenzie. I can keep a secret."

I bet.

"Does Louise have any enemies?" I asked aloud.

"None that I'm aware of."

"Anyone who might be jealous of her celebrity?"

"McKenzie, in a small town like this, you're a celebrity for about a month. After that you're just a woman who teaches art classes in an old church."

A flurry of activity near the entrance of the church attracted our attention. Jeffery Mehren had emerged along with Jennica and a couple other minions. Words were spoken, gestures were made, and the minions disappeared back into the church while Mehren moved to a parked SUV, climbed inside, and did nothing that I could see. A few moments later, the minions started carrying equipment out of the church. Most of it was returned to the van while the rest was moved to the intersection in front of the SUV. Jennica supervised set up while Mehren watched.

"I wonder what they're doing," Peg said.

"Getting ready to film a walk and talk, I'm guessing."

"Walk and talk?"

"You know, where characters in a movie or TV show have a conversation while walking somewhere."

"There's a name for that?"

A moment later, Louise appeared. She had changed her clothes, exchanging her skirt and sweater for jeans and a button-down shirt designed to accentuate her breasts.

"McKenzie," she said. "They told me you were here. Margaret."

"Hello, Louise," Peg said.

Louise handed me a white number ten envelope.

"We need to talk," she said.

"Yes, we do."

"I don't have much time. They'll want to start filming soon. Excuse us, Margaret."

Peg didn't budge, so Louise took my arm and led me away from her and the camera crew. Peg called to me.

"Don't forget those photographs," she said. "I'd be happy to arrange a private showing."

"I'll consider it," I said, but I didn't mean it.

When we were well out of earshot, Louise said, "What were you talking to Margaret about?"

"She told me her name was Peg."

"That's what her friends call her, I suppose."

Okay, not a friend, my inner voice said.

"I think your neighbor is a pervert," I said aloud.

"Well, the winters are pretty long up here. The envelope, McKenzie, it contains the list of students and other people who have been in my house that you asked for. It also—McKenzie, I started thinking after you left. I never actually looked to see if anything else was taken once I realized that the paintings were missing, that was so traumatizing to me. Besides, my computer, my TV, the little jewelry I have, the obvious stuff was still there. After you left, though, I searched more carefully and I discovered that the silver tea set my mother left me was also gone and so were two antique brass candlesticks that my family had brought over from the Netherlands in the 1880s. I have no idea what they're worth. I kept them in a drawer so I didn't realize that they were missing until I actually looked."

"Do you have photographs of them?"

"No, but I have photographs of paintings of them. In the envelope."

I looked.

"I use them sometimes in a class I teach about still life techniques," Louise said.

I studied the photos and announced "Good enough."

"This is great news, isn't it?"

"It gives us something to work with that we didn't have yesterday."

"No, what I mean—doesn't this confirm that the thief might not have known the paintings were there? That he just came into my house to steal whatever?"

"Possibly. We'll see."

Louise glanced over my shoulder. I followed her eyes. Jennica was waving at her. Apparently, they were ready to resume filming.

"You've kept such a low profile about your involvement in the *Scenes from an Inland Sea*, why agree to do this now?" I asked.

"Mary Ann McInnis asked me to. She and a man named Bruce Flonta had agreed to do the documentary, they might even be financing it, I don't know. They both called and asked me to participate. I told them that if I did I would tell the truth. Mary Ann told me to say whatever I wanted. 'The truth can't hurt me any more than it already has,' she said. McKenzie, these people can't know about the paintings."

"They won't hear about them from me. Louise, I wish you would have said something."

"I was afraid you wouldn't have agreed to help me if I had."

"Okay."

"Would it have made a difference?"

"Probably not."

"Perrin Stewart was right. You are a knight in shining armor."

"Stop it. You're embarrassing me."

Still, I was smiling when I said it, so . . .

FOUR

Once I returned to my Mustang, I glanced at Louise's list. She had written down about twenty names complete with addresses and phone numbers. I spent more time studying the silver tea set, though. There was a teapot, creamer, and sugar bowl with a small spoon on top of a rectangular tray with handles. They were fairly plain in appearance and whoever painted it gave the set a faintly yellow tarnish. Yet there was enough ornamentation around the handles and feet to make it easily identifiable. The brass candlesticks should also be clearly recognized, I decided.

I accessed my smartphone and surfed for the names of pawn shops in the area. I found only two. There were, however, a boatload of antiques stores located up and down the North Shore. I figured they were my best bet. I had to decide though, should I go north into Canada or south toward Duluth, checking every store along the way? The answer was easy—south—yet only because I neglected to bring my passport. There was a time when you could cross the border with just a driver's license, but an irrational fear of immigrants had changed all that. The way things were going in Washington, more and more we were headed for a strict federal ID card to be carried by every citizen at all times. Any day now I expected guys in dark trench coats to start patrolling the streets, stopping people at random and demanding "papers please" like they do in all those Nazi spy movies—for our own protection, of course.

I worked my way south, stopping to examine every antiques and collectibles store in every town along Highway 61—Lutsen, Tofte, Schroeder, Little Marais, Silver Bay, Beaver Bay, Castle Danger. It was a glorious drive and I highly recommend it if you're not in a hurry. Three and a half hours after I started I got lucky in a town called Two Harbors.

Originally, it was two separate towns located on Lake Superior, Agate Bay and Burlington, which were located on Burlington Bay. They merged and became Two Harbors at the turn of the last century and like many communities in northeastern Minnesota, it flourished while the iron ore industry did the same. When it faltered, so did the town. Still, it remained a vibrant community with several tourist attractions, a couple of nice restaurants, and three antiques stores.

One of them was called Second Hand Treasures. It wasn't much different from the other antiques stores I had already visited except that instead of an electronic ping that sounded when I opened the door, I was greeted with the tinkling of a bell. Still, no one rushed to see if I needed assistance. I had never been in an antiques store that wasn't laid-back and Nina and I had been in a lot of them.

I made my way to a desk situated in the middle of the store. There was an older man sitting behind the desk and reading a Brian Freeman thriller. I said, "Good afternoon." He waited until he finished a passage before looking up. Can't say I blame him. That Freeman is a spellbinder.

"How can I help you?" he asked.

"I'm looking for a silver tea set."

"I think I might be able to help you out." He stuffed a page marker into the book and set it down as he rose from the desk. "In fact, I got something in just this morning that you might want to take a look at."

He led me deeper into the store to a section that seemed devoted to kitchen supplies including dinnerware, silverware, glassware, serving platters, and pitchers. I saw it even before he pointed it out—teapot, creamer, and sugar bowl with a small spoon on top of a rectangular tray all with a faintly yellow tarnish. I didn't need to compare it to the photograph to know it belonged to Louise, yet I did so anyway.

"You have a picture of it?" the store owner asked. "What's going on? Oh my God, was it stolen? All the years I've been in business I've never bought anything that was stolen. That's the truth, Officer."

"I'm not a policeman."

"What are you?"

It was a question I've been asked many times. I have yet to come up with an adequate response—unlicensed private investigator, semiprofessional busybody, unabashed kibitzer, bored rich jerk. An acquaintance had recently called me a "roving troubleshooter." I liked the label very much but I sounded like an idiot saying it out loud.

"I'm doing a favor for a friend," I said. "Here."

I gave him a good look at the photograph of the brass candlesticks.

"Oh God," he said. "I have these, too."

"Show me."

He did, leading me to a section of the store that was devoted to lights and lanterns. A $135 price tag had been tied to the base of one of the candlesticks with a blue thread.

"Oh God," he said again.

"You say someone brought these in this morning?"

"Yes. He was, oh God, he was waiting for me outside the front door. It was just before ten A.M. I open at ten and he was already here."

How convenient, my inner voice said. *And considerate, too, waiting until this morning to fence his ill-gotten gains.*

"Do you know who sold them?" I asked aloud.

"Yes." He seemed happy to say it. "Yes, of course I do. At my desk."

I picked up the candlesticks and followed him there. Along the way we stopped to retrieve the silver tea set. Its price tag read $379.

He kept a metal box in a drawer. He pulled it out, set it on top of the desk, and opened it. Inside was a large collection of handwritten five-by-eight index cards, some new and some that had faded over time.

"I've always followed the rules that pawn shops are supposed to follow even though I'm not a pawn shop," he said. "Here it is."

He pulled out a card and handed it to me. It contained the name, address, and phone number of the man who had sold the tea set and candlesticks to the antiques store, including his driver's license number and physical description, as well as a complete description of the property, and the date and time of the transaction.

"I didn't know the property was stolen," the man said.

"Can I keep this?" I asked.

"Yes, but no, here."

The shop owner took the card and scanned it into his computer before returning it to his metal box. He printed the scan on an 8½-by-11 sheet of paper and gave that to me. I asked him why he didn't just write down all the transaction information into his computer instead of using an index card and he looked at me like I was kidding him.

"I guess I'm old-school," he said.

"Old-school is a good school."

"Who are you, anyway?"

I told him. He wrote it down.

"I don't want any trouble," he said.

"Neither do I."

"Can I see some ID?"

"Sure."

He transcribed that information, too. Afterward, he gestured at the tea set and candlesticks.

"Take these, too," he said. "I don't want them if they're stolen."

"Let me pay you."

"No, no . . ."

"At least let me give you what you paid for all this stuff."

He thought about it for a moment and offered me a price— $125.

Nice markup, my inner voice said.

After paying, I took the tea set and candlesticks to my Mustang and set them on the floor behind the driver's seat. Once inside the car myself, I found the list Louise Wykoff had given me and checked it against the name on the index card. David Montgomery, third from the top. Louise had indicated that he was a former art student. The address put him on the far side of Grand Marais.

It couldn't possibly be this easy, my inner voice announced.

The end to daylight savings time was still a month and a half away, yet it was already dark by the time I turned onto Eliasen Mill Road. There were no streetlights on the road, which made travel a little dicey, especially when it converted from worn pavement to packed dirt. Finding Montgomery's house, though, turned out to be an easy matter because it was lit up like a shopping mall. Every light had been turned on inside and out, including the yard and garage lights.

I had decided during the drive over there to keep my pitch

simple. Return the paintings of That Wykoff Woman and we'll forget all about this, give me an argument and I'll see you go to prison for five years. I was practicing the speech in my head when I knocked on the door. There was no answer, so I peeked through a window and promptly forgot about the speech.

I returned to the door and twisted the knob. It opened easily. I stepped inside. I was immediately assaulted by the smell of iron and copper. Or maybe it was just the smell I had expected when I saw the pool of drying blood on the floor around Montgomery's head. I based my identification mostly on the size, weight, and hair color that the proprietor of Second Hand Treasures had given me. There wasn't much else to go on.

I kept clear of the blood as I squatted next to Montgomery's body. I didn't touch him but it seemed to me that he had been dead for at least a few hours. Much of the top right side of his head was shattered. I examined the side of his head where the bullet had entered. There was a lot of searing around the hole in his temple and a deep abrasion ring, which told me that the gun had been pressed against the side of his head when it was fired.

I inspected Montgomery's left hand. The butt of a revolver was resting on the palm. However, the fingers were not wrapped around it, gripping it tightly like they would if he had suffered a cadaveric spasm. There was no gunshot residue that I could detect. A watch was wrapped around his left wrist. Typically right-handed people wear their watches on the left wrist and left-handed people wear them on the right wrist.

I began chanting, "Fuck, fuck, fuck," until I covered my mouth with my hand. It seemed so disrespectful to curse like that.

Eventually, I stood, took a couple of deep breaths and looked around as best I could without actually moving. It was not a big house, more like a cabin in the woods. There were no telltale signs of a struggle. All the drawers in the kitchen and the living room that I could see were firmly closed, although a couple of cabinet and closet doors were wide open. The place had been searched, I decided, for something fairly big.

The left side of my brain wanted to search the house myself. The right side wanted to get out of there just as fast as it could. I went with the right side.

My cell didn't work; I was out of range of the nearest tower. I had to drive back toward Grand Marais to get coverage. Along the way I reminded myself that it would be an easy matter to just keep driving. Don't even stop for Nina's donuts. If it was still open when I got there, I could pull off the highway at Betty's Pies just outside of Two Harbors instead and get her a French cherry or a five-layer chocolate pie. She liked cherries. She liked chocolate. Except—Two Harbors . . .

The proprietor of Second Hand Treasures in Two Harbors will remember you, my inner voice said. *He'll remember giving you Montgomery's name and address. The proprietors of all those other antiques stores will remember you, too. So will Louise Wykoff. And Jennica Mehren. And the neighbor, Peg Younghans.*

"Yes, they will," I said aloud.

Besides, you don't actually retire from the cops, do you? You just leave active duty, am I right?

"That's what is said about cops."

You knew you weren't going to take off.

"Dammit!"

Once I got near enough, I used an app on my smartphone to locate a low-slung red stone building on the Gunflint Trail just outside of Grand Marais. A woman in her late forties or early fifties and wearing beige khakis and a black fleece jacket with the words COOK COUNTY LAW ENFORCEMENT CENTER embroidered above her breast greeted me just inside the entrance. She had a pleasant if somewhat tired smile. It occurred to me that she must smile all day long at people who were undeserving of the energy it took and was now giving me her best effort following an eight-hour shift.

"May I help you?" she asked.

"I'm sorry."

"Sir?"

"I need to report a murder."

The smile went away.

"Sir, is this some kind of joke?" she said.

"What's your name?"

She answered as if she wasn't sure she should—"Eileen."

"Eileen, is there anyone on duty?"

The woman summoned a deputy. He was a full decade younger with an expression on his face that suggested he didn't like being disturbed just before his shift ended. His name tag read WURZER.

"All right, all right, what's all this then?" he said. I had to stifle a laugh thinking about all those Monty Python skits making fun of Scotland Yard cops I saw when I was a kid. He noticed the effort and was not amused.

"Sir, have you been drinking?" Wurzer asked.

I told him that David Montgomery was dead.

"Who?" he asked.

I did everything but draw him a picture of the crime scene. He didn't seem concerned. Eileen covered her mouth with a hand and looked away as if what I described was taking place directly in front of her.

"Sir, there are laws against filing false police reports," the deputy said.

I turned toward the woman in the fleece jacket.

"Eileen, are there any adults working here?" I asked.

"Sir?"

"Call the sheriff."

Three minutes later, Deputy Wurzer locked me inside a holding cell.

I spent the next few hours examining my life choices. Except for committing to Nina Truhler now and forever, none of them seemed particularly well thought out.

I was resting uncomfortably on a one-inch thick blue mat stretched over the top of a two-foot high concrete bed with no pillow when the door opened. I stood abruptly. My jeans slipped down and I nearly lost one of my Nikes because they had taken away my belt and shoelaces along with my watch, keys, wallet, and cell phone.

The man who entered the holding cell was old enough to be my father if my father had children in his late thirties. He was taller than me and dressed in a crisp white shirt with dark brown epaulets and a dark brown tie that matched his slacks. There was a five-pointed star above his pocket and a gold pin that spelled SHERIFF on his collar. I noticed that he didn't close the door behind him.

"Mr. McKenzie, I'm Sheriff Bill Bowland," he said. He extended his hand. I extended mine. Instead of shaking it, though, he took me by the wrist and pulled it close. After giving my hand the once-over he said, "Let me see the other." I gave him my left hand to examine.

"Those Smith and Wesson wheel guns kick out a lot of soot," Bowland said. "Your hands are nice and clean. 'Course, you could have washed before coming over."

"What bothers me is that Montgomery's hands were nice and clean, too."

"You noticed that?"

"I did."

"How come you noticed that?"

"Am I under arrest?"

"No."

"Am I a suspect?"

"Of course you are."

"Kinda puts me in a difficult position. I mean, I'd like to cooperate . . ."

"This is where most people try to talk themselves out of trouble."

"Most people are idiots. I'd rather you arrest me and read me my rights so I can call my lawyer because I have no intention of answering any questions without my lawyer present. Actually, I'm kidding. I have no intention of answering your questions whether my lawyer is present or not—if I'm a suspect."

"Spoken like a hardened criminal or an ex-cop who did eleven and a half years with the St. Paul PD before retiring to collect a multimillion dollar reward on an embezzler you tracked down."

I felt better knowing that Bowland had checked me out. 'Course, a lot of cops were angry that I accepted the reward. They say I sold my badge. It occurred to me that he might be one of them.

"I know how bad it looks," I said. "The guy I was hunting is found dead."

"An apparent suicide."

"Yeah."

"What do you think the odds are that a right-handed person would shoot himself with his left hand?" the sheriff asked.

"About the same that he would be holding the gun afterward without having a cadaveric spasm."

"You talk like you've seen this sort of thing before."

"I have seen it before, haven't you?"

"We had a killing down in Tofte about four years ago. After a holiday party, two men bumped into each other in a parking lot. Words were exchanged. One of the men was high on booze and grass. He pulled a forty-five and started shooting. Eventually, he pled guilty to second-degree murder. He's currently doing twelve and a half. Do you know when the last murder in Cook County took place before that?"

"No."

"Neither do I. That's how long it's been. I've already contacted the Bureau of Criminal Apprehension."

"Why?"

I didn't mean to say that out loud, it just kind of slipped out. The sheriff gave me a look that said I was questioning his command and that he didn't like it.

"We don't have the resources for this kind of investigation," he said.

Resources or confidence, I thought but this time was smart enough not to so say.

Don't antagonize the man while you're a guest in his holding cell, my inner voice suggested.

"It's sending a team up from its field office in Duluth, should be here in a couple of hours," the sheriff added. "You can talk to me or wait on them."

"Since I'll probably have to talk to the BCA, anyway . . ."

"My intention is to maintain the integrity of the crime scene, and you, until they arrive. You are not under arrest, McKenzie, but I'm not kicking you loose, either. According to the book I can hold you for thirty-six hours before I need to charge or release you. You can stay here or I can transfer you to the county jail. You decide where you would rather spend the rest of the evening. We have plenty of room."

"I'll stay here. You never know what kind of riffraff you might meet in jail."

"Make yourself comfortable. It's going to be a while."

"Sheriff, I'm sorry about all of this."

Bowland nodded his head like he believed me.

"I knew Dave," he said. "One of the reasons I'm handing the case off. I knew him personally. His little girl played baseball on the team I coached. He couldn't get along with his wife so they divorced, but he got along with everyone else. A nice guy."

"Like I said, I'm sorry. I really am."

Bowland stepped out of the holding cell. This time he did close the door.

FIVE

It didn't occur to me that I hadn't had anything to eat since eleven that morning until about eleven that night. I had expected the BCA to be all over me by then, only no one came to the door, no one bothered to check on me, no one asked if I was hungry.

Just think, my inner voice said, *instead of languishing in a holding cell, you could be at Nina's jazz joint, sitting at a table in the big room, drinking free liquor, and listening to Sophia Shorai singing the blues.*

"Don't remind me," I said aloud.

Funny, though, how things turned out.

Yeah, I told myself. If Louise was correct about the last time she had seen the paintings, Montgomery could have and probably would have unloaded the merchandise he'd stolen anytime during the past week, only he hadn't. Instead, he waited until this morning, one day after I had complained to Perrin Stewart that I didn't have a clue to go by.

Still, I didn't mention my confusion to the BCA when its agents dragged me out of the holding cell bright and early the next morning. Possibly it had something to do with the way the agent woke me from a fitful sleep by shouting, "Hey, you," and half dragged, half pulled me to a conference room.

I was seated at one end of a long table. There was an audio-recording device with a microphone set up in front of me and a video camera set on a tripod pointed at my face. One of the agents started both the recorder and camera before joining his partner and Sheriff Bowland at the other end of the table. The BCA agents looked as if they had pulled an all-nighter. The sheriff, on the other hand, looked refreshed, if not invigorated. The creases on his trousers and shirt were sharp enough to cut butter.

"State your name and address," an agent said.

I remained silent. That seemed to confuse him.

"I said . . ."

"Good manners is how we show respect for one another," I said.

"Are you trying to be funny?"

Apparently, Bowland thought so because he chuckled.

"McKenzie," he said. "This is Agent Larry Plakcy and Agent Patrick Krause from the Duluth field office of the Minnesota Bureau of Criminal Apprehension."

"Which is which?"

"I'm Plakcy," an agent said.

"Good morning, gentlemen. I don't suppose any of you know where a guy can get a cup of coffee. I haven't had anything to eat or drink in almost twenty hours."

"I apologize for that," Bowland said. "Cream? Sugar?"

"Black."

The sheriff left the conference room. I stared at the BCA agents.

"So, guys," I said. "Have you been to Grand Marais before?"

Neither of them responded.

"Beautiful this time of year, don't you think?"

They had no answer for that, either.

"Everyone says you should try the Angry Trout if you're hungry for fish but I recommend Dockside Fish Market right next door. Best fish and chips I've ever had outside of England. And Boston. And Clearwater Beach in Florida. It's really good."

Silence.

Sheriff Bowland returned to the room followed by Eileen, still wearing her khakis and black fleece jacket. Her clear eyes, coiffed hair, and ready smile suggested that, unlike me, she had slept in her own bed. She set a white mug in front of me.

"Thank you," I said.

"Is there anything else I can get for you?"

A couple thoughts sprang to mind, but I said, "No, thank you," just the same.

"Eileen," the sheriff said.

Eileen smiled at me and turned to leave. I took a sip of the coffee. I was surprised how good it tasted and said so as she headed for the door. Eileen stopped.

"I'm glad you like it," Eileen said. "What I do—"

"Eileen," Bowland repeated.

Eileen shrugged and left the room, carefully closing the door behind her.

"Are we ready now?" Plakcy asked. "State your name and—"

"Am I under arrest?" I asked.

"What? No."

"It feels like I'm under arrest. If I am, you should read me my rights."

Krause turned to look at the sheriff. Bowland spread his hands wide and said, "I told you."

"No, Mr. McKenzie, you are not under arrest," Plakcy said.

"So, I'm not legally obligated to answer your questions. I am in fact free to go if I wish."

"Theoretically," Krause said. His voice was low and menacing, the team's bad cop.

"Then say please."

Krause gave me one of those smiles that were meant to scare the bejesus out of a guy.

"McKenzie, you know how it works," he said. "Quit fucking around."

Sound advice, my inner voice said. *All things considered . . .*

I took another sip of coffee before speaking. "What do you want to know?"

"Start with your movements yesterday."

"I left Minneapolis at about eight thirty A.M. I arrived in Duluth at approximately ten thirty where I gassed up my car and had a Yukon Scramble at the Amazing Grace Bakery and Café—do you know it?"

"I know it," Plakcy said.

"I didn't keep my receipts but I paid with a credit card and you have my permission to check my account. I left at about eleven and drove straight to Grand Marais, without stopping, arriving at around one P.M."

I explained about encountering Jennica Mehren and the documentary film crew, meeting Peg Younghans at approximately one thirty, and chatting with Louise Wykoff before leaving on my journey along the North Shore at just before two, arriving at Second Hand Treasures in Two Harbors at five thirty and leaving there at six.

I explained what I had been doing for Louise and why in detail—never lie to the authorities my lawyer keeps telling me. 'Course, I neglected to mention that the paintings I was looking for were actually painted by Randolph McInnis and not That Wykoff Woman. Why complicate matters needlessly?

"I have the photographs Ms. Wykoff gave me in my jacket pocket and the tea set and candlesticks behind the front seat of my car."

"We'll want both," Krause said.

"Did you contact Ms. Wykoff and tell her what you had learned?" Plakcy asked.

"I haven't had the opportunity."

"She has no idea that it was Montgomery who burgled her residence, then?"

"As far as I know."

"When did you arrive at Montgomery's home?"

"It was about seven thirty, seven forty-five."

"Did you touch anything?" Krause asked.

"Front doorknob going in and out. Nothing else."

"We'll want to take your fingerprints anyway."

"They're already on file."

"That's right." Plakcy glanced at Sheriff Bowland when he added, "You were with the St. Paul Police Department."

I was glad the sheriff had told him so I didn't have to.

"I have a question," I said.

"What?"

"Did the county coroner rule that Montgomery's death was a homicide?"

"She has yet to make an official determination."

"What's keeping her?"

"The BCA does not rush to judgment. An exacting post-mortem examination will be conducted, under our supervision mind you."

I bet the coroner will love that, my inner voice said.

"As well as a thorough review of the crime scene before we make an announcement."

"Do you at least have a time of death?"

The two agents glanced at each other before Krause answered "We've been informed that the coroner had established a preliminary postmortem interval of between ten A.M. and two P.M., although that has yet to be confirmed officially."

"So, that pretty much lets me off the hook, doesn't it?"

"Theoretically." Apparently, Krause liked saying that word.

"Montgomery was in Two Harbors selling his swag at ten A.M.," I said. "That took a half hour. It's a ninety-minute drive from there to Grand Marais at the posted speed limits. Add a few more minutes to his house. What are we talking about? Noon plus ten? That should narrow the window somewhat."

"Are you telling us how to do our jobs?"

"I wouldn't dream of it." I took a big sip of coffee, rested my elbow on the table, and propped my chin in my hand before sighing, "Hmm."

"What does 'hmm' mean?"

"Yes, McKenzie," Plakcy said. "Do you have something more to say or are you just making noise?"

"I was wondering—why were all of Montgomery's lights on?"

The agents gave it a few beats before they announced, "We will, of course, investigate your movements to make sure you're telling us the truth. In the meantime, McKenzie, you're free to go."

"I suppose you're going to run to see Ms. Wykoff now," Krause said.

"I think she'd like to know what's going on."

"Fine, you do that—after we talk to her."

"Should we make a race of it, see who gets there first?"

"Should we lock you in the holding cell for another twenty-four hours?" Plakcy asked.

"Or we could arrest you for obstruction of an ongoing criminal investigation," Krause said.

"That would never hold up," I said.

"I don't care." Krause turned toward Plakcy. "Do you care?"

"Not in the slightest."

"What's it going to be, McKenzie?" Krause asked.

"Say please."

I traded Louise's stolen property and her photographs for my belongings and a receipt from Eileen. Her cheerful "Have a pleasant morning, Mr. McKenzie" was a nice bonus. It occurred to me as I headed for the door that she smiled more than anyone I had ever seen who worked inside a police department.

Don't ever change, Eileen, my inner voice said.

Sheriff Bowland decided to walk me to my car. As we were leaving, we bumped into Deputy Wurzer.

"What the hell are you doing?" he asked. "You're not letting him go?"

"No reason to hold him," Bowland said.

"I don't believe this. Give me twenty minutes alone with the sonuvabitch, Sheriff. I'll give you plenty of reason."

Bowland stared at the man for a few beats, not out of anger but surprise, as if he couldn't believe what he was hearing.

"I don't much like that kind of talk, Peter," he said.

"This asshole probably zeroed Montgomery."

"There's no evidence to support that allegation."

The deputy shook his head like a poor teacher who was unable to get through to a dull child, although in this case the student—it was difficult to determine the sheriff's exact age. Studying his face in the bright morning sun made me wonder if Cook County had a mandatory retirement age.

"We did things differently where I came from," the deputy said before throwing up his hands in disgust and walking into the Law Enforcement Center.

"Where did he come from?" I asked.

"Minneapolis."

"That hellhole?"

"It's a long story."

"I bet."

"The BCA and Wurzer—my advice, McKenzie, is to stay away from them both. Stay away from Ms. Wykoff, too, at least until the BCA and I have a chance to interview her."

"Why? Do you think the boys would make good on their threat?"

"Of course they would."

"What about you?"

"Despite what they say in the movies and on TV, a sheriff doesn't have the legal authority to tell someone not to leave town, but McKenzie—don't leave town. Not just yet, anyway."

"I don't know, Sheriff. I think I've already outstayed my welcome."

"I'm relying heavily on the BCA, but it's still my investigation. I'll be asking a lot of questions on my own, including a few more of you."

"Such as?"

"Why *were* Montgomery's lights on?"

"Grand Marais is crawling with tourists. I doubt I can find a room."

"There's a motel out on the highway called the Frontier. I'll give them a call. They should be able to help you out."

"The BCA won't like it, me hanging around."

"Do you care?"

"Not particularly. You should know, though, if I stay, I'm likely to make a nuisance of myself. It's in my nature."

"I'm kinda counting on it."

The owners of the Frontier Motel across the highway from Lake Superior were waiting for me when I arrived. They said they were happy to help a friend of the sheriff. It made me wonder what rowdiness had occurred in their place that Bowland had helped them with.

The motel was shaped like a horseshoe with all of the rooms facing the great lake. Mine was right of center and small, with hardwood floors, walls, and ceiling. I tossed my bag on top of a queen-size bed that took up more than half the space. The remainder was occupied by a small table with two chairs in front of the lone window and an even smaller bureau with a sixteen-inch flat-screen analog TV that picked up five channels. The room was clearly designed for hunters, cross-country skiers, and hikers, people who had no intention of spending a lot of time inside.

There was a two-cup coffeemaker on a small shelf built into the corner. I set it to brew before using the tiny bathroom to shave and shower. I poured one of the cups and drank it while I dressed. The second cup I took with me to the resort chairs arranged in a semicircle in the center of the horseshoe. I sat there and gazed out at the lake.

I decided I liked the bare-bones charm of the motel very much. 'Course, before I met Nina I ate most of my meals off paper plates. I checked my cell phone and was astonished to find that I had bars—*Good for the Frontier,* my inner voice said. I called Nina hoping to catch her at home before she went to Rickie's.

"Hey, you," she said. "I was starting to worry. I thought I'd hear from you last night."

"Things got a little complicated. I'd explain, but you know how much I hate to bore you."

"In other words something nefarious is going on and you don't want to worry me."

"There's nothing to worry about, seriously. I just hate to start telling a story without knowing how it ends. Maybe by tonight I'll have it figured out. How was Sophia Shorai?"

"She was very, very good. She did a cover of 'One for My Baby (and One More for the Road)', but she didn't sing it the way everyone else does, making it a requiem to lost love. She wasn't sad that she lost the boy, she was angry."

"I'm sorry I missed it."

"I'm going to bring her back the first chance I get. Which raises the question—when are you coming back?"

"I don't know. The sheriff told me not to leave town."

"Can he do that?"

"Technically no, but he was so nice about it. Listen, I've been living on coffee for the past twenty-four hours, so . . ."

"Call me tonight?"

"I will."

"Promise?"

"I promise."

"I've heard that before."

Twenty minutes later I was ordering fresh herring, hash browns, eggs, and toast at the South of the Border Cafe. Twenty minutes after that I drove to Louise Wykoff's art academy. If that wasn't enough of a head start for the BCA then too damn bad. Once again I had to park up the street because the academy was surrounded by vehicles including the documentary company's white van.

Before I got halfway to the church, Peg Younghans rushed out of her own house as if she had been waiting for me. She crossed the street and intercepted me on the sidewalk. This time she was wearing a dress, sweater, and heels that made her appear very proper indeed.

"Going to church?" I asked.

"To work in a few minutes. Must look nice for the tourists. McKenzie, did you hear what happened?"

"No, what happened?"

"David Montgomery was killed last night."

"I don't know who that is."

You are the best liar, my inner voice said.

"The sheriff was here this morning," Peg said. "Agents from the Bureau of Criminal Apprehension, too. They think Louise killed him."

"How do you know all this?"

"They have to eat, don't they? At the Blue Water Cafe. They were overheard talking while eating breakfast."

"Who heard them?"

"You don't think I have friends? You don't think they talk to me?"

"What did they say?"

"My friends?"

"The BCA."

"Someone found David's body in his house last night. It looked like he committed suicide, but the agents don't think so. They think he was murdered and the killer tried to make it look like he committed suicide."

"What does that have to do with Louise?"

"I don't know, but they were over here talking to her bright and early, so—something."

She doesn't know that you're involved and she has no pertinent details. Good.

"Just because they spoke to her, that doesn't mean anything," I said. "This guy . . ."

"Dave Montgomery."

"Were he and Louise friends?"

"I don't know if 'friends' is the right word."

"What is the right word?"

"Actually, 'friends' might be the right word after all, friends with benefits."

"You told me yesterday that Louise didn't have any male visitors."

"I said she didn't have *many* male visitors. She's not a cloistered nun, for God's sake."

"How often did you see him here?"

"I couldn't say. Once, twice a month."

"Could he have been one of Louise's art students?"

"I wouldn't think so."

"Still, you don't know for a fact that he and Louise were intimate."

"He was a good-looking boy and divorced in a place where there aren't many good-looking girls who are equally unencumbered. Besides, sometimes I'd get up early in the morning and his car would still be parked in front of her place."

I remembered the description of Montgomery that the owner of Second Hand Treasures had given me.

"Wasn't he about thirty years younger than Louise?"

Peg shook her head like I had insulted her. She set her hand on my wrist.

"McKenzie," she said. "Please."

"How well did you know him?"

"Not very. Just enough to nod and say hello to. I have the

same relationship with just about everyone else in town. At least those that stay here year-round."

"Do you know who his friends were?"

"No." Peg had kept her hand on my wrist, but now she moved it to my hand. "You're not wearing a wedding ring."

"I'm not married."

"Interesting."

I came *this*close to telling her about Nina. I didn't because I decided Peg might be more talkative if she thought I was available.

"I notice that you're not wearing a wedding ring, either," I said.

"I found it cumbersome, even when I was married. You're what? Forty-five?"

"Somewhere in there. You?"

"Old enough to know better, young enough not to care."

"A good age to be."

She let her fingers dance across mine.

Careful, my inner voice said.

"When did the documentary crew get here?" I asked.

"Same time as yesterday."

"Were they loud?"

"Very. I thought they had finished last night, but—you were right about that walking and talking thing. What they did, the director pretended to surprise Louise at her front door and then they walked down the street toward the lake. They did this a half-dozen times before they called it a day and packed up. That was right before sundown. I thought documentaries were supposed to be like TV news. Spontaneous. Or at least unrehearsed."

"What happened then?"

"What do you mean?"

"With Louise."

"I don't know. Went back into the church, I guess. It's not like I spy on her, watch her every movement."

"I need to talk to Louise," I said.

"Right this minute?"

"Before I forget why I came."

"Can't have that."

I gave her my best I'll-see-you-soon smile and moved toward the converted church.

"You remember where I live, right?" Peg said.

I spun toward her as I continued to walk away, smiled, and spun back.

You are such a slut, my inner voice said.

Yes, it was me I was talking to.

I slid inside the doorway without knocking and bumped into Jennica Mehren. She turned and glared at me with such fury that I nearly gasped. She quickly pressed her index finger against her lips, the universal signal for "shut the hell up," and gestured at the interior of the church. There were a half-dozen people inside including her old man, as silent and unmoving as stone even as they directed their cameras, lights, and microphones. Louise Wykoff was sitting on her stool, leaning forward, and gripping the seat with both hands to keep from sliding off. She was wearing a thin black lace dress, bare legs, and no shoes and looked as lovely as she did in one of Randolph McInnis's paintings of her. She was weeping as she choked out the words.

"He was everything to me," Louise said. "Every day that he was gone was empty. I would pray, 'Come back. Please, please come back to me.' And then he would for a few days, or a week or longer, and I'd be so happy that my heart felt like it would burst until he left again. I knew it wouldn't last, couldn't possibly last, yet it did for five wonderful years. Then the accident—a stupid, silly way for a great man to die. I've had good days and bad, thirty-five years of them, but I don't think I've ever been truly happy since before that day.

"Now this. The last thing I had of him taken from me. Stolen. I don't think I've gone more than a few weeks at a time without looking at those paintings and remembering. The hole in my heart now is so great it would have been more merciful if the thieves had killed me. No, no, that's not true. If I was gone, there would be no one left to tell his story, no one who actually knew his story instead of the myth that grew up around *Scenes from an Inland Sea*. The myth that Mary Ann helped create."

His voice had such a low sonorous quality that at first I couldn't tell where it came from. I saw him, finally, standing between two cameras.

"Are you ready to tell the story at last?" Jeffery Mehren asked.

The way I had glanced about must have caught Louise's attention because she was now staring directly at me when she spoke.

"Yes, at last."

She slipped off her stool and started toward me.

"Cut," Mehren said. "Louise, please."

"I must speak to this man. I must find out about my paintings."

The entire company turned to look at me, including Jennica. I nearly gasped again.

The BCA isn't going to like this at all, my inner voice said.

SIX

Louise's apartment above the art academy reminded me of my own place. It was divided into areas—kitchen area, living area, bedroom area. There were large windows with a spectacular view of downtown Grand Marais and the great lake beyond.

"This is where I kept the paintings," she said.

She gestured at a spot against the wall inside a large walk-in closet, the only room with a door besides the bathroom.

"Describe them to me," I said.

She did, telling me that the first painting was nearly all white. Footprints in deep snow in the foreground led to a solitary figure in black, her back to the artist, who was trudging toward Eagle Mountain, the highest point in Minnesota.

"Randolph called it *The Climber*," she said.

The second was painted in the Village of Ontonagon in the Upper Peninsula of Michigan. A naked Louise stood with her back to the artist and leaning against a door frame. Featured within the frame was Ontonagon Lighthouse, built where the Ontonagon River flowed into the great lake.

"I was never sure what Randolph was trying to say with this painting; I'm not sure he knew himself," Louise said. "I liked it very much, though. He called it *Superficial Light*."

The third painting was called *Awake*—Louise had difficulty telling me about it. It showed her lying nude on the far side of a bed, a sheet covering only her legs. The near side was empty, yet the sheets were ruffled and the pillow was dented.

"You were supposed to wonder if the absent lover had just left the subject or if she was waiting for him to come to her."

She called herself the subject, my inner voice reminded me.

"It was Randolph's last painting," Louise said. "I didn't know that, though. I thought it would be his last painting of me."

"How big are they?" I asked.

Louise laughed.

"What's so funny?"

"I don't know. It just seemed an odd question given . . . The first two are the same size—twenty-three-by-thirty inches. *Awake* is forty-four-by-thirty-five inches."

"Not something you can stuff in your pocket."

"Hardly."

"Or a kitchen drawer. Louise, after thirty-five years of keeping them secret, why would you tell the world that these paintings exist now?"

"I didn't mean to. It just kind of slipped out when the sheriff and those BCA agents were questioning me. The one, I think his name was Krause, he frightened me."

"He meant to."

"He kept saying that a silver teapot and brass candlesticks wasn't reason enough to kill someone. My cheap paintings, either. He called them cheap. That's when I said—when I told him that they weren't my paintings. That they were—they're gone, aren't they? Really gone?"

"Yes."

"They weren't inside Montgomery's house?"

"I didn't spend much time there, but I had the impression that the place had been searched before I arrived."

"By who?"

"By whoever knew he had the paintings. An accomplice, per-haps."

"I don't know what to do."

Louise found a corner of the bed to sit on, her hands folded in her lap, her head bowed as if she was lost in prayer and I thought, Damn she's a pretty woman. As pretty as a picture. Most beauty fades upon close examination. Suddenly we see the flaws, the nicks and scratches and blemishes of life. Over time, if we take the time, it's the flaws that we come to appre-ciate most. They're what give beauty its character. Yet That Wykoff Woman had none of these. She remained flawless, even at her age. It made me a little uncomfortable, although I couldn't tell you why.

Her head came up.

"Will you still help me?" she asked.

"Yes, except the paintings will be much harder to find now. There's also the chance that the thief will freak out over all the media coverage and dump them somewhere. Burn them."

"No. Please no . . . But—why does there need to be media coverage?"

"First, you told the Cook County Sheriff and the BCA. That makes it public record. Then you confessed on film in front of a half-dozen members of a documentary crew. Jeffery Mehren is downstairs right now thinking this is the best thing that's hap-pened to him since he won the Oscar."

"They're the only ones who know about Randolph's paint-ings and they won't say anything."

"Are you sure of that?"

"The sheriff, the Bureau of Criminal Apprehension, they won't tell anyone until they're ready to make an arrest . . ."

"Which could come any day now."

"Mehren won't want it to get out, either. Not until his film is finished."

"You watch the news. These things have a way of blow-ing up."

"You'll keep looking, though—won't you?"

"I said I would, only I'm not sure there's much more that I can do. Besides, the BCA is on the case and despite my personal misgivings, they're very, very good at their job. It's what?" I glanced at my watch. "Eleven A.M. Saturday? By this time tomorrow they're going to know everything there is to know about Montgomery. They've probably already requested a subpoena for his phone records. They'll use the cell's GPS to track all of his movements since the beginning of time. Which raises a question—how close were you and Montgomery?"

"Not close at all. He was one of my students."

"Peg Younghans said you were sleeping with him."

Louise came off the bed in a hurry.

"That's not true. That's never been true. Montgomery was divorced, but he wanted to remain close to his daughter so he signed them both up for one of my summer art classes. It was something they could do together."

"Why would he rob you?"

"I don't know."

"Was he hard up financially?"

"I don't know. How would I know?"

"Why would he wait until Friday morning to sell the things he stole?"

"I don't know that, either. Maybe it was the first chance he had."

"What did he do for a living?"

"I don't know. McKenzie, please."

"It bothers me that I was able to identify Montgomery so easily. It's almost as if he wanted me to find him."

"I guess he wasn't a very good criminal."

"Like everything else, it takes practice. Louise, our current problem—whoever killed Montgomery probably has the paintings."

"What will he do with them?"

"Try to sell them, of course. Hmm."

"What?"

"Montgomery would have tried to sell them, too."

Jeffery Mehren had been waiting impatiently at the bottom of the stairs. When he saw me coming down from Louise's apartment he grinned like a kid who had been offered ice cream on a hot day.

"McKenzie," he said. "Did I get the name right? It's Mc-Kenzie?"

"Yes."

"Jennica tells me you're a friend of Louise."

"Also true."

"You're searching for the missing *Scenes from an Inland Sea* for Louise, aren't you?"

"I don't know what gave you that impression."

"Louise's behavior."

"Louise made a mistake, I think, by announcing publicly what has happened. It could make locating the paintings more difficult."

"Then you are looking for them. I would like to be there when you find them. In fact, I'd like to send a crew to film you while you search for them."

"First off, no. Second, hell no. Besides, I've already been warned by the BCA not to interfere in an active criminal investigation. A major art crime like this, I expect the FBI will become involved and they won't like it either, so . . ."

You're giving up way too much information and getting nothing in return, my inner voice said. *Change the subject.*

"I've enjoyed your work, by the way," I said. "*We Gotta Get Out of This Place*, of course, but your other stuff, too. *The Poison in Our Water* I thought was very good, very timely."

"Thank you. I wish the critics agreed."

Since I hadn't actually seen it, or the Vietnam documentary

(68)

for that matter, I tried to sound both knowledgable and innocuous at the same time.

"As fracking becomes a bigger issue, your film will become more important," I said. "Isn't that how it works? The documentarian who's ahead of his time?"

"That's one way of looking at it."

"I'm curious—what made you decide to make a film about *Scenes from an Inland Sea?*"

"Bruce Flonta contacted me . . ."

"The man who bought the collection after Randolph McInnis died."

"Yes. He wanted to do something for the thirty-fifth anniversary of the collection. He's financing the shoot."

"Why? I thought Flonta sold all the paintings to individual collectors and museums."

"He still has a few. My understanding, he also retained the copyrights of all the paintings and drawings that he did sell, which gives him at least a percentage of the profits on any reproductions or exhibits. Capitalism at work."

"I'm surprised that you would agree to make the film, a director of your stature."

Mehren was clearly pleased by my fawning.

"The industry has changed dramatically in the past decade or so," he said. "If you want financing, you need an agenda. There are plenty of individuals, foundations, even corporations that are willing to pay to produce a social documentary, something that promotes or refutes a cause that's important to them. Unfortunately, there's very little interest in funding documentaries that won't necessarily have a significant social impact, what we used to call an art documentary. I appreciate that this particular film was meant to be little more than a commercial for Randolph McInnis's art which Mr. Flonta would profit from. That's all right with me, though. I thought it might be fun. Now, however . . ."

Mehren rubbed his hands together and again I thought of the kid and his ice cream.

"Discovery of three long-lost McInnis paintings—this is an astounding find," he said. "What might have been a fifty-four minute film that we would sell to PBS or Netflix is now going to be a full-length movie that we can take to the festivals, that might get a national release. Especially, if those paintings can be recovered in a timely manner."

"When did you learn about the paintings?"

"Just a couple of hours ago. We returned to the academy at seven this morning and were preparing for a second day of shooting when the sheriff and agents from the bureau—what do you call it?"

"Minnesota Bureau of Criminal Apprehension."

"In California, we call it the Bureau of Investigation. Anyway, they didn't want us listening in when they interviewed Louise. They all but threatened to arrest the entire crew if we didn't 'depart the premises at once' one of them said. Afterward, though, I spoke with Louise. That was probably rude of me because she was clearly distraught. She told me everything, though. She even told me about you. Then she agreed to repeat it all on film. You're some sort of private investigator, is that correct? She hired you to recover the stolen artwork?"

"Like I said, I'm not sure I'll keep looking for the paintings now that the authorities are involved. If I do, though, it won't be in front of a film crew."

"Not an entire crew. Just my daughter and a handheld camera."

"No."

"McKenzie . . ."

"I will not be in your film."

"You might not have a choice."

"Don't you need me to sign a release?"

"If you're a public figure . . ."

"Which I'm not."

"Except, have you ever heard the phrase 'involuntary public figure'? It refers to a person whose behavior and actions result in publicity even though the person did not want or invite public attention."

"C'mon."

"Don't blame me. Blame the United States Supreme Court."

"Another reason to just go home."

Mehren smiled.

"I already know where you live," he said.

The proprietor of Second Hand Treasures caught sight of me as I walked through the door, the bell tinkling overhead. He frowned, looked away, and looked back as if he was hoping I was a mirage that would quickly disappear.

"Please," he said.

The store was filled with tourists looking to buy so I assumed he was imploring me not to make a scene.

A scene for the Scenes. I winced at the words. Sometimes my inner voice says the damnedest things.

"Good afternoon," I said.

The proprietor glanced quickly around him to make sure no one could hear before leaning in.

"I don't need to talk to you," he said. "I don't need to answer any questions. You're not the sheriff."

"That's true. The sheriff should be arriving anytime now, though. Think of it as practice."

"Why should the sheriff—"

He was interrupted by a customer, and then another, and then another. The latter was a senior who purchased a rocking chair that was at least fifty years older than she was. She asked the proprietor to load it into the back of her SUV. I helped. Afterward, we stood outside the front door.

"I'm not trying to jam you up, pal," I said. "I just wanted to ask a few more questions about the man who sold you the silver tea set. I should have asked yesterday only I didn't think of it then."

"What?"

"Did Montgomery try to sell some paintings as well?"

"Paintings? No."

"Are you sure?"

"Pretty sure. He asked, but he didn't. What I mean, after we were done with the tea set and the candlesticks, he asked if I knew anything about paintings, what they're worth. I get it all the time, people coming in believing that the painting that's been hanging in Grandma's living room for fifty years is valuable, at least that's what Grandma told them. They figure it'll be like on *Antiques Roadshow*, that it'll turn out of be painted by some French guy and worth $300,000 or something. What they find out, what I tell them is nearly always the frame is more valuable than the picture in the frame. I told Montgomery to look around the shop. I don't sell paintings. Antique picture frames, now that's a different matter. There's a nice market for that. I said I'd love to take a look at his frames. Only he said he didn't have any frames."

"He never said he had paintings for sale, though?"

"No, he never said that. Just asked about 'em. Why? This guy we're talking about, did he steal some paintings, too?"

Before I could answer, a vehicle drove to the curb in front of the antiques store, the driver halting in a manner that invited a parking ticket. The passenger powered down his window and peered out.

"Don't move," Agent Krause said.

"Are they from the sheriff?" the proprietor asked.

"Worse. The Bureau of Criminal Apprehension."

"I didn't do anything wrong."

"Don't worry. They're more pissed off at me than they are at you."

The agents exited their vehicle and approached like they

thought I might make a run for it and wanted to be sure they could cut off my escape route.

"You should wait inside," I told the proprietor.

He took my advice.

"You've been holding out on us," Plakcy said.

"I have no idea what you're talking about."

"We've interviewed Louise Wykoff."

"So I heard."

"Well?"

"Well what?"

"What do you have to say for yourself?" Krause asked.

"Again, I don't know what you're talking about."

"You deliberately withheld information about those paintings," Plakcy said.

"I told you that Louise Wykoff asked me to recover three paintings that had been stolen from her."

"You didn't tell us that they were painted by Randolph McInnis."

"Oh. That."

"Oh that," Krause said. "We should bust your ass right now."

"Yeah, but then I'd lawyer up and you'd never know what I've learned since we last spoke."

"What have you learned, McKenzie?" Plakcy asked.

"According to the owner of this store, Montgomery asked him if he sold paintings and the owner said no."

"So what? We could learn that ourselves."

"Wait a sec," Krause said. "McKenzie, what does this tell you?"

"Montgomery still had the paintings when he came here yesterday, only he didn't know what to do with them. The tea set and candlesticks he stole, yeah, he knew how to unload those. The paintings? I'm guessing he recognized their value, that's why he grabbed them up. Once he had them, though, he had no idea how to sell them. He didn't have a plan. Now I know you two have never faced this dilemma, but most people when they're confused, what do they do?"

"They ask for advice," Plakcy said.

"Possibly from someone who did have a plan," Krause said.

"I'll see you guys around."

I left the front of the store and moved toward my Mustang. Krause called out to me. I turned to look at him. He held his hand so there was about an inch between his thumb and index finger.

"McKenzie," he said, "you're that far away from real trouble."

I nodded and continued walking to my car.

Hell, that's nothing, my inner voice said. *Wait until it's only a quarter inch. That's when you should worry.*

I pulled away from my parking spot and drove slow enough up Seventh Street for the driver of the Ford Taurus to catch me. When I hit Seventh Avenue, which was also Highway 61, I hung a left, and headed toward Duluth, the opposite direction from Grand Marais. The Taurus followed, probably wondering where I was going, crowding way too close to my rear bumper for it to be inconspicuous.

I'd like to say that I knew it had been tailing me since I left Grand Marais, only I'd be lying. The truth was, I hadn't even noticed the car until I was helping the proprietor load the old lady's rocking chair into the back of her SUV. Even then I probably would have been oblivious if the driver hadn't ducked down, the quick movement catching my eye. My ego claimed it was because the driver was very good at conducting a rolling surveillance. Now that I had the Taurus squarely in my rear-view mirror, though, I realized it was because of my own carelessness.

I followed Highway 61 until I reached the Great! Lakes Candy Kitchen where Nina and I usually stopped when we drove north. I pulled into the narrow parking lot. The tail kept following, parking at the far end of the lot where I wasn't supposed to notice.

I stepped inside the small store and waited behind a half-dozen other customers before buying several small bags of goodies. Afterward, I slipped outside, moved along the edge of the porch in the opposite direction of the Taurus, circled the lot, and came up on the car's blind side. I tapped on the window. I startled Jennica Mehren enough that her head bounced off the ceiling.

She rolled down the window.

"McKenzie," she said.

"Hey, sweetie. I have bags of salty caramel pretzels, peanut clusters, black licorice, assorted truffles, and B-O—N-O—M-O—oh, oh, oh, it's Bonomo—Turkish Taffy."

"Seriously?"

"That was the company's jingle from when I was a kid."

"I'll take the licorice."

"Good choice." I gave her the small bag. "I thought you'd stay with the BCA."

"Dad says you're the story. He said I shouldn't let you out of my sight."

"He's not a take-no-for-an-answer kind of guy, is he?"

"You don't win an Oscar doing that."

"I suppose not. Here's the thing—when there's only one main road like Highway 61 going back to Grand Marais, it wouldn't be all that unexpected for a car to follow behind me for many miles at a time. It wouldn't be something that would make me anxious. At the same time, you don't want to do anything that would draw attention to yourself. My advice—stay at least seven to ten car lengths behind. If a couple of cars slide in between you and me, that would even be better. Remember, you don't have to stay close. I won't be making any abrupt turns. When I do leave the highway, you'll see me signaling far in advance."

"I'll keep it in mind."

"Atta girl."

"I'm embarrassed by all this."

"Why? Because you're following me or because you got caught?"

"It wasn't my idea, I want you to know."

"That's why I'm not upset with you. Your ol' man, on the other hand . . ."

I waved a finger—no, not that one—and moved back to the Mustang while telling myself that Jennica must think I'm really clever.

If only that were true.

I fired up my car, pulled out of the lot, and headed away from Duluth back toward Grand Marais. Jennica followed again, this time doing exactly what I had told her.

"We learn as we go," I said.

SEVEN

I had just finished off the peanut clusters by the time I saw the sign *GRAND MARAIS* • *TOWN CENTER* • *ARTIST POINT* • *BOAT LAUNCH*. I had a lot of time to think while driving toward it. I decided that Montgomery must have known his killer to let him get that close without a struggle. Which meant he was probably from around there. The only way to get a line on him—*Or her,* my inner voice said, *let's not be sexist*—was to speak with Montgomery's family and friends. Unfortunately, the only people I was acquainted with who could introduce me were Louise and Peg Younghans and both women had claimed that they barely knew the man. So, I did the next best thing. I drove to a bar.

Mark's Wheel-Inn catered to the people who actually lived in Grand Marais. You could tell because its prices were reasonable and because it was located up the hill several blocks from the harbor, which meant it might as well be on the moon as far as most tourists were concerned. What's more, it stayed open year-round instead of closing in late October and reopening again in early April like most of its competitors. Nina and I had discovered it the last time we were on the North Shore.

I was surprised by how many cars were in the parking lot until I realized that it was Saturday afternoon during college football season with happy hour prices for beer, wine, rail drinks, chicken wings, and nachos. I stepped inside. The TVs were tuned to the Minnesota Gophers-Wisconsin Badgers football game, although no one seemed to be paying much attention to it. I made my way to the bar. Some of the locals glanced my way but didn't say anything. A moment later they glanced at Jennica Mehren, who had followed me. This time several comments were made, only I didn't hear what was said.

The bartender closed in on my position. He set a coaster down and nodded for me to speak.

"You could get in trouble serving underage drinkers even way up here, right?" I said.

He stared for a few beats as if he was trying to translate what I had told him. His eyes found Jennica who was now positioned a couple of steps off my shoulder.

"Miss," the bartender said, "do you have some ID?"

"What?"

"The drinking age in Minnesota is twenty-one."

Jennica glared at me.

"It's the same in California," she said.

"Do you have an ID?" The bartender repeated.

Jennica's answer was to spin on her heels and stomp out of the bar.

There were a couple of locals sitting at a table within earshot.

"Hey, man," the short one said. "Whaddaya doin' runnin' girls off like that? They could become scarce someday."

"What are you talking about, scarce?" the tall one said. "We're the endangered species 'round here, us men. My wife told me just last night that if we couldn't shovel snow or open jars there'd be a bounty on us."

"Yeah, yeah, yeah," the bartender said. "The way things are goin' lately, I'm surprised women don't chase us down with torches and pitchforks like in them old-time monster movies."

"It's not like we ain't got it comin'," the short man said. "All them stories about sexual harassment and rape and shit—I had no idea. Bill Cosby, really? I grew up watchin' Bill Cosby. America's Dad. Hell, I liked 'im better than my dad. Geezus. And how many since him? I can't even count."

"That guy, that doctor what abused all them gymnasts for like years and years," the taller man said.

"I've never done any of that," the bartender said. "I don't know anyone who has."

"Wasn't it you who was complaining when they started lettin' women announce football and baseball games?"

"That's not the same thing."

"Yeah, it is. Well, it ain't rape, but it is discrimination. Don't you think?"

The shorter man was looking at me when he asked the question, so I provided an answer I hoped wouldn't annoy anyone. After all I was there to make friends.

"It's a new world," I said. "We best get used to it."

The bartender nodded as if he agreed with me.

The taller man raised his glass.

"A toast," he said. "May we all get what we want, but not what we deserve."

"Here, here."

"Gentlemen," I said, "let me buy you a beer."

The bartender served the beers and returned to his place behind the stick. I remained leaning against the bar; my two new friends stayed at their table. We started chatting. No one seemed to mind at all that I was from somewhere else, not even when I said, "I hear there's some excitement in town."

"You talking about the killing?" short man said.

"Dave Montgomery, talk about your sexual harassment," the taller man said.

"He never harassed anyone I ever heard of."

"Not harassed, but he got around."

"That's not the same thing, is it?"

"Have they even decided if it was murder or suicide?" the bartender asked. "I haven't heard."

"I've known Montgomery for a long time," the tall man said. "He wasn't someone who'd shoot himself."

"That's what they say about everyone until they do it," the short man said.

"What is Sheriff Bowland doin' about it is what I want to know," the bartender said.

"That doddering old man?"

"Doddering?" I asked.

"Man's been sheriff since the eighties, but what's he ever done 'cept hassle the high school kids he catches drinkin' in the woods?"

"I heard he brought in the BCA t' take the pressure off hisself," the bartender said.

"Let them take the blame if it all goes to shit," the taller man said. "He's a politician after all."

"I know a little something about how this works," I said. "The first thing they'll do, the sheriff or the BCA, is talk to Montgomery's wife. And then his girlfriends. And then the boyfriends of his girlfriends."

"Good luck with that," the tall man said.

"What do you mean?"

"Like I said—Montgomery got around. I bet he banged half the single women in Cook County."

"Just single women?"

"Well, he wasn't an idiot. There are things you can get away with in the big city that you can't up here. Everyone's got a gun up here."

"You make it sound like Texas or somethin', guys carrying their AR-15s into the local Walmart," the shorter man said. He was looking at me when he added, "It ain't Texas."

"Fuck Texas," the bartender said.

"Have you ever been?"

"Well, no."

"I was in San Antonio once," I said. "Great barbecue. Can't say I saw anyone walking around with an AR."

"Just telling you what I heard."

"So, Montgomery was only involved with single women?"

"Far as I know," the tall man said. "You got the librarian . . ."

"Miss Greyson?" the short man said.

"Yep."

"No kidding?"

"You got Gillian Davis over at the Gunflint Tavern."

"I knew about her."

"Leah Huddleston at the art gallery . . ."

"Which gallery?" I asked.

"Up on Highway 61 near the Dairy Queen. Why?"

"Just curious."

"What about Ardina Curtis over at the casino?" the bartender asked.

"Montgomery was seeing an Ojibwa chick?" the short man asked.

"Yeah, and from what I heard, the brother was not happy about it."

"I'm the BCA and I think Montgomery was killed, the brother is the first guy I talk to," the tall man said.

"Why?" I asked.

"Man has a temper and those Ojibwa, they think you've been trifling with their woman, they take that seriously."

"You think it's a racial thing?"

"Don't know 'bout that. More like a family honor thing."

"What about Louise Wykoff and Peg Younghans?"

"What about 'em?"

"Could Montgomery have been involved with either of them?"

"Nah," the shorter man said.

"I don't know," the bartender said. "Montgomery didn't mind 'em being older, the women he fucked."

"Yeah, okay, but the Wykoff woman? I just can't see it."

"Me, neither," said the taller man. "She's always been so damn proper. Is that the right word, 'proper'?"

"Good as any," I said.

"As for Peggy, she talks a good game yet mostly it's just a tease."

"Remember the reception the Art Colony held back in July right before the art festival began?" the bartender said. "Peg was flirting up a storm; maybe she had too much to drink, I don't know. Anyway, I started flirting back. Woman suffered a full-blown anxiety attack. I'm not exaggerating."

"Sure it wasn't just you comin' on to her?" the short man said. "Fuckin' stop my heart."

"Hardy har har. You"—the bartender was speaking to me—"why you asking about Younghans and Wykoff?"

"Cuz they're the only women in Grand Marais that I've met. How 'bout another beer? Can you guys stand another round?"

"If you're buyin' we're drinkin'," the short man said.

While the bartender took care of us, I said, "After the BCA talks to his girlfriends, they'll talk to his boys. Who'd Montgomery hang out with?"

"I don't know he was tight with anyone since Wayne," the short man said.

"What happened with Wayne?"

"Wayne was Montgomery's best friend going back to grade school . . ."

Not unlike you and Bobby Dunston, my inner voice reminded me.

"Until he caught him in bed with his wife."

Not like you and Bobby Dunston.

"Montgomery screwing everything in sight is not a new phenomenon," the taller man said. "He's been rovin' since God knows when. Jodine put up with it how many years? Then she decided what's good for the goose is good for the gander, am I right?"

"Yeah, but Wayne?" the short man said. "That was pretty rough."

"I think it was meant to be."

"Where's Jodine now?" I asked. "Is she still in town?"

"Nah. Moved to Duluth with the daughter. I heard she's working for the Duluth Art Institute."

"Is that right," the bartender said. "Good for her. She was always one of those artsy types."

"Place is crawlin' with artsy types," the tall man said.

"Only during the summer. Come winter, most are gone, gone, gone."

"Except for Louise Wykoff."

"Except for her."

"What about Wayne?" I asked.

"You mean after he got out of the hospital?" the bartender said.

"He was in the hospital?"

"What can I say?" the taller man said. "Montgomery was a hot-headed fellow."

"Last I heard Wayne moved to Eveleth," the shorter man said.

"What's he doin' in Eveleth?"

"Got a job workin' in the new mine they opened near there. We'll see how long that lasts." The shorter man was looking at me again when he said, "Mining iron ore has always been an up-and-down thing."

"Still," I said, "he sounds like a suspect to me."

"Whaddya know about it?" the bartender asked.

"Like I said, the cops start looking for suspects close to home and then slowly spread out. Think of it like ripples on a pond. This Wayne, you say Montgomery put him in the hospital?"

"That was over four years ago," the taller man said. "Four years since the divorce."

"Some people have been known to hold a grudge."

"That would bother me, if Wayne killed Montgomery, friends the way they were."

"Did Montgomery have any other enemies?"

"I don't know. I don't think so."

"You're asking a lot of questions about people you've never met," the bartender said. "What's that about?"

"Yeah," said the taller man. "You a cop?"

"God no, but let's say that I've had dealings with the police in the past and let it go at that."

"Hell no, I ain't gonna let it go," said the bartender. "Who are you?"

"Just a tourist killing time while my Golden Gophers"—I glanced up at the TV screen—"lose to Wisconsin."

The taller man's head jerked up at the screen.

"How the hell did that happened?" he asked. "They were leading by two touchdowns!"

Clearly, I had outstayed my welcome, so I bid a fond farewell to my newfound besties and returned to the Mustang. I pulled a notebook out of the glove compartment and wrote down everything I could remember about our conversation, especially the names. While I wrote, Jennica Mehren rapped a knuckle on the driver's side window. I rolled it down.

"That was mean," she said.

"What would have been mean is if you were sitting at the bar nursing a drink when the sheriff walked in. The bar owner could have been in serious trouble."

"That's one way of looking at it. McKenzie, I've been waiting here for over an hour."

"So, go home. Who's stopping you?"

"McKenzie . . ."

I slipped the notebook and pen into my jacket pocket and started the car. Jennica stepped back.

"Where are you going?"

I smiled in reply and drove out of the parking lot. I lost sight of her before she managed to get to her own car. Which didn't mean I had lost her. From my condominium in Minneapolis, I could drive sixty miles per hour in a straight line for thirty minutes in any direction and still be in the Twin Cities. I could circle Grand Marais in five minutes, six if I was caught by the town's lone stoplight. Plus, I was driving a black Mustang, not exactly an inconspicuous vehicle even in the Cities. An industrious young lady like Jennica, I figured it wouldn't take her long to locate me. So, I hid among the other tourists in the parking lot next to the Dairy Queen, quickly crossed Highway 61 on foot, and walked the block and a half to the public library. It was a pretty building with gray brick and blue siding. The sign painted on the glass door said it closed at 2:00 P.M. on Saturdays. I cupped my hands against the glass to peer inside and saw a woman moving about. I knocked. The woman came to the door and opened it as if she had been expecting me.

"I'm sorry," she said. "The library is closed."

"I'm looking for Miss Greyson."

"I'm *Ms.* Doris Greyson."

"Ms. Greyson, my name is McKenzie. I'm investigating—Ms. Greyson have you heard what happened to David Montgomery?"

Greyson stared at me while I counted the beats—one, two, three, four . . .

She answered, "Yes," in a soft voice and looked away.

Thank God, my inner voice said. One of the things I did not miss about being a police officer was delivering heartbreaking news to people.

"Were you close?" I asked.

"Close enough."

"I'm sorry for your loss."

"Thank you."

"May I come in?"

She held the door open. I stepped inside the library and she closed and locked the door behind us.

"I heard two versions of the story," Greyson said. "In one, David committed suicide. In the other, he was murdered. I don't know which is worse."

"I'm sure an official determination will be made soon."

She led me deeper inside the building until we were standing next to the reference desk. There was a sign on top of the desk that read SIGN UP FOR INTERNET HERE. Greyson leaned on the desk as if she needed support.

"Why do you want to talk to me?" she asked.

"Your name was mentioned as someone who might be familiar with Montgomery."

"Are you asking if I was fucking him?"

Not a word you'd expect a librarian to use, my inner voice said. *But okay.*

"How well did you know Montgomery?" I asked.

"Besides the fucking part, not well at all. He loved his daughter, doted on her. It was sweet to see them together. All this is going to be very hard on her. Beyond that, though . . . Who are you? You're not with the sheriff's department, I would know."

"My name is McKenzie. I'm investigating the incident privately."

"Incident?" Ms. Greyson repeated the word as if she didn't know what it meant. "Who hired you? Jodine?"

"I'm not at liberty to say."

"It doesn't matter. There's not much I can tell you anyway."

"You could tell me where you were between ten A.M. and two P.M. yesterday."

"I was here."

"Witnesses?"

"A lot of people came in and out, plus my co-workers—why are you asking? Am I a suspect?"

"Not anymore."

Greyson glared as if she wasn't sure she belicved me.

"Do you know if Montgomery had any enemies?" I asked.

"No."

"No one he might have pissed off? Someone he might have been in business with, perhaps?"

Greyson shook her head. At the same time she said, "David advertised himself as a handyman. He did a lot of home repair and small construction projects—plumbing, electrical, carpentry. He could replace your roof or your furnace or your driveway, which put him in a lot of people's homes, so I don't know. We never really spoke about anything like that. His life. My life. David and I never demanded anything more from each other than a few hours of our time.

"You're probably wondering why a man like him would involve himself with a woman nearly twenty years older than he was. It was a matter of commitment. Or lack thereof. Younger women, women David's age, spend a lot of time trying to determine what their future should be. They have plans or they're in the process of making plans: when to get married, when to buy a house and bring two-point-five children into the world, when to put their youth behind them. David wasn't interested in participating in the process. He liked older women—me—because we already have the future figured out and have determined that a permanent relationship isn't necessarily part of it. I've done marriage and I have no compelling reason to try it again . . ."

Not unlike Nina.

"Now a temporary relationship with the duration of, say, a Sunday afternoon, that's an entirely different matter," Greyson said.

"I've been told that you weren't the only woman he—that Montgomery was involved with," I said.

"No, I wouldn't think so."

"You don't seem upset by the news."

"Not in the slightest."

"Perhaps his other partners weren't as open-minded."

"When David discovered that his wife was sleeping with his best friend, he beat up on Wayne, yet he never touched her."

"Meaning?"

"If someone was angry that I was sleeping with David, they would have come after me, not him."

"I was a police officer for a long time. That's not necessarily how it works."

Greyson gave it a few beats before she responded. "I have no idea who he might have been sleeping with besides me. He never spoke about anyone else while we were together."

"Gillian Davis?"

"It's possible."

"Leah Huddleston?"

She shrugged.

"Ardina Curtis?"

"I don't know who that is."

"Peg Younghans?"

"I wouldn't put it past her."

"Louise Wykoff?"

Greyson snorted at the suggestion.

"Now that would shock me," she said. "That would shock me to my core."

"When was the last time you saw Montgomery?"

"Tuesday evening."

After the paintings were stolen, my inner voice reminded me.

"We were together for only about an hour," Greyson added. "I had an early morning."

"How did he seem?"

"Happy."

"Happy? Did he tell you why?" Greyson's eyes snapped toward me like I had just insulted her. "I mean for a reason besides that."

"All he said was that it was a beautiful day."

"Was it a beautiful day?"

"No, now that you mention it. It was cold and raining."

I thanked Ms. Greyson for her time and left the library. I moved cautiously back to the highway while searching for Jennica. I didn't see her, but I saw a black-and-white SUV with a light bar on the roof and SHERIFF COOK COUNTY painted on the door. It was two blocks up and coming toward me. I turned around and walked quickly enough in the opposite direction to put plenty of distance between my back and the street, yet not so rapidly as to draw attention to myself. At the same time I threw a glance over my shoulder. Deputy Wurzer was behind the wheel. He didn't notice me, though, and kept driving until he hit Broadway and hung a right. I felt a little silly, hiding from the police, only I didn't trust him. When he was out of sight, I spun back around and went to my car.

Northern Lights Art Gallery was located near the Dairy Queen, as I had been told. I could see its sign over the roof of the Mustang as I unlocked the door. I glanced around for both Jennica and Wurzer and not seeing either of them, I relocked the car door, walked the hundred and fifty yards to the entrance, and stepped inside. The gallery was filled with customers. They moved slowly, examining each painting, print, sculpture, carving, ceramic bowl or vase, photograph, and article of jewelry as if they were curating for, well, the City of Lakes Art Museum. Yet except for a few coffee mugs, a couple of hand-painted greeting cards, and a trout knife with a handle made from a deer antler, I didn't see anyone buy anything.

There were a few paintings by Louise Wykoff hanging on the walls and I spent most of my time studying them until the crowd thinned out. I don't know much about art, but I know what I like—the line was attributed to Mark Twain, although I doubt he actually said it. I have used it myself, though, often substituting the word "art" for food, music, theater, ballet, or whatever other subject I was woefully ignorant in. I can say, however, that I really liked Louise's paintings, especially the one of a French voyager working at a blacksmith's forge. I was wondering what Nina might say about the $3,500 price tag when a woman moved to my side.

"That's my uncle," she said.

"Your uncle?"

"My uncle Frank. He's a reenactor."

The expression on my face must have revealed my confusion because she continued.

"The National Park Service restored the North West Company's trading post up in Grand Portage I don't know how many years ago. Turned it into a national monument. This is the fort where the voyageurs would take the furs they collected in Canada, load them onto boats, and send them across the great lakes to the St. Lawrence River and eventually to Europe. Every August, reenactors from across the country dress in period attire and gather at the post for what is called the Grand Rendezvous and pretend for three days to be living in the late eighteenth century. It's actually quite extraordinary. My uncle is one of the reenactors. He conducts blacksmithing classes. Louise painted him from photographs she took."

"She makes me believe she was actually there in the 1790s."

"I wouldn't put it past her; the woman's been around forever."

The woman slapped a hand over her mouth and for a moment she was thirty years old going on ten.

"Do you know Louise?" she asked.

"I do."

"Don't tell her I said that."

"I promise."

"We should all look that fabulous when we're her age."

"How old do you think she is?"

"I'm just digging this hole deeper and deeper, aren't I?"

"Don't worry about it."

She offered her hand.

"I'm Leah Huddleston," she said.

No kidding? my inner voice said. I thought Leah would be another woman fast approaching retirement age.

"I'm McKenzie," I said.

"Oh. You're not what I expected at all."

"You were expecting me?"

"Peg Younghans said you might be stopping by."

"Did she?"

"When she spelled me for my lunch break. Minnesota state law requires that small businesses give employees sufficient mealtime if they work more than eight consecutive hours, and I always take an hour at exactly eleven thirty whether the boss likes it or not."

"Who's the boss?"

"I am. Peg said you were working for That Wykoff Woman. Should I say what she called you?"

"Please do."

"She said you were Louise's boy-toy."

"I don't know if I should be flattered or insulted."

"Knowing Peg, I'd say flattered."

"Knowing Peg, if she was male they'd call her a dirty old man."

"She does seem fixated by all things sexual."

"How long have you known her?"

"I inherited her when I bought the gallery four years ago. She works part-time in the summer. Terrifically punctual. You could set your watch to her. During the winter, though, we're open eleven to five, three days a week and I have that covered."

"You're not a native."

"I am, actually. I grew up here, went to Cook County High School. Go Vikings. Fear no one. My family moved to Chicago, though, halfway through my junior year. I enrolled at the Chicago Academy for the Arts and caught the bug. Later I graduated from Columbia College. Worked in a couple of galleries. When Northern Lights went up for sale, I jumped at it. I love Grand Marais. The hustle and bustle of the summer. The quiet and solitude of the winter."

"Good for you."

"What can I do for you, sir? Peg says that you're looking for some of Louise's paintings that were stolen?"

"It's possible that they were stolen by David Montgomery."

Leah closed her eyes and shook her head as if she did not want to believe my accusation, yet didn't necessarily disbelieve it. She moved slowly to the counter she kept at the far end of the gallery. I followed her.

"Poor David," she said. "Peg said that even though it looks like he committed suicide, the sheriff thinks he was murdered. She said that Louise might have done it."

I was upset by the suggestion and probably my voice revealed it.

"Absolutely not," I said. "Louise was surrounded by a dozen witnesses when Montgomery died."

"Thank God."

"In any case, the authorities haven't yet officially determined if it was suicide or murder."

"Peg is the worst gossip."

"I got that impression."

"I hope—what do I hope? If David committed suicide you wonder what you could have done to prevent it, what you could have done to help him. If he was murdered, you wonder which one of your neighbors, your friends, is a killer. Oh, God."

"I was told you dated him."

"I did. A couple of times last February. 'Course, everyone in town knew about it. There are only a few places in Grand Marais that are open in the winter so it's kind of hard to keep a secret. The problem—he was—David thought all he had to do was play his flute and women would shimmy and shake for him. When I say flute, I'm speaking metaphorically."

"Yeah, I got that."

"I came of age in Chicago, though, and I know charmers and I know snakes and he was more the latter than the former. I wanted nothing to do with his flute. That seemed to surprise him."

"Apparently, others weren't as discriminating."

"There's something like fifty-one hundred people living in all of Cook County, mostly along the lake. There aren't many opportunities to meet people unless you travel."

"Do you travel?"

"As often as possible. When you say 'others,' who do you mean?"

"You tell me."

"No. I'll leave that to Peg."

"You say you haven't seen Montgomery since February."

"Of course I saw him. It's Grand Marais. I haven't spent any time with him, though, if that's what you mean."

"He wouldn't have come to you with the paintings then."

"If he had, I would have contacted the sheriff in a heartbeat. I like Louise and I want her to like me. I want her to let me keep selling her work."

"Okay."

"Don't tell her I said she was old."

"I won't."

"Besides, what would I have done with the paintings? Hang them on a wall in a store located less than six blocks from Louise's front door? Exhibit them next to the paintings she actually commissioned me to sell? David couldn't have been that dumb."

"I have a hypothetical question for you, and please don't be insulted. If you did have the paintings and you wanted to sell them, where would you take them?"

Leah answered as if it was a question she had been asked a thousand times. "Canada."

"Why Canada?"

"Because it's not here."

"That makes sense. How would you get them across the border?"

"There are a thousand places you can cross the Pigeon River in a small boat. In the winter, you can walk across it. Or just drive across at the, what's it called—Grand Portage Port of Entry. I've gone to Canada and back a thousand times and between the CBP and the Canadian Border Service the trunk of my car was searched maybe twice."

"Do you think Montgomery might have had the same thought?"

"I have no idea what was in his head. I am sorry he's dead, though. I really am."

EIGHT

I found Jennica resting against the Mustang. She glanced at her watch as I approached like she was annoyed that I had kept her waiting, yet didn't want to say so out loud.

"I've been wandering all over town trying to find you," she said.

"I hope you're a better filmmaker than you are a stalker."

"Time will tell."

I glanced at my own watch.

"Are you hungry?" I asked.

"I could eat."

"C'mon, sweetie. I'll buy you some fish and chips."

"Are you deliberately trying to be sexist when you call me sweetie?"

"No offense. As I grow older I find that more and more I call the women I like sweetie."

"You like me?"

"I gave you my licorice, didn't I?"

I led Jennica to the Gitchi-Gami State Trail, which was a fancy name for the sidewalk that meandered alongside the lakeshore, and we started following it to the Dockside Fish Market. The sun was setting fast and for a few minutes Superior held a warm orange glow that forced us to stop and look until it was slowly absorbed by the dark water.

"Pretty," I said.

"Reminds me of home, the way the sun sets on the ocean."

"Home is California?"

"Uh-huh."

"Why aren't you in school?"

"I'm supposed to be. I was all set to start my junior year at the School of Theater, Film and Television at UCLA and then this project came along. It was unexpected and a lot of my father's usual crew was committed to other projects so I asked him, begged him, actually, to let me step in. 'There are a lot of baristas with film degrees,' I told him, which is something he told me a thousand times growing up. That and how he learned everything he needed to know working for Roger Corman on low-budget indies. Finally, he gave in, which made my mom even more angry than she was when I got my tattoo."

"This is your first time working on a documentary?"

"Dad let me work with him in the past but I was mostly a gofer, you know, go-for this, go-for that, help out here, help out there. This is the first time I've been allowed to make decisions. I can always go back to school starting in the winter term, no big deal."

"Roger Corman, huh?"

"I met him, talked to him. He is the nicest man."

We got lucky at the Dockside. There was one small unoccupied table remaining on its veranda and Jennica took charge of it while I ordered our dinners off the blackboard behind the counter. Dusk became hard night while we ate and talked. I liked that she so obviously loved her family. I got the impression that she would set a fire for her father, but she'd walk through it for her mom. I called her sweetie again and then apologized, but she said not to. Sweetie was fine.

We were the last to leave; the Dockside staff had locked the doors and was in the process of cleaning up when we finally returned to the sidewalk and started following it back toward downtown.

"You said before that this project was unexpected," I said.

"Mr. Flonta called my father like two weeks ago."

"Two weeks?"

"He said he wanted to do something for the thirty-fifth anniversary of *Scenes from an Inland Sea*. He said there was no time to lose. Let me tell you, McKenzie, to put all this together in that short of time is almost a miracle, if I do say so myself."

The way she was smiling made me think that Jennica considered herself one of the miracle workers.

"Why the thirty-fifth anniversary?" I asked. "Why not the thirtieth? Why not the twenty-fifth? Why is there no time to lose?"

"Something I learned a long time ago living in Hollywood, people with money want what they want when they want it and people like my father and me, too, if you want to know, are happy to give it to them—if they pay us enough."

"How much is enough?"

"A realistic budget for a feature-length documentary, if you go by the industry's standard rates, you're talking a low of $300,000 to more than a million. You can do it for much less. Heck, you could make a doc for $20,000, a two-person filmmaking team, few interviews, fewer locations, no third-party material like music or film footage. Technology has made it possible to do more with less. Only then we're talking about a labor of love and not business. What I was taught, $3,000 to $4,000 per finished minute of film is the minimum starting point."

"What is the budget for this film?"

"I doubt Dad would want me to tell you. Let's just say it's at the high end and let it go with that."

"So, two weeks ago Flonta called your old man and offered to give him a budget of a million bucks or more to make an art film about the *Scenes from an Inland Sea* with the understanding that he starts the project immediately. After traveling all the way from California, you arrive in Grand Marais just in time to be told, on film mind you, that not only had Randolph McInnis painted three additional canvases that no one has ever seen, but they've gone missing, which could very well transform your simple commercial documentary into a rip-roaring action-adventure mystery destined for a national release. Some people have all the luck."

We covered a lot of sidewalk before Jennica said, "Stranger things have happened."

"You're going to stop following me now," I said. "For one thing, I'm going into a lot of bars that I'll have you thrown out of, which will be embarrassing for both of us. For another, I'll become annoyed enough to call you something besides sweetie."

"What exactly are you doing, anyway?"

"I'm trying to find out about David Montgomery."

"Find out what?"

"I'll know it when I hear it."

"I'll promise to stop following you if you make me a promise in return."

"What he asked reluctantly."

"That you let me interview you on film."

"You interview me, not your old man?"

"Exactly."

"I'm sure he'll like that."

"He won't, but Mom will. She's always saying I should assert myself more."

"Does that include tattoos?"

"Maybe not that much."

"*If* I find the paintings, I'll ask my client for permission. If she says yes, then I'll give you the interview." *Although I'm pretty sure she'll say no*, my inner voice added. *In fact, I guarantee it.* "That's the only promise I'll make."

"Louise Wykoff is your client, am I right?"

I shrugged. Jennica grinned and held out her hand. I shook it.

"Done," she said.

"You drive a hard bargain, sweetie."

"I'm liking more and more that you call me that."

It was Saturday night in Grand Marais and the Gunflint Tavern was hopping. Gillian Davis was far too busy to talk to me when I arrived, but she promised that she would when she went on her break.

The Gunflint was divided into three levels. The first had a bar and TVs tuned to whatever sporting event was popular at the moment. The second featured a much larger bar and tables galore for diners. The third was an outside terrace with a live band. Perhaps "band" was being too generous. It was just two guys playing guitars and singing Gordon Lightfoot songs. They were pretty good, though, the craft beer was great, and the view of the harbor was spectacular, so I settled on a stool next to the railing and waited.

The duo finished its set with "The Wreck of the Edmund Fitzgerald," a prerequisite, I suppose, if you're going to play a gig on the North Shore of Lake Superior. They did a nice job of it. When they sang the final line, "Superior, they said, never gives up her dead when the gales of November come early," I found myself looking up at the clear, warm September night sky. I shivered just the same.

Gillian appeared at the top of the wooden staircase. She glanced around until she saw my wave and came toward me. That's when I noticed for the first time the tall and short men I met at Mark's Wheel-Inn earlier. They were sitting at a table with two other men on the far side of the terrace and watching me. They looked like they hadn't stopped drinking since I left them.

"McKenzie?" she said. "Did I get that right?"

"Yes."

Gillian climbed onto the stool next to mine.

"I'm sorry I kept you waiting so long," she said.

"Not at all. I appreciate you sparing time to see me."

"It's all right now. Before—we're always pretty busy until nine. Afterward, business will start tapering off. It's not like the Cities where the band doesn't even start playing until nine. What do you think of the music?"

"Much better than I expected."

"I'm seeing one of the singers."

"They're quite good. Can I get you anything?"

"Thank you, no. McKenzie, you said you wanted to talk about David Montgomery."

"I was under the impression that you were seeing him."

"That's old news."

"How old?"

"Four months."

"So, May?"

"Started in April; ended in May. I work here April through October. Gunflint is one of the few businesses that stays open all year-round, but they don't need as much help in the winter so I go down to the Cities. My parents are in the Cities. As bad as winter is down there—actually it's worse in Minneapolis than it is up here in GM. I looked it up once. The average temperatures are nearly the same, but Grand Marais gets forty-three inches of snow and Minneapolis gets fifty-five. It's because GM is located right on the lake and the lake is warm, I mean compara- tively. The town of Finland, I have a friend who lives in Fin- land; it's only six miles from the lake and they average ninety inches of snow. The thing is, though, winter in the Cities lasts about a hundred days. Here it seems to go on *forever.* There is absolutely nothing to do. Probably why David shot himself, looking at another endless winter."

"If he shot himself."

"I know of at least a half-dozen people who have killed them- selves up here or tried to in just the past few years. No one has been murdered since, like, forever."

"Have you spoken to Montgomery recently?"

"Oh, yeah. Like I said, we started seeing each other in April right after I came back up, but I knew it wasn't going anywhere right away. David wasn't looking for a serious relationship. Neither, was I, truthfully, but I sure wanted more than 'meet me at the Frontier Motel in an hour.' I mean, c'mon. I have no complaints, though. It was fun while it lasted. We stayed friends, just without benefits. Besides, there are only so many places where you can get a drink, you know? So many places you can hang out."

"When did you see him last?"

"Oh wow, that would have to be—Tuesday? Yeah, Tuesday night around ten o'clock or so."

The night Louise Wykoff discovered her paintings were missing. It was also just after he spent time with Ms. Greyson.

"I remember the way he was grinning like he just got away with something," Gillian added. "I asked what. He said a gentleman never tells, which made me think he just got laid. I think he wanted me to ask who, but I didn't. I mean, why would I care? Anyway, David was in a chatty mood so in between serving my other customers we talked. It was cold and raining so it was a slow night and I had plenty of time. I asked if he had been working. Handyman work is pretty spotty, I guess. Anyway, he said that just that day he had replaced Louise Wykoff's water heater and I'm like—what?"

What? my inner voice echoed. *Funny she didn't mention that to you.*

"I asked—were you with That Wykoff Woman?" Leah said. "And he was like, 'No. God no. I wish.'"

"Did you believe him?"

"I did cuz even if David wouldn't come right out and say it, he'd want you to know if he had done Louise. He'd want to brag about it. Heck, if I did her, I'd want to brag about it, too. I always figured the reason she stays pretty much to herself is because she doesn't want people talking about her, so . . . It's not like we're BBFs, though, and tell each other our deepest, dark-est secrets. I mean, Louise might be a real party girl when there's no one around to see."

"You said that handyman work was spotty up here."

"Well, to hear David talk about it . . ."

"Do you know if he was having financial problems?"

"Nope. At least it wasn't something he ever talked about. He had an ex and a daughter and I think he sent them money, I don't really know for sure, though. You should ask Jodine. She'd know."

I flashed on something Louise had told me when we first met—the local newspaper, the *News-Herald* I think she called it, had reported that burglaries in Cook County had doubled in the past few years.

"I was just wondering if he might have taken things from the homes his job put him in."

"You mean steal?"

Gillian looked as if I had just called her friend an obscenity and she wasn't happy about it.

"No," she said. "No, I don't believe that. I don't believe David would do that. Besides, from a practical standpoint, you work in people's homes and things start going missing, even if you didn't take them that would probably kill your business, wouldn't you think? It wouldn't matter if you were guilty or not. People would start talking . . . Well, wait. I wonder. If people were talking . . . David killing himself, maybe . . . I don't know. I heard somewhere that most suicides are spontaneous. That people decide to kill themselves and then they do it within like an hour of making the decision but if they would only wait an-other hour, they'd probably talk themselves out of it. What I mean—what if something happened that David decided he couldn't live with even though, if he took the time to think about it, maybe he could?"

"The question is, what thing?" I said.

"Yeah, that's a question. Listen. I need to get back to work."

"All right, thank you. Thank you for your time."

"No problem."

My eyes followed Gillian as she crossed the terrace toward the staircase. The table where my pals from Mark's Wheel-Inn was empty now. I wasn't paying much attention to that, though. Instead, I noticed that Gillian gave a wave to the two guitar players as she passed the small stage. They both smiled broadly and waved back and I wondered, She's seeing only one of them, right?

I hate to leave in the middle of a set; it seems so disrespectful to the musicians. Except I had been working on only a few hours of sleep and it was catching up to me. I made a production out of dropping a twenty in the tip jar as I crossed the terrace, though, hoping that would make up for my rude behavior. I descended the long wooden staircase to the sidewalk, paused to take one last look at the harbor, and started moving toward the parking lot next to the Dairy Queen.

I didn't make it.

"There you are," a voice said from the shadows.

I kept walking without altering my speed half a step.

"Hey, I'm talking to you."

Both the short man and the taller man that I had met earlier emerged from the shadows followed by their two friends.

"Hey, guys." I kept walking. All four of them were behind me now. "What's going on?"

"Where do you think you're going?" the taller man asked.

I hung a right without answering and kept moving down the block.

"Running around town asking questions about Dave Montgomery, who are you?" the shorter man said. "Dammit, stop walking."

I did when I reached a streetlight. I turned to face the four men. We were now standing directly in front of the Dairy Queen, one of the few places in Grand Marais that was still open at a quarter to ten.

"You guys want to talk?" I said. "Why don't we step inside? I'll buy the Dilly Bars."

"Not here," said one of the men I didn't know. He was wearing a Twins baseball cap, which should have made us allies but didn't.

"Where else can you get a Dilly Bar?" I asked.

He didn't reply.

"Seriously," I said. "Why are you guys following me?"

"We want to talk to you," said the taller man.

"You could have talked to me at the Gunflint."

"In private."

The man in the baseball cap started circling like he wanted to get behind me. I brought my hand up as if I was drawing a gun and pointed at him.

"You're making me nervous," I said. "Who knows what mischief might ensue if I become nervous?"

I don't know if it was because of my message or the convoluted way I stated it, yet he stopped moving.

"You've been asking questions all over town about Montgomery," the shorter man said.

"I'm trying to find out if he killed himself or if he was murdered. You have a problem with that?"

"Yes," said the man in the ball cap.

"Why? Are you involved?"

"No."

"What's your name?"

He didn't answer.

I pulled the notebook and pen from my pocket.

"Name?" I repeated.

The notebook seemed to frighten him.

"What do you want to know that for?" he asked.

"I want to know all of your names in case I'm called to testify."

"What are you talking about?" the shorter man asked.

"The Bureau of Criminal Apprehension will want to know who's interfering in this investigation. They'll want to know why."

The fourth man, who had remained silent all this time, turned and started walking away.

Okay, now it's three to one, my inner voice said.

"You don't scare me," said the ball cap.

"You scare me. Tell me why? Why do you want to keep me from finding out if Montgomery was murdered?"

"No one said that," the taller man told me. He took a few steps backward and my inner voice asked, *Two to one?*

"Going around town accusing people," said the shorter man. "This is our town."

"Are you afraid I'll accuse you?"

The man wearing the baseball cap balled his fists and raised them chest high. He started moving toward me.

"Asshole," he said.

Here we go.

I dropped the notebook and pen and moved into an American stance, deliberately facing ball cap sideways, my feet at forty-five degree angles about a shoulder's width apart, knees bent, my left hand up around my chin, the right poised along my ribs. If my posture told ball cap that I knew some karate, it sure didn't frighten him any. Or the shorter man, who brought his hands up like he knew how to fight, too.

A bright light flicked on, capturing all of us. I brought my hand up to keep it out of my eyes. The others squinted at it, too. At first I thought it was flashlight. As it began to circle us, I realized it was a light mounted on a digital camera.

"Keep doing what you're doing," Jennica said. "Don't mind me."

We all stopped and watched her while at the same time trying to protect our eyes.

"Pretend I'm not here," she added.

"Who are you?" ball cap wanted to know.

"I'm Jennica Mehren. I'm with the documentary crew that's filming here in Grand Marais."

"There's a documentary?" the shorter man said.

"Didn't you know?" I asked.

"Let's get out of here," said the taller man.

"No, please," Jennica said. "Go 'head and beat up on McKenzie. This is great stuff."

The man in the ball cap shoved my shoulder hard as if he meant to comply with the woman's request and then stepped backward.

"Another time, asshole." He pointed at Jennica. "You put me on film and I'll sue."

"Everyone says that yet no one ever does," Jennica said.

The men all started moving back toward the harbor. I heard some muttering yet couldn't make out what was said. I retrieved my notebook and pen. Jennica turned off her light and lowered her camera.

"Hello, Jen," I said.

"McKenzie, hi. What was all that about?"

"Alcohol-infused paranoia, I think. They wanted to know what's happening in their town and I pushed back too hard. If they had asked while we were at the Gunflint I might have told them. Accosting me on the street, though . . . Don't think I haven't noticed—you said you would stop following me. You lied."

"Yeah, and you were going to grant me an on-camera interview after telling my father never, ever. I'm pretty, McKenzie. I'm not dumb."

"No, you're not. Dumb, I mean."

"You can still call me sweetie, though."

"Sweetie, I have a room at the Frontier Motel. I'm going there now."

"Should I follow you?"

"Absolutely not."

Jennica thought that was awfully funny.

"Are you sure?" she said.

Yeah, like she can't think of a better way to spend the evening than with a man who was literally old enough to be her father.

"Pretty sure," I said.

"Good night, McKenzie. See you in the morning."

The parking lot at the Frontier Motel was two more or less straight lines behind the rooms. I found a slot directly in front of mine. There was a soft light above the door that allowed me to see the number and little else. I went to unlock the door. When I did, I heard the sound of a car door opening behind me. My first thought—ball cap.

I spun to face the noise. The car door was shut and with it the vehicle's overhead light. A shadow moved toward me. I recognized her voice before I saw her face.

"Took you long enough," Peg Younghans said.

"Geezus, you scared the hell out of me."

"Scared?"

"Startled. What are you doing here?"

"Waiting for you. I thought you might want to discuss those photographs I told you about. I would have called your cell, except I didn't have the number."

"How did you find me?"

"There's only about two dozen places where a visitor can stay in GM. The Frontier was number thirteen on the list that I called."

"How resourceful of you."

If she can find you, anyone can, my inner voice said.

Peg stepped within the small circle of light. She was wearing a trench coat, which I thought was appropriate, all things considered. If she was wearing anything beneath the trench coat, though, I couldn't say.

"About those photographs . . ." she said.

I tried to keep it friendly.

"You tempt me," I said. "Only I never mix business with pleasure."

Peg pulled at my jacket like a tailor trying to see if it fit properly.

"Are you sure?" she asked, only not the way Jennica had. Peg was dead serious.

"This is the part of the program where I should tell you that I'm in a committed relationship."

"Boy or girl?"

No one had ever asked me that question before and it kind of threw me. Again, Peg was serious. She didn't so much as grin.

"Girl," I said.

"Girlfriend, but not wife?"

"It's complicated."

"Tell me—you bonded yourself to someone else. Does it give you stability? Does that make you stronger?"

"I don't know what you mean."

"Most people feel more secure when they're in a pair. It's like they're afraid to stand alone."

"It's not something I've given much thought."

Not something you want to discuss with her, either.

"Should we talk business, then?" Peg asked.

"Please."

"Are you going to let me in?"

"No."

"Chicken?"

"Let's just say it's a small room with a big bed and I make no claims to virtue. Besides, you make me feel outnumbered."

"That might be the best brush-off I've ever heard."

"Brush-off?"

"Let's not forget how old I am."

"If I thought you were old we wouldn't be standing out here."

"Telling a girl no while making her feel good about it, that takes some skill, McKenzie. I think you and David would have gotten along very well."

"You said before that you didn't know Montgomery."

"I knew his reputation. I doubt I ever spoke more than a dozen words to him. I know that Leah Huddleston spent some time with him. She claimed she was not enriched by the experience."

"I got that impression, too. Ever hire Montgomery to fix something around the house?"

"My house? There was never a need."

"Do you still insist that Montgomery and Louise were intimate?"

"Weren't they?"

"Louise says no."

"I saw his car parked at her place many times. What does that tell you?"

Peg wanted me to call Louise a liar. Instead, I said, "It tells me that Montgomery's car was parked near her place many times."

"In a murder investigation, don't the police check the GPS on the victim's phone to determine everywhere he's been?"

"Sometimes."

"Then that will show that he parked on the street where Louise lived, won't it?"

"It should, yes."

"Then we'll see, won't we?"

"You're pretty determined to prove that Louise was involved with Montgomery, aren't you? Why?"

"Somebody killed him."

"It wasn't Louise. She was surrounded by a half-dozen documentary filmmakers when Montgomery was shot."

"I hadn't thought of that. McKenzie, since you're not going to let me in—"

"No."

"I should be going."

"Okay."

"It's too bad. I wore my sexiest nightie. It's lavender. Do you want to see?"

"Better not."

"Then I'll say good night."

"Drive carefully."

"Not me, McKenzie. My motto—drive fast, take chances."

"You're an interesting woman, Peg Younghans."

"You have no idea."

Ten forty-five on a Saturday night and I was alone in a Grand Marais motel room eating what was left of the salty caramel pretzels I bought from the Great! Lakes Candy Kitchen. I had the TV on and was watching halfheartedly while a Duluth sportscaster explained how the Gophers lost to Wisconsin instead of how the Badgers beat them.

I grabbed my smartphone and started surfing the net. I found a couple of websites that listed crime statistics for Cook County. Turned out, it was a great place to be sheriff—no homicides, armed robberies, aggravated assaults, arsons, human trafficking or prostitution beefs reported in the previous calendar year, plus only eight motor vehicle thefts, fifteen DUIs, twenty drug arrests, twenty DCs, and two rapes—and both rapes were cleared. But burglaries? The numbers were all over the place, yet with a little adding and subtracting I decided that the *News-Herald* was correct; the number of burglaries had doubled in the past four years from an average of about sixteen incidents to thirty-two while the clearance rate declined from thirteen percent, just above the national average, to less than eight.

Not exactly a crime wave, my inner voice said. *The number of burglaries—that's a slow weekend in Minneapolis.*

Still, I wondered why there was an uptick and what the ratio was between tourists and residents. Plus, how many crimes were committed in the winter when people left their homes and cabins unattended while they escaped to warmer climes? The *News-Herald* didn't say. Neither did anybody else.

Montgomery divorced his wife four years ago, my inner voice reminded me. *Gillian Davis says he's been sending his ex and his daughter money ever since. Is this where he got it?*

I had finished the pretzels and started working on the assorted truffles when I logged off the internet and started scrolling through my phone contacts. I tapped the icon for Rickie's because Nina nearly always left her cell in her office when she was working. A woman's voice said, "Rickie's, how may I help you?" I recognized the voice, Jenness Crawford, the weekend manager.

"Jenness," I said. "This is McKenzie. Is the boss free?"

A minute later, Nina said, "Are you all right?"

"I'm fine. Why do you ask?"

"You're actually calling me when you said you would. When was the last time that happened?"

"C'mon, I'm not as bad as all that."

There was music in the background.

"Who's in the big room tonight?" I asked.

"Patty Peterson and the Jazz Women All-Stars."

"I love those guys."

"You love everybody who plays jazz."

"Mary Louise Knutson on piano showing Bill Evans's ghost how it's done. What's not to love?"

"Let me put you on hold for a sec. I want to go to my office."

When Nina picked up the phone again, I could hear nothing but her voice and that was fine. She asked me about my day and I told her. When I finished, I said, "What do you think?"

"I am so glad that I didn't go to Grand Marais with you."

"That boring, huh?"

"I like the girl with the camera, though."

"Jennica is great. She reminds me a little of Erica without the tats. How is Erica, anyway?"

"Fine as far as I know. She's like you. She never calls when she's supposed to. Tell me more about the woman who showed up at your door wearing nothing but a lavender nightie."

"Peg was wearing a trench coat. I took her word about the nightie."

"Reminds me of my mother."

That caused me to sit up in bed. In all the years I'd known her, the only thing Nina had told me about her mother was that she didn't want to talk about her mother.

"She was the Whore of Babylon, too," Nina said. "I couldn't count the number of times she left the house late at night when I was a kid in school. 'Don't wait up,' she'd say. One time she was gone for three days. When she came back she said, 'Miss me?' like she had gone off to the corner store for a gallon of milk. You know what's truly sad, McKenzie? I didn't miss her. Not at all. I knew how to take care of myself; she had made sure of that. Good for Mom. As for the rest—I sometimes wonder if that's the reason I married so young, if I was looking for the attention and affection that I didn't get at home. We both know how that worked out, too, don't we? Okay. Call me tomorrow. Let me know when you're coming home."

"I will."

"And don't brood."

"Brood?"

"Right now you're wondering about all the things I never told you about myself. Really, McKenzie there aren't that many and they're not that interesting. Besides, it's not like you don't keep secrets from me."

"Never. Well, almost never."

"Good night, McKenzie. I'll tell Mary Louise you said hi."

NINE

I had my second cup of morning coffee in the same resort chair positioned in the center of the horseshoe as the day before.

In Minnesota during that brief passage of time when summer gives way to fall, there are days of pure grace with the sun, clouds, wind, and temperature reaching a golden balance. On days like that you don't want to do much of anything except sit back and enjoy, yet instead I was studying the traffic on Highway 61 as it passed between the Frontier Motel and the great lake beyond. I did not see the same vehicle more than once, nor was anyone parked along the shoulder in either direction that I could glimpse from my perch. I was a little disappointed. I was sure that Jennica Mehren would be watching and waiting for me to make a move.

Finally, I did. After returning the now empty coffee cup to the room, I climbed into my Mustang. Less than a minute later I was on Highway 61, only I was driving northeast toward Canada and not southwest toward Grand Marais.

Seven miles from the border I found Grand Portage, an unorganized territory, whatever that meant. It contained not only the community of Grand Portage, but also the Grand Portage Indian Reservation, called *Gichi-onigamiing* in the Ojibwa language. The Grand Portage Lodge and Casino was located on the reservation near the lake. Next to it, and also operated by the Ojibwa, was the Grand Portage Trading Post where you could buy everything from groceries and gas to fishing rods and grass seed. Between them was the Grand Portage Art Gallery.

I parked near the front entrance of the gallery. The trading post was open from six A.M. to eleven P.M. on the weekends and, of course, the casino never closed. I doubt its front door even had locks. The art gallery, however, opened at ten A.M. and if you couldn't find anything you liked by five thirty, you were out of luck.

I had arrived nearly a half hour early and decided to take a walk and enjoy the day. Soon I found myself on Casino Road where it met Marina Road that led to the Grand Portage Marina, which was also owned by the Ojibwa. I was wondering how much the tribal members each earned from all of this entrepreneurship when I noticed the distinctive black-and-white Cook County Sheriff's SUV parked on the shoulder about a hundred yards down the road. It was behind a tan-colored two-door. It could have been a Toyota; it could have been a Honda. It was hard to tell from that distance. My first thought, Traffic stop.

Deputy Wurzer got out of the black-and-white and moved toward the two-door. He did it sloppily, approaching on the driver's side instead of the passenger side, swinging his arms like he was marching in a parade, walking away from the vehicle instead of hugging the body so he could watch the driver through the side view mirror.

"Don't you get it?" I heard myself saying aloud. "Traffic stops are among the most dangerous things you can do. Read the damn statistics."

Only it became apparent that Wurzer knew exactly what he was doing and to whom. He yanked open the driver's side door and pulled at the driver. The driver was taller than Wurzer with a full body and long black hair. He came out of the vehicle and shoved the deputy. Wurzer shoved back. The Ojibwa—I assumed he was Ojibwa—looked like he was going to take it up a notch when Wurzer stepped back and rested his hand on his service weapon. The Ojibwa gave him the finger. Wurzer waved his own finger at the Ojibwa, but did not take his other hand from the butt of his gun. The Ojibwa threw his hands in the air in exasperation, but not surrender. More words were exchanged. The situation de-escalated. Wurzer removed his hand from his weapon. The Ojibwa folded his arms across this chest.

Maybe they're discussing the weather, my inner voice said.

Eventually, the Ojibwa made a yeah-I-get-it gesture with his hands. Wurzer spread his own hands wide. The Ojibwa gestured some more, turned, and slid back into his vehicle, shutting the door behind him. Wurzer leaned on the door, hanging his ass out into the traffic, if there had been traffic. More words were exchanged through the open window. Finally, the deputy pushed himself upward and stepped away from the two-door. The Ojibwa drove off. Wurzer watched him go. When the two-door was far down the road, the deputy turned and walked back to his own vehicle. He looked up when he reached the bumper and saw me.

And froze.

I was too far away to read his expression, yet I was fluent enough in body language to know that he was not pleased that I had witnessed the traffic stop. He climbed into the SUV. I turned and walked back toward my own car. I walked quickly. Still, if Deputy Wurzer had wanted to overtake me, he could have. He didn't.

It was five minutes to ten when I returned to the art gallery. I tried the door anyway and was surprised when it opened. It was pleasantly warm inside, yet not nearly as pleasant or warm as the voice of the woman behind the counter.

"I'll be with you in a moment," she said.

"Take your time."

I spent the next few minutes drifting through the gallery until I stopped at a glass case which contained a lot of beadwork. The artist was identified as Marcie McIntire. Above the case were several prints of landscape paintings by a man called George Morrison, whose Ojibwa name was Wah Wah Teh Go Nay Ga Bo, which meant Standing in the Northern Lights. The woman stepped next to me.

"George was from here," she said. "He was born on the rez in 1919."

The woman was tall with lustrous straight black hair and eyes that reminded me of Belgian chocolate.

"He graduated from Grand Marais High School in 1938 and the Minnesota School of Art, what is now the Minneapolis College of Art and Design, in '43. He won the Van Derlip Traveling Scholarship, studied at the Art Students League in New York and, after receiving a Fulbright scholarship, studied in Paris and at the University of Aix-Marseilles. He was awarded a John Hay Whitney Fellowship in 1953."

"I have no idea what any of that means. The way you say it, though, makes me think Mr. Morrison was quite an artist."

The woman thought that was funny. She offered her hand.

"Ardina Curtis," she said.

I shook her hand.

"What does that mean in Ojibwa?" I asked.

"Ardina Curtis. Actually, Ardina is from the Latin. It means ardent, eager."

"McKenzie," I said.

"What can I help you with?"

I gestured at the beadwork.

"Is Ms. McIntire also from the reservation?" I asked.

"Uh-huh."

I expected more, but didn't get it.

"I take it you're not as impressed with her," I said.

"Is beadwork a true art form or simply a craft or folk art?"

"I'm the last person you should ask that question. I suppose like most things it's in the eye of the beholder. I, for example, insist that a chili cheese dog with chopped onions is real food."

"There's no accounting for taste."

"Exactly my point."

"What can I show you, Mr. McKenzie?"

"McKenzie is fine. Do you have any Louise Wykoff?"

"Now there's an artist. Right this way."

We didn't travel far, only to the other side of the gallery. Ardina had three of Louise's paintings hanging on the wall, all of them featuring Ojibwa models.

"Louise is originally from Duluth, if I'm not mistaken," she said. "She's lived in Grand Marais for decades though, so we claim her as one of our own. I like her very much. She has a quality about her that I find fascinating. Not aloof so much as . . ."

"Distant?"

"No, more like—detached. Like she's not connected to the world the way the rest of us are. She floats above it. Yet her paintings are very grounded. In many ways, her work is reminiscent of Eastman Johnson."

"That's the second time I've heard his name. I'm afraid I don't know anything about him."

Ardina looked at me as if she was concerned about the quality of the schools I attended.

"Among other things, Johnson was one of the cofounders of the Metropolitan Museum of Art in New York," she said. "In his day he was known as the American Rembrandt."

"So he was a big deal?"

"Oh, my God."

"How is he like Louise Wykoff? Or vice versa?"

"In the mid-1850s, Johnson spent time in Superior, Wisconsin, what is now on the other side of the bridge from Duluth. I guess he had people living there. While he was in Superior, he spent a lot of time with a man named Stephen Bonga who was married to an Ojibwa woman and had an Ojibwa family. Through Bonga, Johnson was able to convince a great many Ojibwa to sit for him and he painted them as he saw them. As people. There were no war bonnets, no loincloths, no half-naked maidens; none of the noble savage stereotypes that existed at the time and for God knows how long afterward. Maybe that's why he didn't sell the paintings during his lifetime, because they ran counter to the prevailing attitude people had of Native Americans. They're now owned by the St. Louis County Historical Society and are on display in Duluth. Louise has been doing much the same kind of work for the past few years, often creating these very intimate portraits of everyday Ojibwa living their lives.

"She's really come into her own as a painter. Every artist has an individual style, a technique; a way of putting themselves on canvas. It isn't necessarily something they think about as much as it's something they develop over time. It took years for Louise to reach that point. Before it was all Randolph McInnis. Do you know McInnis?"

"Yes."

"Then you must know about Louise's relationship with him and the *Scenes from an Inland Sea*."

"I do."

"Her early work resembled his later work, the work he displayed in the *Scenes*. Style—technique—is what distinguishes you from other artists, and what keeps your work looking professional, cohesive, and focused. The greatest artists throughout history had styles that were incredibly distinctive and unique. Take someone like Van Gogh as an obvious example. If you've seen one Van Gogh painting, you can spot another from a mile away. If you looked at Wykoff's earlier work, though, all you saw was McInnis. Over time, Louise was able to break away from that and find her own voice. 'Course, once you find a style that works for you, that doesn't mean you stop. The creative process doesn't end. At least it shouldn't."

"What about Louise? Do you think she's a one-trick pony?"

"No. Well, we'll see. Historically, the most compelling artists have been the ones who are constantly reinventing and transforming themselves. Monet. Degas. Diebenkorn. I'm anxious to see what she does next. Am I boring you?"

"Not at all."

"I've been told I have a tendency to lecture people, especially when it comes to art."

"Lecture away."

"I think I've gotten it out of my system for a while. Did you want to buy a painting?"

"I'm afraid this is where I confess that I'm here under false pretenses."

"Oh?"

"I know Louise personally," I said. "She asked me to help find some paintings that have gone missing from her studio."

"She was robbed? That's crazy."

"It gets worse."

"How?"

"I'm told you were involved with David Montgomery."

I couldn't have hurt her more if I had slapped her. Ardina abruptly turned away, showing her back to me and hiding her face. Her shoulders heaved and I thought I heard a whimper.

"Ms. Curtis?"

She held a hand up, asking for silence. I gave it to her. She reminded me of an athlete who took a hard hit yet didn't want you to know how much he felt it.

"David was my friend," she said, her back still to me.

"More than a friend?"

"Yes."

"I'm sorry for your loss."

She held her hand up again.

I waited.

"I keep thinking of his daughter, Jamie; what she must be feeling," Ardina said. "Jodine, too."

That has to be your next stop, my inner voice said. *Talk to Jodine Montgomery in Duluth.*

"Did you know David?" Ardina asked.

"No, ma'am. We never met."

"You would have liked him. He was . . . charming."

"Yes, ma'am. So I've been told."

"Why are you asking about him?"

"I'm afraid to hurt you again."

"McKenzie . . ."

"He was the one who stole the paintings."

"No."

"We're pretty sure."

"Why? Why, McKenzie? Why would he do that? It's not like jewelry. A TV. It's not like he could sell the damn things out of the trunk of his car."

"Ma'am . . ."

"Don't call me ma'am!" Ardina was shouting now. "I'm twenty-eight years old. Do I look like a ma'am to you?"

"No, ma . . . No."

"I don't believe it, McKenzie. I don't."

"How well did you know him?"

"I . . . I cared about him a great deal."

"Yes, but how well did you know him?"

"We met years ago. He was a friend of my brother's. They started hanging out after David's divorce. David and I became involved in June."

After Leah Huddleston and Gillian Davis, but while he was still seeing Doris Greyson. Do the woman a favor and keep your mouth shut about it.

"McKenzie, does this have anything to do with his death?" Ardina asked.

"Honestly, I don't know."

"I don't believe he killed himself."

"Neither do I."

Ardina closed her eyes. Her lashes knocked the tears free. They trailed down her cheeks.

So far she's the only one who's shown genuine sorrow at Montgomery's passing.

The door to the art gallery was pulled open and the Ojibwa I had seen earlier with Deputy Wurzer hurried across the threshold.

"Hey, sis?" he said.

I was surprised by the greeting. It's the kind of thing you hear in movies but I've never heard someone say the word in real life before.

The Ojibwa was surprised to see his sister weeping. He crossed the gallery in a hurry and put his arm around her shoulder.

"Sis?" he said.

His eyes fell on me and I knew what he was thinking, which is why I brought my hands up and took several steps backward.

"What did you do?" he asked.

He released Ardina and moved toward me.

"Did you hurt my sister?"

Ardina grabbed hold of his arm and pulled him back.

"No, Eddie," she said. "It's not like that. He—we were talking about David."

Eddie Curtis, my inner voice said.

"Oh," Curtis said. "Oh." He wrapped Ardina in his arms. "I'm sorry. It'll be all right. Everything's going to be fine. Don't worry."

Which was exactly the kind of harmless and wholly inadequate nonsense I would have mumbled if I were him. Experience had taught me, though, that it didn't really matter what you said. Being there is what's important. After a few moments, Ardina regained her balance and dried her tears.

"Okay?" Curtis asked.

Ardina nodded.

"I'm sorry, McKenzie," she said.

"Please don't be. I'm the one who should apologize."

"Apologize for what?" Curtis asked.

"He said that they think David stole some paintings from Louise Wykoff," Ardina said.

"Why would he do that?" Curtis pointed at me. "Why would he do that?"

"You were his friend?"

"That's right."

"Was he having any financial difficulties?"

"You mean besides paying his ex her damn alimony?"

"No," Ardina said. "David wasn't paying alimony. Jodine didn't want any. He was paying child support and he was happy to do it. He loved his daughter. That's what he told me."

"That's not what David told me."

"What did he tell you?" I asked.

"None of your damn business."

"We're pretty sure Montgomery stole from Louise. Did he take from anyone else?"

"You know what? It's time for you to get out of here."

"Eddie," Ardina said.

"No, sis. He barges in here, throwing insults around about David. You, get out."

I reached into my pocket for my notebook and pen and started writing.

Hey, it worked before.

"What are you doing?" Curtis asked.

"Writing that you refused to be interviewed. In case I'm called to testify."

"So people will think I have something to hide?"

"Do you have something to hide?"

"I have an idea. Shove that little notebook up your ass."

A few minutes later I was driving south on Highway 61 past the Judge C. R. Magney State Park when I spied the approach

of a Cook County Sheriff Department vehicle in my rearview.
I glanced down at my speedometer. I was surprised that I had
been actually driving the speed limit for a change. The driver
of the SUV didn't seem to care. He came up so fast and so close
that it frightened me. His push bumper brushed the rear of the
Mustang and I wondered, Is he trying to force me off the road?

The SUV backed off quickly though, if you count one car
length as backing off. The overhead was turned on and he hit
the siren.

The siren is unnecessary, my inner voice said. *He's just trying
to mess with you.*

I angled the Mustang onto the shoulder and slowed to a stop.
I turned off the engine and rested my hands on top of the steering wheel. Using the side view mirror, I watched Deputy Wurzer
exit the SUV.

Kinda knew it was him, didn't you?

Wurzer moved toward the driver's side door. Once again the
word "sloppy" came to mind.

When he reached my open window I said "Good morning,
Deputy. Is there something wrong?"

"Speeding," he said. "Careless driving. Failure to stop. I don't
see a seat belt."

I pulled the strap off my chest a few inches and let it slide
back into place.

"Yeah, okay," I said. "I get it."

Wurzer sniffed the air.

"Is that marijuana I smell?" he asked. "If I search your car
will I find two ounces of the bad thing in your trunk? Two
ounces is felony weight. Five years, $10,000 fine."

"I'm aware."

"I could bust your ass for whatever the fuck I want and make
it stick."

"I said I get it."

There weren't many vehicles on the highway, but they came
steadily, each slowing as they approached the SUV with its

flashing overhead light. I smiled at the drivers, giving a wave to a few. Wurzer couldn't help but notice.

"Trying to make friends, McKenzie?" he asked.

"As many as possible."

"Think they'll do you any good?"

"You can never tell. Someone might pull out a phone hoping to get a video of police corruption they can upload."

"You oughta know all about that."

"I oughta?"

"Think I don't know you, McKenzie? Back when I was with Minneapolis we used to talk about you all the time. You're the SPPD who recovered all that cash some jack-off embezzler siphoned, returned it to the insurance company for fifty cents on the dollar. How much was that, anyway? I heard $10 million."

"That's a huge exaggeration."

"How much did you get?"

"Only three million and change."

"Only three million dollars and change. Half the guys thought you won the lottery, lucky fucking you. The other half thinking you sold your shield. A three-striper I know called you a mutt. Whaddya think of that?"

"I've been called worse. Why aren't you still with the MPD?"

"I like it up here. The air is clean and you can see the stars at night."

"Both big pluses. If you knew I was on the job, why did you try to jam me up for Montgomery's death? 'Give me twenty minutes alone with the sonuvabitch,' you said."

"Think because you once carried a badge that should give you special privileges?"

"Perish the thought."

"I don't like it when some fucking buff interferes in police work; I don't give a damn how long you've been on the job."

"Tell it to Sheriff Bowland."

"That clown? He was smart enough to hire me. Other than

that . . . He got old in a hurry; you know what I mean? Took like a year. He's past it now, man."

"Maybe so, but if you have a problem, tell him."

"I'm telling you."

"The sheriff wants to find out who killed Montgomery. He thinks I can help."

"Is that why you were talking with Ardina Curtis?"

"She knew Montgomery. Her brother knew Montgomery. Did you know Montgomery?"

"Yeah, I knew him."

"Yet, when I went to the Law Enforcement Center Friday night to report that he had been killed, you said, 'Who?'"

"You got something to say, McKenzie, or do you just like the sound of your own voice?"

"Just connecting the dots. Tell me about Eddie Curtis."

"What about him?"

"Are you friends?"

"Deputies aren't supposed to have friends?"

"All that pushing and shoving you guys were doing. It looked to me like you were getting ready to pull on him."

Wurzer's hand slid to his firearm.

"Like now," I said.

I smiled at another driver and gave her the thumbs-up as she rolled slowly past us.

"Step out of the vehicle," Wurzer said.

"No."

"What did you say?"

I threw a thumb at the SUV behind me.

"I notice that you have a camera mounted on your rearview mirror," I said.

"You know what? I think it's malfunctioning."

"Yeah, that's what I thought. Call for backup. I'll get out of the car when your backup gets here."

"You'll do what I tell you."

Wurzer reached for the door handle and pulled up, only it was locked.

"Why?" I asked. "So you can tune me up? Maybe give me a wood shampoo."

"You know all the slang."

"I invented the fucking slang, asshole." Probably I shouldn't have shouted, but the deputy was starting to annoy me. "You want to hang paper on me, go right ahead. You want to put the arm on me, we can do that, too. Once your backup gets here with a camera that's working."

"I should pull you in for violating the jackass ordinance if nothing else."

"It didn't need to go down this way, Deputy. You could've just come up to me and talked like a man. But no, you had to get all large and emphatic. You had to get badge-heavy. Is that why you're not in Minneapolis anymore? You kept stopping, arresting, or threatening everyone in sight?"

He stared at me as if he was reviewing his options. There must have been a lot of them because it was a full thirty seconds before he said, "Move it down the road, mutt."

"You first."

Wurzer smirked because he knew what I was thinking, that he'd give me a head start and then run me into a ditch.

"Don't worry about it, McKenzie. The next time you see me, you'll see me."

I wasn't entirely sure what hc meant. Wurzer seemed satisfied that it was a good exit line, though. He moved back to his vehicle, silenced the light bar, and pulled onto Highway 61. He spun his tires as if he wanted to spray the Mustang with gravel, but all he churned up was dust. I gave him a full five minutes before I followed.

Jodine Montgomery was sitting behind a small desk in the same room that hosted the Eastman Johnson collection. She did not look up when I entered, even though it seemed as if we were the only two people in that wing of the Duluth Art Institute. Possibly she was too absorbed by her work to notice me. Or it could have been that the classical music they pumped into the exhibit hall masked what little noise I made. I listened hard, yet could not identify the work.

Still, my inner voice said. *Music. In an art museum. Take that, Perrin Stewart.*

I approached the desk and said, "Excuse me."

The woman glanced up and smiled.

"May I help you?" she asked.

"Jodine Montgomery?"

"Yes?"

"My name's McKenzie."

"Let me guess. You want to talk about my ex-husband."

"If it's not too much trouble."

"I'm very uncomfortable with this. Whatever my personal feelings toward David . . . Look, I've already spoken with agents from the BCA."

My hand slipped into my jacket pocket and fingered the notebook and pen I had there. I decided, though, she deserved better than that tired gag.

"I apologize." I reverted to my most relaxed and reassuring voice, the one I honed through countless interviews conducted during my illustrious career as a police officer—okay, maybe not illustrious. "I'm deeply sorry for intruding on you during your grief. Unfortunately, things have changed since you were interviewed by the police."

"In what way?"

I surprised myself by telling her the truth, explained about the missing *Scenes from an Inland Sea.* Jodine stood up.

"That's impossible," she said.

She began pacing the room. I had the impression that, like me, she preferred to think on her feet. As she paced I noticed Eastman Johnson's oil paintings and sketches hanging on the walls. I discovered a charcoal and crayon sketch titled *Objib-way Girl* that was particularly striking.

How is it you've never heard of this guy?

"The authorities believe that David stole *Scenes from an Inland Sea?*" Jodine asked.

"They do."

"That's—that's insane."

"Do you know Louise Wykoff?"

"Yes. Not well. I doubt anyone in GM knows her well. She stays pretty much to herself. We've spoken a few times over the years, though. We have a couple of her paintings right there." Jodine gestured to a spot on the wall near the door. "Her work blends in nicely with Johnson's. Some people can't even tell them apart. Anyway, she seemed very nice. I can't believe it. Do you know what those paintings must be worth? Randolph McInnis? But no. No. I don't believe it. David was a cheat. He wasn't a thief."

"Do you think your ex-husband knew Louise?"

"I know what you're asking, McKenzie. I want to say no. On the other hand, David had cheated on me with so many women over the years, why not her, too?"

"How long have you and David been divorced?"

"Just over four years now. McKenzie, David was not a bad guy. Yes, he cheated on me. It was like he couldn't help himself. He never hit me, though. He never abused me. He wasn't a drunk or a druggie or a compulsive gambler or whatever. He treated our daughter like a royal princess. Once the divorce was final and I stopped wondering where he was putting his dick, we got along fine. He never missed a child support payment. He was always there when it was his turn to take Jamie for the weekend."

"It must have been hard on him, though."

"It was hard on me, too."

"When was the last time you two spoke?"

"Friday morning."

"Last Friday morning?"

"Wild, isn't it? He called early, right after Jamie left for school. He wanted to know if it was all right with me if he took her to Kakabeka Falls in Canada during his next weekend. It's about ninety minutes from GM, a nice day-trip. He's not allowed to take Jamie out of the state much less out of the country without my permission and he wanted to know if I objected before he mentioned anything to Jamie about it. Like I said, not a bad guy."

Wait a sec, my inner voice said. *Leah Huddleston told you that if she had the paintings, she would take them to Canada, crossing the Pigeon River at the Grand Portage Port of Entry. If you were CBP or the Canadian Border Services Agency and you had a car passing through with a pretty little girl in the passenger seat and her proud daddy behind the wheel, would you bother to check the trunk of their car?*

"Did you agree to let them go?" I asked aloud.

"Yes. Why not? Then Saturday morning they told me that he was dead. Apparent suicide. I still haven't been able to explain it to Jamie. That's one of the reasons I'm working today, so I don't have to explain it. How do you explain it to a child? She keeps asking, 'Why? Why?' David . . . he seemed fine when I spoke to him. Happy even. He said all the crap he pulled when we were married, he was going to make it up to me. He said the same thing when we were married so I didn't actually believe him. Yet he sounded—McKenzie, he sounded sincere. I don't know what to tell Jamie. My biggest fear is that she'll blame herself because that's what people do, don't they? They blame themselves when someone commits suicide. Why didn't I see it coming? Why couldn't I help? My second greatest fear is that she'll blame me, that she'll decide that her father killed himself because I left him."

I came *this*close to telling Jodine that her ex-husband might have been murdered instead, yet decided against it. Would that have made the conversations with her daughter easier or harder?

Especially since I had nothing to offer in the way of proof, except for my own suspicions.

"I'm sorry for your loss," I said.

"Unfortunately, it's not just my loss. It's also my daughter's. David—how could he do this to her?"

TEN

It was a two-hour drive from Duluth to Grand Marais. During the trip, I used the Mustang's SYNC System to make a hands-free phone call. It took a couple of trics before I was able to reach Sheriff Bowland. He told me he and the agents from the BCA were gathering at the Blue Water Cafe. He said to meet them there. I said I would.

Parking in Grand Marais on a glorious Sunday afternoon was about what you'd expect. I ended up in a space near Drury Lane, an independent bookstore that was painted to resemble a child's dollhouse, and walked the block and a half to the café. I intercepted the sheriff, who had parked even farther away than me. Once again, I was impressed by how impeccably he dressed and how old he appeared.

My inner voice admonished me. *What do you expect? Andy Griffith?*

"What do you know about an Ojibwa named Eddie Curtis?" I asked.

"I don't know an Eddie Curtis."

"Really?"

"What do you think, that I know everyone in Cook County?"

"Has your department had any professional dealings with the man?"

"Like I said, I don't know."

"Deputy Wurzer would know."

"Why?"

I described their confrontation on Marina Road in Grand Portage.

"When did this take place?" Bowland asked.

"Shortly before I had my own confrontation with Wurzer on Highway 61."

I explained that to the sheriff as well.

"No guns were pulled or punches thrown," I added. "Wurzer made it clear, though, that he was unhappy that I had seen him and Curtis together."

"I'll look into it. In the meantime, stay away from Wurzer, at least until I have a chance to talk to him."

"How did he end up here, anyway?"

Bowland sighed as if it was a sad story that he was tired of telling.

"It's about money, McKenzie. Isn't it always? The average salary for a police officer in Minneapolis is $64,000. Do you think I can pay that? In a county with a population of fifty-one hundred? With a limited tax base? There's not a lot of money to hire what we need so we end up having to make do with what we have. A man like Wurzer, he was dismissed from the Minneapolis Police Department for"—the sheriff halted on the sidewalk, closed his eyes, and spoke as if he was reciting a line from memory—"the intentional, reckless, or negligent withholding, hiding, altering, fabricating, or destroying of evidence relevant to a legal proceeding."

He opened his eyes and continued walking.

"Something to do with a botched raid and a fence the county attorney was trying to build a case against," Bowland said. "For most departments that would raise a bright, red flag. For me, though, for small town and county police forces like mine, that made him affordable."

"He helped a fence?"

"I don't know the details. The MPD likes to keep its secrets. Wurzer wasn't particularly forthcoming about it, either, and I didn't press. All I saw was a man who went through the Minneapolis Police Academy, who had eight years on the job, and who was willing to move to Grand Marais and work for the money I paid him. I've kept a close eye on him, don't think I haven't. Except for the occasional disrespectful remark about the bodunk way I run things and a couple of complaints about what one DUI called an overbearing attitude, I haven't had any problems with him."

"How long has he been here?"

"Just over four years."

Agent Krause shook his head when I entered the Blue Water Cafe with the sheriff as if I was the last person he wanted to see. Plakcy grinned at me.

"Why is it that when we go to interview someone you've been there first?" he asked.

I gestured at Krause and said, "I don't have any deadweight to lug around."

Plakcy looked at his partner and laughed. Krause not so much.

"What are you doing here?" he asked.

"I was invited by the sheriff."

"We're all on the same side," Bowland said.

Krause clearly didn't agree. You could hear it in his voice when he said, "It's your county."

The BCA agents had grabbed a booth just inside the front door of the café with a view of the park that sprawled in front of the harbor. It was three thirty in the afternoon, yet the agents were both eating breakfast. Plakcy had ordered pancakes.

Krause was working on a Denver omelet. They made room for us and Bowland and I sat.

"Well?" Krause said.

"Well what?"

"If you want information, McKenzie, you damn well better have plenty to give us. You go first."

I told them every move I'd made and every person I had spoken to, including Peg Younghans at the Frontier Motel the night before. I also offered support for Louise's theory that the theft of the McInnis paintings was a random act by pointing out that property crimes in Cook County had doubled in the past few years. I could tell that Sheriff Bowland didn't like me mentioning that, yet he didn't disagree.

"Your theory is that Montgomery used his job as a handyman to target his vics?" Krause asked.

"I don't know if they're his victims or not. It shouldn't be too hard to figure out, though. Just contact anyone who's filed a complaint in the past few years and ask if Montgomery had worked for them."

"Not too hard at all," the sheriff agreed. The way he said it, though, made me think he wished he had thought of it himself.

Maybe Deputy Wurzer was right, my inner voice said. *Maybe the job is past him.*

"On the other hand," I said, "according to his ex-wife, Montgomery had planned a day-trip to Canada next weekend. She said he was going to take his daughter to see the Kakabeka Falls."

No one spoke for a few moments until Agent Plakcy said, "My little girl likes waterfalls, too."

"Just telling you what I heard."

"Something to consider, isn't it?" Plakcy added.

"You know, I appreciate this, fellas. You're suspicious of me, I get that. I'd be suspicious of me, too. You're listening, though. Most cops have little regard for the things I have to tell them and here I am, a taxpayer in the thirty-seven percent bracket."

"Well, at least we know who to send the bill to," Krause said.

The waitress appeared and asked the sheriff and me if we wanted to see a menu. We both settled for coffee. After it was poured, I asked, "What did the county coroner say?"

"She ruled that Montgomery died of a single GSW to the head, specifically the left temple," Plakcy said. "The bullet followed an upward ten-degree trajectory and exited through the top right of his skull. She remarked that the force he had used to press the barrel of the gun against his temple was significant. Very deep bruising. She also said she's seen it before, suicides that were very angry with themselves."

"I wonder why he was angry."

"Maybe he heard that you were trying to track him down," Krause said.

"Does the coroner have an official time of death?"

"She now says the closest she can estimate is between twelve thirty and one P.M."

"So Montgomery was dead *before* I started to track him down."

Krause glared for a moment, yet said nothing.

"What about a right-hander shooting himself with his left hand?" I asked.

"The coroner said it happens about five percent of the time," Plakcy answered.

"Without dropping the gun?"

"Twenty-six percent of the time."

"I thought it was way less than that. Fingerprints on the gun?"

"Smudged."

"The shell casings inside the gun?"

"The same."

"C'mon."

"It is what it is."

"On the other hand, there are a few facts that don't seem to jibe," Krause said.

"Such as?"

"The GSR test results. There were trace amounts of gunshot residue on Montgomery's hand, but the coroner doesn't trust it. She said the patterning was off, like someone might have been holding his hand when the gun was fired."

"Except she won't swear to it," Plakcy added. "She said the evidence is inconclusive."

"What else?" I asked.

"There were two spent cartridges in the gun, yet only one bullet hole," Krause said. "Could be the killer shot Montgomery, wrapped his hand around the gun, and fired a second round through the open doorway."

"Or it's possible Montgomery fired a round God knows when and where and never reloaded," Plakcy said. "At least that's the counterargument."

"The handgun was unregistered. We can't prove who it belonged to. However, Montgomery possessed a small arsenal, mostly hunting rifles and shotguns. They weren't registered, either. In Minnesota they don't need to be. You do need to register your handguns, though, and he did. Two handguns, two registrations, just as the law prescribes."

"An inconsistency," I said. "Don't you love 'em?"

"You'll love this then, too," Plakcy said. "Montgomery had ammunition for every weapon in his gun cabinet, only none of it matched the S and W that killed him."

"I don't suppose there was any evidence of forced entry."

"None."

"Given all of this, what did the coroner decide was the manner of death?"

"Undetermined."

"Meaning she's leaving it up to you."

"Us?" Krause said. "Hell, McKenzie, if it wasn't for you we wouldn't be here. We wouldn't be investigating Montgomery's death as a homicide. Would we?"

He glanced at the sheriff as if he was seeking confirmation. The sheriff looked at me.

"It was you calling it a homicide that made me think it was a homicide," he said.

"What do you think now?" I asked.

The sheriff shook his head and said, "I don't know. Could you have been wrong? Could I have been wrong? My original conclusion was based on Montgomery shooting himself left-handed; on him still holding the weapon. If that's a common thing . . ."

"Assuming it was murder . . ."

"That's what we've been doing," Krause said.

"Who do we know who is capable of staging a suicide?"

"You mean besides anyone who's ever watched reruns of *CSI*?"

The sheriff's eyes grew wide with anger. He knew what I was suggesting. He didn't say anything, though, and I didn't pursue the matter. What was I going to tell them? That there's this ex-MPD I don't like who doesn't like me, who knew Montgomery, but who said he didn't? Despite having been a cop, or perhaps because I had been a cop, I'm not necessarily a big proponent of the thin blue line. Yet I was loath to cross it unless I had what the justice community deemed unassailable evidence, so I tucked the thought away.

Meanwhile, Sheriff Bowland turned in his seat to stare out the window.

"I don't know," he said.

"There are only a few reasons why people kill," Plakcy said. "Remove drugs and booze and a lack of impulse control from the equation and the reasons become even fewer."

"What have you decided?" I asked.

"We need to find those fucking paintings," Krause said.

"Find the paintings, find the killer," Plakcy said. "Or not."

"Yeah," Krause said. "Or not."

"Wait a minute," Bowland said. "You don't think it's the same case?"

"The lights in Montgomery's house," I said.

"You keep bringing that up. What about them?"

"We believe someone must have arrived on the scene shortly before McKenzie did," Plakcy said. "Just after the sun had set. He or she—"

"Or them," Krause added.

"Found Montgomery dead and promptly searched the house, turning on all the lights as they went. There were no drawers opened, no flower pots overturned because what they wanted wouldn't have fit in a drawer or a flower pot."

"The smallest of the paintings is twenty-two-by-thirty inches," I said.

"Closet doors were opened, though, and so were the cabinets," Plakcy added. "We could tell by how the bedspreads were wrinkled and dust was disturbed that the bed, sofas, and chairs had all been looked under. There was plenty of evidence that the garage and shed were searched, too. We figure the suspect either left just before McKenzie arrived or hid until after he left."

"Unless it was McKenzie," Krause said.

"It wasn't," I said.

"I'm inclined to believe you."

"Really? That's the nicest thing you've ever said to me."

"Shut up."

"It's highly unlikely," Plakcy said, "that the person or persons unknown who murdered Montgomery—if he was murdered— would return to the scene of the crime six hours after it occurred and turn on all the lights. Meaning there were at least two people who knew about the paintings."

"Or the person who zeroed Montgomery didn't know about the paintings and killed him for some other reason."

"Or Montgomery really did commit suicide."

"Would you kill yourself if you had paintings worth God knows how many millions hidden beneath your bed?" I asked.

"I don't know," Krause said. "It's entirely possible that he killed himself *because* he had paintings worth God knows how many millions hidden beneath his bed."

"Ninety percent of the time we know whodunit five minutes after we arrive at a crime scene," Plakcy said. "This time, though . . ."

"This time you actually have to earn that huge government paycheck," I said.

"Don't you hate it when that happens, Sheriff?" Plakcy asked.

Bowland nodded, but didn't speak.

"Did you have the chance to access Montgomery's cell phone records yet, determine his movements?" I asked.

The agents both nodded.

"And?"

"He did exactly what you said he did on Friday," Plakcy said. "He drove to Two Harbors and, after selling the tea set and candlesticks to the antiques dealer, drove straight home."

"Where someone he knew was waiting for him," Krause said.

"Something else that should make you happy, McKenzie— Louise Wykoff lied to us about her relationship with Montgomery."

"How so?"

"He was parked outside Louise Wykoff's home on Tuesday from nine A.M. until three in the afternoon."

"He was fixing her water heater," I said.

"Are you sure of that?"

"That's what I was told."

"By who? Wykoff?"

"No. A waitress at the Gunflint Tavern that Montgomery was friendly with."

"All right, I'll give you that for now."

"Still," Krause said, "I wonder what he was fixing from nine until midnight Wednesday and from seven until eight on Thursday night? Any ideas?"

"Before you answer," Plakcy said, "know that according to Montgomery's phone log, Louise also called him."

"Louise called Montgomery and not the other way around?" I asked.

"Yep."

"When? Tuesday to fix her water heater?"

"Nope. On Thursday. One half hour before he parked his car outside her house."

"I don't understand. Louise was being filmed by a documentary crew when Montgomery was killed," I said aloud. "That gives her a perfect alibi."

"Just like you," Krause said.

"So why deny she had a relationship with the man?"

"Pride," Sheriff Bowland said. "She's the Wykoff woman. Do you think she wants her neighbors to know that she was playing bedroom tag with a low-life player like Montgomery?"

"I still don't believe it."

The two agents glanced at each other.

"What do you call it when you become personally involved with a suspect?" Plakcy asked.

"Stupid," Krause replied.

"I'm not personally involved," I said.

"Of course not. You've been running errands all over northern Minnesota for her because—why exactly?"

"I'm just a friend of a friend."

"That cxplains it."

I might have said more in my defense except Bowland's phone went off, distracting me.

"This is the sheriff," he said. "Hi, Eileen." I pictured the woman dressed in beige slacks and a black fleece jacket that I had met earlier. "What do you mean CNN wants to interview me . . . ? Who else . . . ? KBJR?"

"KBJR is the NBC affiliate in Duluth," Plakcy said.

"What do they want to talk about?" the sheriff asked his cell phone.

At the same time, I nudged the sheriff's elbow and pointed out the window at the park across the street. A TV van with CBS 3 NEWS painted on the side was breaking several parking laws while a cameraman and a woman with impossibly blond hair prepared to film a live remote with the harbor at her back. Meanwhile, Jeffery Mehren was standing off to the side with Jennica and the rest of the documentary crew preparing to film the TV news crew. Tourists were gathering in a semicircle to watch.

I don't know if the sheriff was talking to his cell phone, us, or the world at large.

"This is not good," he said.

ELEVEN

"Dammit, Louise," I said. We were standing in the art school area of her converted church. Representatives of CNN, CBS, and NBC had left just minutes earlier. "You contacted the media?"

"Don't be angry with me."

"I'm not nearly as angry as the BCA. What were you thinking?"

"I was thinking that Perrin Stewart was right. The world needs to know about Randolph's paintings. They need to be seen."

"I told you before—publicity makes the paintings harder to recover. Didn't you believe me?"

"The police haven't done anything."

"It's been less than two days. Give them a chance."

"This way, the world will know the paintings exist and that they belong to me. That'll make them harder to sell."

"You don't want to make them harder to sell. Don't you get that? Listen to me—this is a true story. A sculpture made by Matisse was stolen from a Swiss museum in the early 1990s. Twenty-five years later—twenty-five, Louise—an auction house contacted the Art Loss Register to report that a man was attempting to sell it. The man claimed that he bought the sculpture in a thrift shop for something like one percent of its actual value a few weeks after the theft had taken place in the same town where the museum was located. He said he thought the sculpture was a copy but later came to think differently. He was unable to provide documentation to prove that his story was true. However, neither could the authorities provide evidence stating that it wasn't true. Follow me? Eventually, the man returned the sculpture to the insurance company that covered the loss for an undisclosed amount of money. You can bet, though, it was for a helluva lot more than one percent. What's stopping our thief from doing the same thing? What's stopping him from stashing the paintings in an attic and waiting for ten, twenty, or thirty years before trying to sell them, all the while pretending that he bought them at a flea market?"

"But they belong to me."

"They were never displayed, they were never insured, and twenty years from now, will you even be around to argue your case?"

When I was a rookie cop, I once had to knock on a door and tell the woman that answered that her daughter had been killed by a drunk driver. I can still hear her screams of agony and loss. Louise sounded just like her. Her voice was filled with such pain and she collapsed, just as the mother had done. I caught her before she fell and gently lowered her to the floor. She folded her body into a fetal position and wept. I held her in my arms. After a while, she ceased crying and started breathing normally. She remained on the floor, though, and I continued to hold her.

"I'm surprised the BCA hasn't arrived by now," I said. "The agents have questions to ask."

"What questions?"

"About your relationship with David Montgomery."

"I told you—"

"He fixed your water heater Tuesday."

"That's right. I forgot."

"The man spent six hours working in your house the day you discovered your most valued possessions were stolen and it didn't occur to you that he might have been involved until this moment? Not even after you learned that he had been killed?"

"What are you suggesting?"

"He was also parked outside of your house Wednesday and Thursday night."

"Why?"

"You tell me."

"I can't."

"You called him around six thirty Thursday night."

Her body stiffened in my arms, yet she did not reply.

"What did you talk about?" I asked.

Louise shook her head slowly.

"I don't know how to explain any of this," she said.

"Believe me, the BCA will ask you to try."

"McKenzie, I appreciate that we barely know each other. You're Perrin's friend not—not mine. But, McKenzie, tell me, please, what should I do?"

"Don't worry. We'll think of something."

I was hungry when I left Louise, so I stopped at the Crooked Spoon Café. It had an enclosed rooftop bar called the Crooked Lookout. I must have caught a seam between the early evening and later evening dinner crowd because I managed to find an unoccupied table in the corner with a nice view of the harbor. The TV news crew had vanished along with Mehren and his filmmakers. A waitress appeared and I ordered pan-roasted salmon and an ale from the Castle Danger Brewery just outside of Two Harbors. I liked the ale so much that by the time the waitress returned with my salmon, I was ready for another one.

I was about three bites into the salmon when the chair across from me was pulled out and Jennica sat down.

"Hello, McKenzie."

"Hey, sweetie."

"Mind if I join you?"

"Not at all. Do you mind if I keep eating?"

Her response was to prop her elbows on the table, rest her head in her hands, and ask, "Are you married?"

"Nope."

"Why not?"

"The woman I love more than life itself was in very bad, very abusive marriage and it soured her on the institution, so now we live together in a $450,000 condominium with a view of the Mississippi River in downtown Minneapolis and probably always will unless she decides to move somewhere else in which case I have no doubt I'll go with her."

"That explains it, then."

"Explains what?"

"Why you didn't hit on me last night when you had the chance."

"Here I thought it was because I'm a gentleman."

"What does that have to do with anything?"

"I'm also about twenty-five years older than you are."

"You know where I'm from, right? In Hollywood, men hooking up with women young enough to be their daughters is a common occurrence. When was the last time you went to the movies, anyway? All the male actors are fifty and all the females are twenty."

"I'm not from Hollywood. Besides, what would your father say?"

"He wouldn't say anything. He'd just shoot you. 'Course, he's not from Hollywood, either. He grew up in Kansas City. Thinks the sun rises and sets on the Royals."

"What baseball team do you root for?"

"Los Angeles Angels."

"Not the Dodgers?"

"Screw the Dodgers."

"I knew there was a reason I liked you. I like your father, too. Where is he, by the way?"

"Downstairs waiting for a table. He's buying dinner for the entire crew. We're leaving first thing tomorrow morning."

"Before you get an ending to your movie?"

"We're not done. There's plenty more to shoot. Besides, we can always come back."

"I wish you good luck. Both you and your father."

She stood.

I stood.

"Take care, Jennica."

"What?" she said. "I'm not sweetie anymore?"

"You'll always be a sweetie to me."

She shook my hand, smiled, and said, "See you around, Mc-Kenzie."

I lingered over my dinner, which didn't make my waitress happy. My table was prime real estate and she was losing revenue on it. While I dawdled, I found a Wi-Fi network and checked on my Minnesota Twins. They were slugging it out with the Cleveland Indians for a playoff berth. The Royals, meanwhile, had faded after the All-Star break and were in the process of giving their September call-ups a lot of playing time.

Too bad for Mehren, my inner voice decided.

I left the waitress a tip big enough to make up for my dis-courtesy and made my way downstairs. Mehren and his crew had been seated at a large table across the dining room. They seemed to be having a good time. Jennica saw me and gave a wave. Mehren witnessed the wave and excused himself. He walked toward me with his hand outstretched so I felt obligated to wait on him.

Mehren shook my hand and said, "Before you leave, may I have a moment?"

"Sure."

We stepped outside. The Blue Water Cafe was just across the street. In Grand Marais everything was just across the street.

"I know you don't want to be in my movie," Mehren said. "However . . ."

"What?"

"I've spoken to Mr. Flonta about you. He said if you have something tangible to contribute to the film, he'd be happy to make it worth your while."

"Fortunately, I'm independently wealthy so that kind of offer doesn't mean as much to me as it used to."

"I know that about you. I also know that you'll occasionally involve yourself in a criminal investigation to help a friend. All I want to do is film it."

"Are we friends?"

"You and my daughter seem chummy and she's one of the producers."

"Stop it."

"Seriously, if you do find those paintings, I'd make it worth your while to talk about it on film. If money doesn't interest you, we'll think of something else."

"Did Jennica tell you that she and I had made a deal?"

"She did. She also told me that she and her camera kept you from taking a beating."

"No. No beating. It was only two against one. Anyway, listen—tell Jennica that I'll keep my promise even though she broke hers."

"You will?"

"Sure."

"Give her an interview, but not me?"

"That's the deal."

Mehren thought that was funny. While he laughed, he said, "My daughter. I knew I should have sent her back to school. All right, okay, that's the deal. Thank you."

"Don't thank me. I haven't found the paintings yet. The way things are going, I probably won't."

"I have a great deal of faith in you."

Geezus, my inner voice said. *That's exactly what Perrin Stewart said. It's how you got into this mess.*

"Just between you and me and the light post, though," Mehren said. "Why do you think Louise changed her mind about contacting the media?"

"Why does anyone contact the media? She wanted attention."

"I'm in the attention business, McKenzie. It still doesn't make sense to me."

"See you around, Hollywood," I said, just to be obnoxious. "Too bad about your Royals."

"Kansas City won the World Series a couple of years ago. What has your team done, lately?"

He had me there.

I decided that Deputy Wurzer was onto something about the stars. You could only see the largest of them in the city because there was so much light pollution. Yet on the North Shore, even the tiniest was bright enough that you felt you could reach out and touch it.

After parking my Mustang, I passed through my room, going from the back door to the front door, into the horseshoe, down the gently sloping hill, and across Highway 61 to the lakeshore, all so I could get a better look at the stars.

That's when they came at me, like guard dogs with their vocal cords cut, attacking without barking out a warning first. I felt the hard blow to my solar plexus before I even knew they were there. I collapsed onto the gravel and sand. Two men pulled me up by my arms. A third said, "McKenzie."

My first reaction was embarrassment. How could I have been so careless; how could I have not have known of their approach? I had been paying attention ever since I joined the cops. What the hell was wrong with me now?

My second was fear. The man had used my name, which meant I hadn't stumbled into a random mugging although, seriously, how many random muggings were there on the North Shore of Lake Superior?

These are not the guys from the Dairy Queen, my inner voice told me, although their goal appeared to be the same. I found that out when the third man moved close enough to me that I could smell the tobacco and beer on his breath.

"You shouldn't poke your nose into other people's business," he said.

I knew what was coming and I tried to move my arms to protect myself, but his two companions held them fast. I tensed my stomach muscles and that helped some as he hit me just above my belt line.

He enjoyed it so much that he drove his fist into my stomach a second time. My knees buckled and I began to retch. I would have fallen if the men holding my arms hadn't kept me upright.

The third man stepped close again. He grabbed a fistful of hair and yanked upward. My head went with it until my face was close to his face.

"What did I say?" he asked.

"I shouldn't poke my head into other people's business."

"What do you say?"

"All right."

"Huh?"

"You want me out of it, I'm out of it."

"You trying to be cute?"

"I'm trying not to get hurt any more. Listen, I'm way too old for this shit."

They must have thought that was funny because all three of them chuckled.

"You're not as tough as I was told," the third man said.

"Who told you I was tough? No one who knows me."

"Just to be sure . . ."

The third man hit me again, this time in the face.

I muttered a few obscenities. Apparently, he thought I was swearing at him because he hit me again. I could feel my teeth loosen and my mouth fill with blood.

The other two men released my arms and I crumpled onto the lakeshore. I rolled immediately into a ball to protect my head and my groin from the kicks that I knew were coming. My experience, guys like these always kick you when you're down.

That's when she screamed, a woman who was walking on the beach hand in hand with her boyfriend beneath the starlit sky.

She screamed more than once.

Truthfully, I lost count of how many times she screamed while her boyfriend stood there with what I assumed was a perplexed expression on his face.

The three attackers disappeared into the night almost as silently as they had come.

The boyfriend tightened his grip on his girlfriend's hand and pulled her toward the lights of the Frontier Motel, not bothering at all to see what condition my condition was in. I didn't blame him. In fact, I would have done the same thing—make sure the person I cared most about was safe before I started caring about someone else.

By then the woman's screams had attracted the attention of my fellow motel guests. Some came to their windows and looked out. A few more enthusiastic types actually stepped out of their rooms and approached the screaming woman who by now had stopped screaming.

I managed to get to my knees. After a few moments, I was standing. I stumbled across the lakeshore to the highway and across the highway to the gentle slope. That's where a few guests reached me.

"What happened?" they asked.

"Are you hurt?" they asked.

A woman I recognized as one of the motel's owners pulled

one of my arms around her shoulder and slid her arm around my waist and began helping me to my room.

"I called the sheriff," she said.

The woman and her boyfriend watched from a distance.

"Are you the one who screamed?" I asked.

She nodded vigorously.

"Thank you."

I sat on the corner of the bed while the woman who owned the motel tended my wounds, mostly with ice and antiseptic, as if she had done this sort of thing many times before. She didn't ask me who or what or why, only where, and once she was satisfied that the attack didn't occur on Frontier Motel property, she stopped asking questions altogether.

After a few minutes, the door was knocked on and Deputy Wurzer entered my room. I chuckled when I saw his face even though it hurt both my stomach and mouth to do so. He smiled in return.

"Thank you," he said. "I'll take it from here."

The woman nodded and made for the door.

Wurzer asked, "Are you all right?"

"Fit as a fiddle and ready for love," I said.

The woman frowned as she stepped outside, but then I sometimes have that effect on people.

"Seriously, McKenzie," Wurzer said. "Are you all right? I wouldn't want to be accused of refusing medical attention to a suspect."

"I'm a suspect?"

"No one outside is sure who started the fight."

"It wasn't a fight, Deputy. It was a beatdown."

"You're saying someone taught you a lesson? Well, well . . ."

"Is that what they call felony assault up here in Cook County?"

"Can you identify your assailants?"

Again I flashed on the guys outside the Dairy Queen.

"No," I said. "It was too dark. There were three of them, though; men about my size. Only one spoke. I doubt I'd recognize his voice if he walked through the door right now and asked who ordered pizza. It could have been you for all I know."

"Me? I was at the Law Enforcement Center drinking Eileen's coffee when the call came in."

"I'd be surprised if you weren't," I said. "I notice you're not writing anything down."

"Tell me something worth writing down."

"I lied."

"What do you mean?"

"The man who hit me. He said I should stop poking my nose in other people's business. I told him if he wanted me out of it, I'd stay out of it. I lied."

"Of course you did. What business, exactly?"

"What do you think?"

"You tell me."

"Are you trying to be funny?"

"Do I look like I'm trying to be funny?"

"I'm investigating Montgomery's murder. What else?"

"Sheriff Bowland told me an hour ago that neither the county coroner nor the BCA are convinced that Montgomery was murdered. He said there's a good chance that his death will eventually be ruled a suicide. Which means tuning you up can only work against the killer—if there is a killer. So, yeah, what else? Who have you pissed off besides me?"

"I don't know."

"Think about it."

Could this be about the burglaries? my inner voice asked.

"I don't know," I repeated.

"The men who came at you obviously knew you were staying at the Frontier. Who knew that?"

That's a law-dog question. Is Wurzer actually trying to do his job?

"It wasn't a secret," I said.

The deputy grabbed my chin and turned my face so he could get a good look at it. I knocked his hand away. He smirked.

"You think you're so damn smart, doncha?" he said.

"Actually, I have very serious self-esteem issues."

"I told you not to interfere in police business. You didn't listen. As far as I'm concerned, you got what you deserve." Deputy Wurzer stared at me for a few more beats, shook his head, and made for the door. "Some people need more than one lesson. Some people get more than one lesson."

"Oh, I learned my lesson, Deputy. I learned it well."

His response was to smirk yet again.

"If you think of something useful, give me a shout," he said. "I don't much care what happens to you, McKenzie, but a tourist getting mugged is bad for the town image."

I stepped into the bathroom and fiddled with my teeth. None of them were broken. The left side of my face was swollen, though, and while there weren't any broken bones, I was sure there would be bruising in the morning. I absolutely knew I could expect a black-and-blue stomach, yet that seemed more or less intact, too.

"You were lucky," I told my reflection.

My reflection didn't argue with me.

I double-checked the locks on the doors, closed the blinds, turned off the lights, and lay down on the bed without removing my clothes. I pressed an ice pack against my face, but not against my stomach. It was about that time of night when I should be calling Nina. I decided against it, though.

I'll make up some story in the morning, I told myself.

I closed my eyes. Sleep began pulling at me almost immediately.

My cell phone rang.

My eyes popped open.

"All right, Nina, all right." I reached for the cell and swiped right. "This is McKenzie."

"McKenzie, we need to talk."

It was a woman's voice but not Nina's.

"Who's calling, please?" I asked.

"I'd like to see you as soon as possible."

"Who is this?"

"Oh. That's right. We've never been introduced. I'm Mary Ann McInnis."

TWELVE

Kenwood was originally developed when millionaires still believed it was acceptable to erect their mansions next door to each other instead of several football fields apart. The neighborhood was more or less nestled between Cedar Lake and Lake of the Isles and designed, according to the Minneapolis government website, for "discriminating residents," which meant that there was no poverty whatsoever within its borders unless you considered a six-figure income living on the edge.

The mansion I wanted was more than a hundred years old and had a nice view of the Cedar Lake East Beach. I parked on the street, climbed the concrete steps to a portico, and knocked on the door. The door was pulled open by a woman all of five feet tall with long gray hair worn in a ponytail and wearing a sweatshirt that swore her allegiance to the Minnesota Lynx women's basketball team.

"You can't use the doorbell?" she said. "You need to knock? Here."

She stepped onto the porch and pressed the button on the door frame. Inside I heard four bells chime the melody known as the Westminster Quarters. It was the same tune you hear in London when the clock tower at the Palace of Westminster where Big Ben hangs marks the hour. The music was so deep and sonorous that you might have thought it was the real thing.

"That is so cool," I said.

"Go 'head. You know you want to."

I pressed the button and listened to the chimes again.

"I never get tired of that," she said. "Are you McKenzie?"

"Yes, ma'am."

"Don't call me ma'am. Ma'am is an archaic term coined by men to disparage older women."

"I didn't know that."

"Neither did I until my granddaughter explained it to me. Personally I think she's full of hooey. The word doesn't seem to bother the Queen of England, does it?"

"Not that I'm aware of."

"I'm Mary Ann McInnis. Shake my hand."

I did.

"Are we going to be friends, McKenzie?"

"I hope so."

"Then you can call me M. A. M-A, not to be confused with 'Ma.' Are you a drinking man, McKenzie?"

"Yes, M. A."

"Thank God. Come inside."

I did. Directly in front of me was a grand staircase reminiscent of the one Clark Gable carried Vivien Leigh up in *Gone with the Wind*. At the top of the stairs was a photograph of the actor Nastassja Kinski during her sex-symbol days. She was very young and very nude and wrapped in a boa constrictor.

Okay, not in Kansas anymore, my inner voice said.

To my right there was a lot of furniture plus a grand piano strategically arranged around a fireplace large enough to roast a side of beef. To my left was another sitting area, only this time the furniture was arranged around a bar. I had never seen an actual bar inside a house before except in the movies. *The Philadelphia Story* came to mind.

Mary Ann went to the bar. I followed her. Along the way I discovered a dining room with a table large enough to seat twenty and another room that I wanted to call a library because it was filled with books even though the books were in stacks scattered around chairs and tables and not arranged on shelves.

"What time is it?" she asked.

"Noon."

"Beer or wine?"

"Beer."

I was delighted when she pulled two Summit EPAs out of a refrigerator behind the bar. She popped the caps off the bottles with an opener that had a handle designed to resemble a baseball bat and gave me one.

"My philosophy, you can drink anything you want in the morning as long as you mix it with tomato or orange juice," Mary Ann said. "Noon until four it's beer or wine. After four it's every man for himself."

"Rules to live by."

"Cheers."

We clinked bottles and drank.

"So, McKenzie," Mary Ann said. "What happened to your face? Run into a door?"

I fingered a line of purple and blue along my jaw that looked like a goth cosmetologist had painted it there. It was my stomach that ached though. A palm full of Advil and black coffee early that morning had alleviated some of the pain, but not by much. The beer worked better.

"More like the door ran into me," I said.

"But you should see the other guy, am I right?"

"I'm sure his hands are very sore."

"You're not going to defend your honor or at least your ego? You're not going to tell me that you didn't see him coming?"

"I didn't see him coming. I should have, though."

"Perrin Stewart likes you very much. She says you're the least pretentious man she knows."

"The way things have been going lately, I wish she liked me less."

"I called her yesterday after I saw the report about Randolph's paintings on the news. I asked her what she knew about it. She told me everything."

"Yeah, I figured."

"You don't fault her for that?"

"It doesn't make much sense to keep Louise Wykoff's secrets if Louise isn't going to keep them."

"I want those paintings."

"I figured that, too."

"They don't belong to the Wykoff woman. They belonged to my husband, which means they now belong to me."

"You certainly have a valid claim."

"Only you refuse to accept it?"

"Let's just say I appreciate Louise's point of view as well."

"What you appreciate is that Louise is sexy as hell. Don't worry. I don't hold that against you. It's what men do."

"You misjudge me."

"I doubt it. You know, McKenzie, I was pretty once."

"I believe you."

"No, you don't. Come with me."

Mary Ann led me into the library that really wasn't a library. It was another sitting room with a wall of windows facing south. It looked as if Mary Ann had once read a book there, set it down, read a second book, and when she was finished set it on top of the first book, and then repeated the process about six hundred times. We negotiated the stacks until we came to a wall filled with family photographs and a single portrait. The portrait was of Mary Ann. It had been painted by Randolph McInnis and it gave off the same vibe as the paintings he had done of That Wykoff Woman.

"Wow," I said.

"This was painted in 1959 after I started sleeping with Randolph. I discovered later that it was not uncommon for him to paint portraits of the women he slept with, although it was uncommon for him to marry them. Louise wasn't the first by any means and if Randolph hadn't frozen to death in that damn ditch, she wouldn't have been the last. She was the prettiest, though."

"That's debatable."

"Ha. Aren't you the charmer? But I know where I rated in Randolph's hierarchy. This was done twenty years before Louise Wykoff was even born. I was cherry when I first did it with Randolph and drunk, a coed—they called us coeds back then—studying business administration even though I doubted I'd be permitted to be anything more than a secretary. Such were the times I grew up in. Randolph eventually put me in charge of the empire, mostly because he had so many disagreements with the man he had hired before me. I was always grateful for that. It gave me a reason to get up in the morning and I thought it would protect my place in the hierarchy. That and our son. Silly girl. I was forty-five by the time my sixty-five-year-old husband got around to twenty-five-year-old Louise and in his eyes, I was fading fast. Old age is tough, especially on women. Even on women with all the money in the world. Louise, though—she just keeps rolling along, doesn't she? Age doesn't seem to bother her at all. If Randolph had lived, who knows? She might've been the one drinking beer with you."

Mary Ann took a long pull from the bottle and I liked that she had done nothing to hide the years; that she hadn't resorted to tucks and lifts and injections and hair dyes. When she smiled, her entire face smiled. When she frowned, you could see every line, crease, and crevice that she had earned over eighty years. I liked that she had greeted me in a sweatshirt. I liked that she drank beer from the bottle. I liked that she spoke of her life without sentimentality.

"I like you." I didn't mean to actually speak the words. They just kind of slipped out.

"McKenzie," Mary Ann said. "Oh my."

She took my arm and we retreated back to the bar.

"You like me, huh?" Mary Ann said. "So what's it going to take to get you on my side in this thing?"

"Does there need to be sides?"

"Have you any idea what those paintings are worth—the missing *Scenes from an Inland Sea?* My granddaughter says we're trending. I'm not entirely sure what that means. It sounds profitable, though. Plus I keep getting calls from CBS, CNN, MSNBC, Bloomberg, Reuters, the Associated Press, *Time*—they all want to do stories; they all want quotes, mostly I think, because they're so damn tired of covering those nitwits in Washington. This must be a nice change of pace for them. I might not be up on social media, McKenzie, but the mainstream media, publicity, that I understand very well." Mary Ann lifted a fist straight into the air and pulled it down quickly. "Cha-ching. So, McKenzie. Let's cut to the chase, shall we? Do you know where those damn paintings are? Can you get them? Will you get them for me?"

"No. Possibly." I held my hand flat and gave it a waggle. "Meh."

"What the hell does 'meh' mean?"

"May I tell you a story, M. A.?"

"Should I drink another beer while you tell me this story?"

"I would."

She opened two more bottles and slid one over to me. I drained my first Summit ale and took a sip of the second.

"Once upon a time," I said, "a three-hundred-year-old Stradivarius violin valued at more than five million bucks was stolen from the concertmaster for the Milwaukee Symphony Orchestra. The FBI's Art Crime Team was brought into the case almost immediately because it thought that the Strad would be transported across state lines. Only it wasn't. The crime was all about the reward money—$100,000. Instead of trying to move it on the black market, the thieves attempted to trade it back to the insurance company that covered it. They were caught, the violin was recovered, the thieves were sentenced to seven years in prison for receiving stolen property, and the concertmaster got his Stradivarius back."

"And the moral to this story is . . . ?"

"Always, always, always follow the money."

"I don't understand."

"There are only a handful of people in the entire world who could sell the *Scenes from an Inland Sea* on the black market and I guarantee none of them live in Grand Marais. In my opinion, the thieves didn't have a plan when they snatched the paintings and probably still don't. We should provide them with one."

"What are you suggesting?"

"You should offer a reward for information leading to the safe return of the *Scenes from an Inland Sea*. We'll use the word 'information' because it allows you to argue that you're not negotiating with criminals, which of course you are."

"I know all that, McKenzie. This isn't my first rodeo. But why me?"

"The paintings weren't insured. There's no insurance company involved."

"Why? Me?"

"Louise doesn't have the money."

"Too bad for her. Wait. You don't actually expect me to pay these thieves for my own property, do you? Then turn around and give it to That Wykoff Woman? Hell no."

"First, I'm hoping we can avoid actually paying the ransom, but if it comes to that—yes. Pay them. As for the rest, I'm hoping you and Louise can reach an understanding."

"Why? I don't need her, McKenzie. Come to think of it, I don't need you, either. I can take your plan to the FBI, see what they have to say. Or I could hire private investigators or mercs or whoever it is you hire for this sort of thing."

"Except . . ."

"Except, what?"

"I've made enough of a nuisance of myself in Grand Marais that the thieves probably already know me. Anyone else, they'll automatically think is a cop. Granted, that might not matter. What does matter—there's only one person in the world who knows what the paintings actually look like, who can identify them as being the real deal."

I ignored my inner voice when it said, *You can authenticate the paintings. Louise already described them to you, plus you know their exact dimensions.*

"You're saying we need to be sure, before money changes hands, that we're not buying forgeries," Mary Ann said.

"We need to do it at a glance, too. Once things start popping, it's doubtful we'll have much time."

"Shit." Mary Ann took another pull of her beer and slammed the bottle down so hard on the bar that I had to marvel at the tensile strength of the glass. "I'd tell you, McKenzie, that I don't want that woman in my life, but the sad truth is she's been a part of my life for thirty-five years. Shit." Mary Ann began shredding the label on the beer bottle as if she hated it. "I've only spoken to Louise once since the *Scenes from an Inland Sea* was introduced and that was last week. Bruce Flonta decided— do you know Flonta?"

"We haven't met, but I know of him."

"Flonta wanted to film a documentary about the series and he asked me to participate. Apparently, he also asked Louise because she had the audacity to contact me through Perrin Stewart and ask if it was all right if she told the truth. Like she even knows what the fucking truth is. When Randolph went up to Duluth he was on vacation for God's sake. People don't act the same while on vacation as they do at home. It's all fun and games when you're on vacation."

When she finished tearing the beer label, Mary Ann glared at me.

"Goddammit, McKenzie," she said. "What kind of arrangement are you suggesting?"

"That's entirely up to you two."

"Let me guess. I'm supposed to go all the way up to Grand Marais and negotiate with the bitch."

"Actually, she's here."

"In Minneapolis?"

"She's staying with Perrin Stewart."

"Since when?"

"Since about ten this morning."

"You brought her down, didn't you? Aren't you a clever boy?"

"I don't know how else to get the paintings back."

"I'm not even sure I want the goddamn things back, now."

"Oh, M. A., of course you do."

I turned from the bar toward the staircase. A young man skipped down the steps with the swagger of youth, college age, perhaps grad school. Like Mary Ann, he was dressed casually in a sweatshirt with a CalArts logo and faded jeans as if he wanted you to think he was a struggling student. His shoes gave him away, though, black Yeezy Boost from Adidas with SPLY-350 stitched in red upside down on the outside. When I was his age I once bought a car that cost less than his shoes.

"I thought you left," Mary Ann said.

"I came back."

"McKenzie, this is my grandson Mitchell." I thought she rolled her eyes when she spoke his name, but I couldn't be sure.

Mitchell crossed the room and we shook hands. His hair was full of product and his facial hair looked as if it had been trimmed by Japanese gardeners, yet I didn't hold that against him.

"You must recover the missing *Scenes from an Inland Sea*, you simply must," he said.

"Why must we?" Mary Ann asked.

"To guarantee a comfortable retirement for your progeny."

"Fuck that."

"M. A., your language."

"I'm eighty years old and rich. I can talk any goddamn way

I want. McKenzie, my son Mark wanted nothing to do with the family business. He became a financial analyst and moved to New York. Good for him. This young man, however, fancies himself a great artist like his grandfather."

I gestured at Mitchell's hoodie.

"CalArts?" I asked.

"I attended the California Institute of Arts in Valencia, California. It's one of the best art schools in the country."

"It's also on the other side of the continent from his parents," Mary Ann said.

"That, too," Mitchell said.

"Unfortunately, Mitchell is a better illustrator than he is an artist."

"You mean like Andy Warhol, Norman Rockwell, Richard Corben, Frank Miller, Jack Kirby, Edmund Dulac, and Maurice Sendak?" Mitchell asked.

"Jack Kirby, the comic book guy?" I asked.

"Don't you start."

"Okay, college boy," Mary Ann said. "What do you think those missing paintings are worth."

"I don't know, but not too long ago Sotheby's sold a Nicolas Lancret at auction for two-point-two million bucks."

"I don't know who that is," I admitted.

"Neither does anyone else."

"All right, McKenzie," Mary Ann said. "Call the bitch."

After I made the phone call, Mary Ann excused herself and went upstairs. Mitchell stayed with me at the bar and complained about his grandmother's taste in beer.

"Are you familiar with Insight Brewing?" he asked. "I had a beer there yesterday, it was so fruity—grapefruit, tangerine slices, mango. Delicious."

That, I decided, I *would* hold against him.

We settled into an uncomfortable silence. Mitchell broke it when he asked, "Are you familiar with my grandfather's work?"

"Yes."

"The *Scenes*, of course, but also his earlier efforts?"

"Yes."

"The *Scenes* was the only thing he did that was worthwhile. Before that, it was all about the Benjamins. M. A. would argue differently, of course."

"You call your grandmother M. A.?"

"She insists. That's her brand. M. A. understands branding. She understands commerce. She understands what sells. What is art anyway? Ask fifty people and you'll get fifty arguments, but what sells—now that's a different matter. In France, buyers seem to like half-naked people. In puritan America, not so much. Some people want to see the brushstrokes, others don't. Yet there are more commonalities than there are differences.

"The majority of people throughout the world, for example, like the color blue. They prefer spring to the other seasons, outdoor paintings to indoor paintings, and rivers, lakes, and forests over cities. It doesn't take a genius then to grasp that the most popular paintings are landscapes with open spaces filled with low grasses and diverse greenery interspersed with trees; paintings that include the presence of water, indications of animal and birdlife, and a path, riverbank, or shoreline that extends into the distance. That's what Randolph McInnis painted with minor variations over and over and over again. They sold like crazy, too. It's also why he was never truly embraced by the art critics. He became rich and rock-star famous selling work they considered insipid at best."

"Until *Scenes from an Inland Sea*," I said.

"Until *Scenes*."

"What do you think made the difference?"

"I never met my grandfather, of course. I only know him from what my father and my grandmother told me and they don't always agree. If I had to guess, though, I'd say he found a muse that encouraged him to do his best and most creative work. That's why I'm hanging around. I want to meet the woman my grandfather fell so thoroughly in love with."

The Westminster Quarters announced Louise Wykoff's arrival ten minutes later. Mitchell pulled the front door open and did exactly what I had done when I first met her. He stared.

"I'm Louise Wykoff," she said. "I believe I'm expected."

"Yes, yes, of course. Forgive me. Please come in. I'm Mitchell McInnis."

Mitchell didn't see the woman standing behind Louise until he nearly closed the door on her.

"I'm sorry," he said. "You are . . . ?"

"Perrin Stewart."

"The ah, the ah, the person from, the ah, City of Lakes Art Museum."

Smooth, kid, my inner voice said. *Very smooth.*

"My grandmother has spoken of you," Mitchell added. "Please come in."

The three of them stood just inside the doorway and stared at one another while Mitchell struggled to find something clever to say. I remained at the bar and watched. Perrin gave me a little wave. Louise gave me nothing.

"Good afternoon," Mary Ann said.

Eyes turned to where she stood at the top of the staircase and followed her as she slowly descended. Gone were the jeans and sweatshirt, replaced with a red and navy blue dress that I just knew you couldn't buy off the rack at Nordstrom. Her hair was piled on top of her head and she was wearing makeup, including a flavor of lipstick that I was sure you could find in one of Mitchell's beers. She still looked her age, yet she also looked like a woman who had many millions of dollars squirreled away.

"Hello, M. A.," Perrin said. "You look fabulous."

"You're very kind, Perrin. Thank you. And you must be Louise Wykoff. I recognize you from the paintings."

"I apologize for the intrusion, Mrs. McInnis."

Louise lifted her hand. Mary Ann turned her back on it and moved toward the sitting room where the fireplace was located.

"Mr. McKenzie," she said. "Would you care to join us?"

Here we go.

By the time I reached the room everyone was sitting comfortably except Perrin. She looked nervous as hell. I grabbed a spot next to the piano. I wished that Mary Louise Knutson was sitting at the piano and playing slow and quiet; something by Hoagy Carmichael perhaps. It just seemed like that kind of moment.

"It's been a very long time since I've had the opportunity to tell you how sorry I am for the way things worked out after the *Scenes* were exhibited," Louise said.

"If I actually believed you were sorry, dear, I might take your apology to heart," Mary Ann replied. "Only you're not sorry, are you?"

"No, I'm not. I was merely attempting to be polite."

"Please don't do anything out of character."

"In fact, if I was able to contribute even the tiniest amount to Randolph's legacy, that makes me very happy indeed."

"Is that what you think you did—contribute to his legacy?"

"People know the *Scenes from an Inland Sea* more than they know any of the work that came before it. They know me more than they know you."

"It must have given you great pleasure these many years then to hear people speak of you the way they did; to have them wonder about you. That Wykoff Woman. Me? I'm merely the wronged woman. Hardly anyone speaks about me—unless they're also speaking about you. Funny how that works."

"Grandmother, must we do this now?" Mitchell said.

Mary Ann glared at him for a few beats. I had no idea what

she was thinking, yet from her expression I concluded that they were not happy thoughts. Finally, she forced her mouth into a smile that didn't quite reach her eyes.

"As Miss Wykoff noted earlier, it's been a long time. It is *Miss* Wykoff, correct? You've never married? Pity. Such a pretty girl. Mr. McKenzie, I believe you arranged this meeting. What's on your mind?"

"A public announcement should be made in your name offering a reward for information leading to the safe return of the missing paintings. The announcement should include the number of a burn phone that I've activated."

"Burn phone?" Mitchell asked.

"Just a cheap phone I picked up at Target. Something we can toss after we're done with it. Something that can't be traced to my front door. After we make the announcement I'll go back up to Grand Marais and we'll wait to see what happens. If the thieves bite, we'll make arrangements to swap the reward for the paintings. If possible, we'll manage it in such a way that will allow us to not only recover the artwork, but capture the criminals."

"I don't care anything about that," Louise said.

"I do. A man was killed, remember? However, if the thieves take precautions that preclude capture, we'll pay the money and call it a day."

"Why pay the money?" Mary Ann said. "If they have the paintings that means they stole them."

"What if the guy says he found them in a Dumpster behind the local Dairy Queen? You'd have to prove he's lying."

"I don't want to pay for what was stolen from me."

"I don't blame you, but here's the thing—publicaly stating that you are offering a reward for something is basically considered a legally binding contract. If you offer a reward in return for an object, for the paintings, and someone provides you with that object, you are obligated to follow through. If you refuse to pay the reward, the person in question has every right to take you to court. You need to make the decision right now that you're going to pay up, like it or not."

"McKenzie has done this sort of thing before," Perrin said.

"Perhaps one day you'll tell me about that," Mary Ann said. "All right. How much money?"

"We need a figure that will convince the thieves that a swap is worth the risk," I said.

"That would be . . . ?"

"At least a quarter of a million dollars."

"The paintings are worth ten times that much at least," Mitchell said. "Twenty times. Perhaps thirty."

"Not to the thieves," I said. "Not if they can't sell them at auction. I think $250,000 is more than enough bait."

"In cash?" Mary Ann asked.

"Hard to say. The thieves might demand an electronic transfer of the funds from your account to an account overseas. They might decide to deal in Bitcoin or some other cryptocurrency. It depends on how sophisticated they are."

"You're betting that they're not sophisticated."

"I've been wrong before. It's best to plan for every contingency."

"All I know is that you're betting with my money."

"Yes, ma'am. Sorry. Yes, M. A."

"What will the FBI or the BCA think of all of this?" Mitchell asked.

"They won't like it and they'll tell us so in no uncertain terms. They might even make some noise about the penalty for receiving stolen property. They won't interfere, though, especially if we promise to give up whoever tries for the reward."

"Can you guarantee that I'll get my paintings back?" Louise asked.

"I can only guarantee to do my best."

"They're not your paintings, dear," Mary Ann said.

"They are mine," Louise said. "Randolph gave them to me."

"So you say."

"I do say. They were the last things he gave to me before he— before he . . . You don't care. You only want the paintings so you can sell them."

"That's what Randolph painted them for."

"Who are you going to sell them to? Bruce Flonta?"

"If he's interested."

"So he can put them in storage somewhere?"

"You've always been naïve."

"Storage?" I asked.

"Many people today buy art as an investment," Mitchell said. "They don't necessarily want to hang it on their walls or exhibit it in a museum. All they care about is keeping it safe until it grows in value and they can resell it for a profit. So, a lot of art ends up being stored in these vast warehouses usually located near international airports called 'free ports.'"

"Free ports?"

"If you buy a painting in London and send it to a free port in New York, it doesn't actually enter New York. Instead, it ends up in a kind of customs-free no-man's-land between countries. It's all about tax evasion. You don't have to pay taxes on the artwork until you actually take it out of the warehouse. These free ports weren't created to be tax havens, of course. They were originally designed in the nineteenth century to promote the trade of commodities like grain and tea, and later manufactured goods. Producers were allowed to store their goods until someone bought them, then they paid their taxes. Now, though, people use them to store not only artwork, but also gold, jewelry, wine—whatever they want to avoid paying taxes on. They're also used to hide illegally acquired assets and launder money. Isn't that right, M. A.?"

"Is that what they taught you at that fancy California college?" Mary Ann asked. "You know everything about art except how to make it."

"Randolph's paintings need to be seen," Louise said.

"Exactly what the art world needs—more nudes."

"Ladies," I said, "we don't actually have the paintings, yet."

"No, we don't." Mary Ann set her eyes on Louise. "McKenzie said he needs you to describe the paintings."

Louise shifted her eyes to me. The way she nodded ever so slightly I was given the impression that, since she had already told me what they looked like, she understood I was looking out for her interests as best I could given the circumstances.

"I know why I'm here," she said.

"Well then, describe them, dear. Better yet, you're not a completely incompetent artist. Perhaps you can favor us with a few sketches."

"I will describe them to McKenzie and no one else."

Mary Ann smiled like she had when I first met her and turned to Perrin Stewart.

"She's a smart girl," Mary Ann said.

"We're all smart girls," Perrin replied.

"Still, I insist on having an agreement in place that specifically outlines what will be done with the paintings once they are in our possession."

"They're mine," Louise said.

"Then you pay for them."

"If I could, I would."

"There are three paintings," I said. "How 'bout you each take one and we'll cut the third in half?"

"McKenzie, please," Perrin said.

A long pause followed while Mary Ann and Louise glared at each other. Finally, Louise said, "That's acceptable to me."

"What is, dear?" Mary Ann asked.

"I'll take one painting, you take one, and the third we'll put on permanent exhibit at the City of Lakes Art Museum in both of our names and share the tax deduction."

Perrin's eyes brightened, yet she said nothing.

"Finally, a spark of common sense," Mary Ann said. "I get first choice."

"No," Louise said. "I demand first choice. There's one painting that means—when Randolph painted it—I get first choice."

"Were you wearing clothes in that one?"

Louise stood.

"It's my final offer," she said. "Take it or leave it."

"Sit down, little girl."

I wondered when was the last time someone called Louise a little girl, if ever. I doubt that's what she was thinking about, though. Her fists clenched and her perfect eyes became tiny dots. She leaned toward Mary Ann and snarled, actually snarled. Mary Ann smiled in reply.

"I accept your offer," she said. "Sit down."

Louise sat, only she wasn't happy about it. She perched on the edge of a chair as if prepared to spring upward again at the slightest provocation.

"I'll have contracts drawn," Mary Ann said. "It won't take long. Then—how do we go about making our intentions known, McKenzie? Please understand; I will not be present at any sort of press gathering. I will not consent to be interviewed. It's bad enough that I will appear a fool without adding the trappings of a clown. Louise, you do it—with my blessings."

"No."

"I would think you'd relish the opportunity to . . ."

"I said no."

Mary Ann smiled some more. "Somewhere I think Randolph is having a good laugh over all of this."

"Yes," Louise said. "I'm sure that he is, too."

"I'll make the announcement, M. A.," Perrin said, "if I have permission to speak in your name."

I got the impression that Mary Ann didn't savor the idea of anyone speaking in her name. She nodded, though, and said, "You have permission to speak in the name of the estate of Randolph McInnis." She sighed deeply and asked, "Should we drink to our partnership?"

"I don't drink," Louise said.

"Of course not. How silly of me."

"I will share a pot of tea with you, though."

"Why not, dear? We've shared so much already."

THIRTEEN

I announced that there was something I needed to check out that may or may not have anything to do with the paintings, we'll see, and made ready to depart. Both Mary Ann and Louise looked at me with alarm, like a couple of heavyweights who suddenly realized that there would be no referee available to guard against low blows. Perrin Stewart wasn't happy about it, either. My departure made her the only neutral party in the room. Mitchell, on the other hand, thought watching Mary Ann and Louise snipe at each other was more fun than an HBO epic fantasy.

Twenty minutes later, I was at the Minneapolis City Hall and Hennepin County Courthouse. Apparently, when it was built in 1906, eleventh- and twelfth-century Romanesque architecture was a big thing. It had rose granite walls, a copper roof with green patina, two towers including one with a four-face clock, stained glass windows, and a five-story rotunda featuring a statue carved of marble from the same quarries used by Leonardo da Vinci and Michelangelo. It also contained Room 108, which was actually a suite of offices that served the Minneapolis Police Department's assault, robbery, narcotics, forgery/fraud, sex crimes, and homicide units, among others.

I was held up in the reception area until a uniform escorted me down a long, white marble corridor to a dark brown wood door. Once past the door, the elegance of the building was replaced by the furnishings of civil employees hard at work— metal desks, rolling office chairs, and a hat rack that held no hats. I was led to the cramped office of Lieutenant Clayton Rask and was left alone at the open door. Rask was reading something and did not look up. I knocked tentatively on his door, yet he refused to acknowledge my presence for a good thirty seconds. We had that kind of relationship.

Finally, he said, "What?"

"Good afternoon, LT."

"You want something, McKenzie?"

"Do I need to want something?"

"Yes, and it had better be important if you're coming to my office and disturbing my work."

"Here I thought we were pals."

"You want to go out and get a beer, talk baseball? I can do that, especially if you're buying. You didn't come here for that, though, did you?"

"No."

"You carry an ID that says you're a retired St. Paul police officer, but as far as I'm concerned, McKenzie, you're nothing but a buff. If you hadn't been helpful to me in the past, I'd throw your ass out of here."

"About that . . ."

The way I figured it, Rask owed me a favor for past courtesies. Either he agreed or he thought that I might be useful to him yet again, because he leaned back in his chair, laced his hands behind his head, and said, "All right, I'll bite. What do you want?"

"Officer Peter Wurzer."

Rask gave me another slow count, this time about ten seconds, before responding.

"Close the door," he said.

I did.

He gestured at the chair on the other side of this desk.

I sat.

"You trying to be an asshole?" Rask asked.

"Who? Me?"

"Why are you asking questions about Wurzer?"

"You recognized the name so quickly."

"What about him?"

"He's working as a deputy up in Cook County."

"That's the North Shore, right? Grand Marais, Lutsen?"

"Yes."

"So?"

"I'm trying to get some intel on him. The sheriff up there told me Wurzer did eight years with the MPD before he was retired. The sheriff was a little vague about why he was retired. That was four years ago, which is why I'm surprised his name was so top of mind."

"This is important because . . . ?"

"Things have gone missing in Grand Marais."

"You're not talking about those paintings, are you? You're involved with that? Why am I surprised?"

"Paintings, yes. Other things as well. Burglaries are up about one hundred percent countywide. It started going up after Wurzer was hired."

Rask sniffed like he was examining the contents of a long-forgotten Tupperware container.

"They said he was dirty," he said. "I still don't believe them."

"Who's they?"

"They, they, they—you were a cop. You know who they are. Why am I telling you this?"

"Because you like me?"

"No, that's not it. I liked Wurzer, though. I met him not long after he took the oath. He wanted to know what it would take to get into plainclothes; what he needed to do to work his way up to homicide. He was serious about it, too. It wasn't just because he wanted to be a TV cop. So I gave him some advice."

"You were his rabbi?"

"No, no, nothing like that. I just kind of kept an eye on him."

"What happened?"

"Remember that fence that works out of the Phillips neighborhood calls himself the Lord?"

"El Cid?"

"Aka Dave Wicker, yeah. He was involved in the Jade Lily heist if memory serves."

"I remember."

"A joint task force tried to build a case against him back in the day, take him down for receiving stolen property, flip him, see who else they could gather up. Someone tipped Wicker, though, and he skated. The brassholes were very unhappy about it. Apparently, there were a lot of man-hours invested in the case. They looked for someone to blame. Eventually, IAD fingered Wurzer, busted him for *selective enforcement,* if you believe that shit, and sent him on his way. I didn't believe it, that he was taking from El Cid. Besides, the man was driving a unit out of the Third District at the time; he wasn't even on the task force."

"What do you believe?"

"Between you, me, and the closed door? I think Wicker was someone's CI, probably still is, and that someone wanted to cover his asset without telling anyone he was covering his asset."

"Who? You said it was a joint task force. MPD? County? State? Feds?"

"I don't know. Could be anybody. I tried to look into it. Made some noise. I was told to keep quiet, that the MPD didn't need the black eye. Keep it in-house, they said. Anyone ever tells you to keep the truth in-house, McKenzie, it's because they're more worried about the house than the truth. You know what I'm saying."

"You're saying someone on the task force gave Wicker the heads-up, leaving Wurzer to hold the bag."

"Did I say that?"

"Not in so many words."

"Then don't go around telling anyone that I did. What's your interest in Wurzer again?"

"There's an ongoing criminal investigation in Grand Marais that I got sucked into. Deputy Wurzer is adamant that I stay out of it."

"Why should he be different than the rest of us?"

"I was wondering if he had a reason besides a dislike of kibitzers. Now I feel bad."

"Why? Because you thought he was bent? Hell, McKenzie, maybe he is. Maybe *they* were right. I'd like to think, though . . ."

"Yes?"

"You'd at least give him the benefit of a doubt."

"Wurzer, yeah. Not Wicker."

"I don't need this to become a thing, McKenzie."

"If it does, LT, I was never here."

The Phillips neighborhood, located more or less in the center of Minneapolis, wasn't ethnically anything in that it was ethnically everything. African, Asian, Native American, Hispanic— you name it, Phillips had it. Forty percent of its population was born outside the United States, twenty percent spoke a language other than English; twenty-five percent lived below the poverty line. Unfortunately, wherever immigrants and the very poor congregate, you also have gangs, drugs, and a soaring crime rate. 'Course, if could have been worse. It could have been the north side.

I parked across the street from a low-slung building with brown brick, closed drapes, and iron bars on the windows. I knew it was a bar because I had been there before, yet no one else would have. There was no name above the door, no neon lights flashing the logos of pasteurized beers from St. Louis or Milwaukee, no sign saying it was open. Only a black-and-white notification taped to the window that read NO FIREARMS ARE ALLOWED ON THESE PREMISES. I once ran the address through the Hennepin County property tax website to find out the name of the owner or at least who was paying the taxes on the property. It told me "no records found" and provided a list of tips to improve my search. None of them worked.

I stepped inside. The lights were low. A young man was sitting at a table near the center of the room with an unobstructed view of the front door. The light from the tablet he was reading gave his pale skin an eerie sheen. I held my breath while his eyes locked on mine for a few beats. He grinned. I gave him a nod. I didn't know his name but he knew mine and guessed why I was there. Just in case, though, he turned his head slightly and rested his eyes on the opened pages of the Minneapolis *StarTribune* that was lying on the table within easy reach, making sure I saw him do it. There was a sawed-off shotgun beneath the newspaper. I gave him another nod.

There were a few other patrons in the bar, yet none of them noticed our little drama. Most were sitting in old-fashioned wooden booths, the kind with high backs that you can't see over; working men and two women enjoying happy hour shots with beer chasers and free salted-in-the shell peanuts. A couple of shells crunched under my feet as I made my way to the booth just to the right of the table where the sentry sat.

Dave Wicker was leaning against the wall of the booth and typing on a smartphone with one finger. I watched him do it. Like Lieutenant Rask, he ignored my presence for a good thirty seconds. At least this time I could hear Tony Bennett singing softly from invisible speakers.

Finally, Wicker set the smartphone on the table next to the other three phones he was using. There was also a white mug filled with coffee. He picked up the mug, took a sip, set the mug down.

"The fuck, McKenzie," he said.

"El Cid."

I used the name because Wicker liked it, the Lord; a nickname that he had given himself, pilfering it from Rodrigo Díaz de Vivar, the Spanish knight and mercenary credited with driving the Moors out of Spain in the eleventh century.

"I thought I made it clear the last time, I don't like you," he said.

"How long are you going to hold a grudge, anyway?"

"To the end of fucking time."

"All I did was present you with the opportunity to return some stolen property to its rightful owners. You didn't spend five minutes in jail."

"That's because I made a couple of deals."

"Isn't that your life? Making deals?"

"It's not the cops or the deals, McKenzie. It's the principle of the thing. You gave me up."

"I didn't give you up. Lieutenant Rask yanked your name out of me."

"You could have lied."

"Have you met Lieutenant Rask?"

"You owe me, McKenzie."

"Yeah, okay," I said, although I didn't mean it.

"Fuck you want, anyway?" Wicker asked.

I slid onto the bench across the table from him.

"*Scenes from an Inland Sea*," I said.

"You too, huh? I've had a dozen calls from all over the country since the story of the lost paintings went viral, calls from people who wouldn't have given me the time of day a week ago. They all want the paintings."

"You are the most highly regarded facilitator between Chicago and the West Coast."

I said "facilitator" because I knew Wicker liked the word better than "fence."

"I take it you also want them, the McInnis paintings," Wicker said. "What I would like to know—what makes you think I have them?"

"Peter Wurzer."

"Who?"

Wicker's reaction to the name told me nothing. There are certain tells—facial tics, and eye movements—that reveal when someone is lying the same way they reveal when a poker player is bluffing. Wicker had none of them. Which didn't mean he wasn't lying, only that he was good at it.

"Officer Peter Wurzer," I said.

"I don't know who that is."

"That surprises me considering the man took a fall for you."

"What are you talking about, McKenzie?"

"I've been reliably informed that if it wasn't for Wurzer, a joint task force would have punched your ticket to the Minnesota Correctional Facility in Oak Park Heights."

"When?"

"About four years ago."

"I honestly don't know what you're talking about."

Maybe he doesn't.

"Wurzer is working as a deputy for the Cook County Sheriff's Department based in Grand Marais. Rumor has it that he might have been involved in the theft of the *Scenes from an Inland Sea*. If that's true, where would he take them if not his old friend?"

Wicker found a spot on the table to stare at for a few beats while he came to a decision.

"Should I tell you a secret, McKenzie? This Deputy Wurzer—I don't know who he is. We have no relationship, professional or otherwise."

"He isn't dirty?"

"I don't know what he is, only that I had nothing to do with him."

"So, you're saying he was an innocent cop that someone tossed in the jackpot to protect you."

"Ain't none of us innocent, McKenzie."

"Tomorrow morning the Randolph McInnis estate will publicly offer a reward for information leading to the recovery of the paintings no questions asked, $250,000. You're welcome to try and collect."

Wicker thought that was funny.

"Sure," he said. "I'll also let you have the Oppenheimer Blue for fifty bucks."

"Clean money. Easy profit."

"Tell it to the IRS."

I slid off the bench and stood next to the booth.

"That it?" Wicker asked.

"If you hear anything about the paintings, you're going to call me."

"Why would I do that?"

"Because I'm really pissed off about what happened to Wurzer."

"Don't know why I should care if some mook . . ."

"He was a cop."

Standing up for Deputy Wurzer? my inner voice said. *Where the hell did that come from?*

"What do I care?" Wicker said.

"Word on the street is that you're a snitch." I said it loud enough that more than one of our fellow patrons turned to look. Wicker noticed it, too. "The only question is, are you informing to the FBI or the BCA?"

"You sonuvabitch."

"People are saying, your colleagues, your customers—they're saying that's why the joint task force failed to indict four years ago. That's why you didn't pay the price when the Jade Lily went missing two years ago. They're saying you can't be trusted."

"Who's saying that?"

"No one, yet."

To survive much less flourish in his chosen profession, Cid

needed to negotiate with the most dangerous thieves as well as the least scrupulous customers. The fear of betrayal, of being ripped off, of being arrested, was always present so it was important to demonstrate a certain amount of fearlessness. The name "El Cid," the barroom office, the barely concealed bodyguard pretending to read his tablet while carefully watching me, was meant to convince associates that Wicker was not someone to trifle with. Yet there I was—trifling with him.

"You're making a serious mistake, McKenzie," he said.

As if to prove it, Wicker's bodyguard carefully set down his tablet and rested his hands palm down on the table next to the newspaper.

"You say I owe you," I said. "Well, Cid, you owe for what happened to Wurzer. You owe big-time and I'm not the only one who thinks so." I didn't use the name Lieutenant Rask, yet I was sure Wicker heard it just the same. "You tell me something valuable about those fucking paintings, we'll call it even."

I stepped over to the table and stood in front of the bodyguard like I was made of highly polished bulletproof glass. To this day I can't tell you what I was thinking.

"You got something you want to say to me?" I asked.

The bodyguard glanced at Wicker sitting in the booth and back at me. He slowly shook his head.

I turned and walked from the bar. I didn't realize that I was holding my breath until I hit the street.

Nina had not been pleased to see me in my battered and bruised state. She added plenty of insults to my injuries, mostly along the lines of my inability to behave like a normal human being. It was a conversation we've had many times in the past. Most men probably would have become bored if not infuriated with it by now. I took it as an indication of how much she cared.

"I love you," I said.

"Don't change the subject," she told me. "I'm angry."

I gave her fresh bakery from World's Best Donuts.

"This helps," she said. "But only a little bit."

That was this morning, though, when I first arrived home from GM. Now it was early Monday evening and we were walking hand in hand from our condominium in downtown Minneapolis to the Stone Arch Bridge with the intention of crossing the Mississippi River and going to Pracna on Main, which billed itself as the "the oldest restaurant on the oldest street in Minneapolis." More and more I'd noticed that Nina had been gravitating toward what's old—antiques, vintage clothing, retro-style furniture. When we traveled, we rarely stayed at the best hotels unless the best hotels were built a hundred years ago. Not that I was complaining. If life expectancy for a male in the United States is seventy-nine, I've been on the downward slide for nearly half a decade now so, yeah, I hope she embraces what's old and getting older like crazy.

We were just about to enter Gold Medal Park off of South Second Street when a black Lincoln Town Car pulled to a stop directly in front of us. My first thought, El Cid.

I grabbed Nina's arm and pulled her behind me.

A man got out of the driver's side of the Lincoln and quickly circled it until he reached the back passenger door. He was dressed more like an accountant than a limo driver and looked young, a college graduate but just barely. He pulled open the door and said, "Get in."

I made sure I was standing between the car and Nina.

"No," I said.

"Aren't you McKenzie? Get in."

I moved Nina cautiously to my right and forced her down the sidewalk while continuing to keep myself between her and the Lincoln.

"You never get into the car no matter how much candy the stranger offers," I told the driver. "Didn't your mother ever tell you that? That's what mine told me."

The driver looked as if that was the most ridiculous advice he had ever heard.

We kept walking. My hand on Nina's forearm was so tight that she forced me to release her.

We were a good car length past the Lincoln when I heard a voice.

"Mr. McKenzie, are you really going to make me chase you down the street?"

An old man, dressed to impress, had emerged from the back of the Town Car. He used a cane to help propel himself forward. The driver attempted to steady him; the old man shrugged his hands away. For a moment I felt relief—*Okay, not El Cid.* Yet that lasted only for a moment.

"McKenzie," the old man repeated.

I stopped while still making sure Nina remained behind me. The old man smiled as if he had won something and moved a few steps forward. Despite his age, he projected the confidence of a guy who didn't feel the need to explain who he was or what he did to a single soul on the planet.

"Do you know who I am?" he said.

"I'm going to guess—Bruce Flonta."

"Very good. Now guess how I know who you are?"

"Jeffery Mehren."

"I'm sure you now know why I'm here."

"You want me to audition for *Jeopardy!* I love that show."

"I'm a serious man, Mr. McKenzie."

"Of course you are. Why else would you accost me on the street instead of picking up a phone?"

"I did. My calls went unanswered."

I glanced at Nina. Her shrug told me everything—in this age of caller ID, no one answers an unrecognized number.

"You have my attention, Mr. Flonta," I said.

"Step into the car and I'll tell you what I have in mind."

I gestured toward a bench in Gold Medal Park.

Flonta spoke to me the way an exasperated parent might speak to a child while explaining yet again that there are no monsters in the closet or under the bed.

"You are being unnecessarily dramatic," he said. "I mean you no harm."

Yet—I heard the word even though he didn't speak it.

"If I knew something more about you besides your name I might believe you," I said. "But I doubt it."

"Then I shall be blunt. The *Scenes from an Inland Sea* that were stolen from the Wykoff woman rightfully belong to me. I want them."

"How do they belong to you?"

"I bought the entire collection from Mary Ann McInnis in 1983 except for those few pieces that were specifically identified in our contract. These three paintings are part of the collection. They're mine."

"I'm sure a long, drawn-out, and obscenely expensive civil court case involving you, Louise Wykoff, and Mary Ann McInnis will decide the issue."

"Not if I control the paintings first. Possession is nine-tenths of the law."

"So it's been explained to me."

"I have been made aware through Mr. Mehren that you have been retained to recover the paintings for the Wykoff woman. I will pay you handsomely to deliver them to me instead."

Flonta was smiling. It occurred to me that he hadn't stopped smiling since he emerged from the Lincoln. I found it extremely disconcerting. In my mind, the only people who smile that much are either professional liars—think politicians on the campaign trail—or insane.

"Let me guess again," I said. "This is where you tell me that everyone has a price."

"Are you telling me that it's not true?"

"No. It is true. Everyone does have a price. It isn't always money, though."

"What's your price, McKenzie?"

"I'm not sure. What can you offer that will make it all right for me to betray the people I promised to help?"

"I am merely providing you with a potentially lucrative business proposition."

"I respectfully decline."

"Just so you understand—we are enemies now."

"Why? Why are we enemies?"

"You've insulted me to my face."

"Because I declined your so-called business proposition? That's a reason to go to war? What are you going to do if the grocery store runs out of brats, invade Germany?"

"Watch your back, McKenzie."

"Oh, for God's sake."

With the assistance of his driver, Flonta climbed back inside the Lincoln Town Car. The driver shut the rear door and circled the car to the driver's side door. He opened the door, yet before sliding behind the wheel he gave me a playful smile, one that I translated to mean, "Do you believe this shit?"

A moment later, the Lincoln pulled away from the curb and headed down the street. Nina tapped me on the shoulder and spoke her first words since Flonta stopped us, "Can we go to dinner now? I'm really hungry."

At nine o'clock the next morning, Perrin Stewart conducted a press conference in a meeting room at the City of Lakes Art Museum during which she revealed that the estate of Randolph McInnis, in order to recover and protect what is clearly an American art treasure, was now offering a reward of $250,000 for information leading to the safe return of the three *Scenes from an Inland Sea* that had been taken from the home of Louise Wykoff in Grand Marais, Minnesota. None of the twenty-four-hour cable news networks carried the conference live, yet by ten all of them were broadcasting recordings of the announcement. My TV remote allowed me to rewind and re-play programs and I did several times, mostly to make sure that it was Jennica I had glimpsed briefly off to the side and yes, it was Jeffery Mehren kneeling in front of the podium and aim-ing a camera upward at Perrin. Well, well, well . . .

After the initial report, the networks began adding film of the McInnis exhibit on the third floor of the museum as well as a shot of Louise's own painting. Still later, the segment was ex-panded to include a summary of the now decades-old contro-versy surrounding the Wykoff paintings and the relationship of artist and model as well as in-studio debates by a panel of ex-perts over the wisdom, legality, and ethics of negotiating with criminals or terrorists depending if you were watching CNN or Fox. Eventually, the story would take up ten to twelve minutes of every hour of programming for the remainder of the day.

My burn phone began ringing almost immediately. The call-ers fell into three categories.

The first was comprised of TV and print journalists, talk radio hosts, podcasters, and, to my surprise, online bloggers—I had never read one so I didn't know they were that big of a thing. I declined to identify myself or answer any of the ques-tions they asked. I also insisted that they not call again and blocked their numbers in case they tried.

The second group consisted of ordinary citizens, if I could use that term, who felt the need to voice their opinion on the McInnis estate's wholehearted endorsement and reward of criminal activities whether I cared to hear it or not. I was par-ticularly impressed by the number who wanted to see me dead and or in hell. I mean—really?

The third and decidedly much smaller group was looking for a quick payday. Usually the conversations went along these lines:

"Yes," I'd say when I answered the cell.

"Who's this?" they'd ask.

"Who's this?" I'd repeat.

"Wouldn't you like to know?"

"Why are you calling?"

"I have your precious paintings and if you ever want to see them again you'll pay the money you promised. No tricks."

"That's the deal."

"If I even think I see a cop I'll burn them."

"Fair enough, but I want to see the paintings."

"You'll see them *after* I get the money."

"There are three paintings."

"I know how many there are."

"How big are they?"

"What?"

"What are the dimensions?"

"I don't know."

"Go and measure them. I'll wait."

"I'm not going to measure them."

"I'm going to hang up now. If you really do have the paintings, go get a tape measure and figure out their dimensions. When you have the sizes call me back. If they're accurate we'll talk."

As I said, this went on for most of the day. Despite my up close and personal experience with the dark side as a police officer and what I do now, I have a more or less optimistic view of the world. Only I was becoming increasingly angry and frustrated by what I decided was a telling exemplar of the greed and stupidity of my fellow man. I loved the condo Nina and I shared yet after a few hours I felt it closing in around me. I came *this*close to tossing the burn phone off the balcony. After a few hours more, I came *this*close to tossing myself off the balcony.

Around four P.M. though, the calls slowed and then ceased. My first thought—there was something wrong with the cell phone. I paid only $19.99 for the damned thing, after all. I soon received calls from Perrin Stewart, Louise Wykoff, and Mary Ann McInnis in quick succession on my regular cell phone. Perrin was first.

"Turn on CNN," she said.

I did and discovered Bruce Flonta conducting a press conference of his own. The background suggested a hotel in Minneapolis that I could see from my balcony. He was telling the same reporters that had gathered around Perrin Stewart that the missing *Scenes from an Inland Sea* rightfully belonged to him, a fact that he would prove in court should that be required. In the meantime, Flonta said, "I will pay $500,000 for the safe return of the paintings to me."

This time I didn't need to rewind the program to see both Jeffery and Jennica Mehren and their cameras. Father and daughter seemed to be having a wonderful time.

I had to laugh. Perrin didn't think it was funny. Neither did Louise when I spoke to her. Mary Ann, on the other hand, thought it was hysterical.

"We'll run an auction on national TV," she said. "Wolf Blitzer can act as auctioneer. What are my bids, what are my bids, twenty-five, twenty-five, thirty, thirty-five over here. No, no, not Wolf. We'll get Anderson Cooper. I know his mother, Gloria Vanderbilt. It'll be great fun."

"I'm glad to see that you haven't lost your sense of humor. Perrin and Louise are beside themselves."

"I always had a feeling this would end up in court. I'd really like to avoid that if at all possible, though. Tell me, McKenzie, what are we going to do? I've spoken to my attorneys and they say there's nothing they can do about Flonta trying to outbid my reward offer. They say nothing can be done period until someone actually takes possession of the paintings in which case the police might or might not get involved and the lawsuits can commence. You're not a policeman, however, and you're not a lawyer so, I ask again, McKenzie, what are we going to do?"

"We could make a deal with Flonta."

"Why would I want to do that? The man's a schmuck."

"He also has more money than we do. Or am I mistaken about that?"

"I have no idea. I would guess, though, based on my past dealings with the man, Flonta would be willing to pay a lot more for the paintings that I would. I mean, look what he paid the first time. What a nitwit."

"So, a three-way split? You each take one painting?"

"Won't Perrin be happy to hear that? Why would Flonta want to partner with us, though?"

"We have something he doesn't."

"Louise."

"We also have the exact dimensions of the paintings."

"If we have the dimensions, why do we need Louise?"

"We just do."

"You're a romantic, you know that, McKenzie?"

"She called me first. Besides, if Louise is compelled to make a separate deal with Flonta . . ."

"All right, all right. Should I give Flonta a call or will you?"

"He already told me that he was my enemy, so . . ."

"Why would he do that?"

"Because I said no when he asked me to betray you guys and join his side."

"McKenzie. You are a romantic. Okay, I'll call him tomorrow morning; let him get a taste of what it's like to be on cable news first. I don't expect the conversation to go well, though. In the meantime, seriously, what are we going to do if he turns us down?"

"I'll think of something."

"I have a great deal of faith in you."

"I wish people would stop saying that."

FOURTEEN

The population of Grand Marais had declined significantly by the time I returned Wednesday afternoon, yet I expected it would ramp up again for the weekend. The kids had gone back to school, which made weeklong family vacations iffy, yet the weather was still warm and the autumn leaves remained resplendent. In a couple of weeks that would change. The leaves would fall and so would the temperature. Soon after, the gales of November would come slashin' just like Gordon Lightfoot's song promised, followed by an abundance of ice and snow. Most of the restaurants and other businesses would close and the remaining inhabitants would prepare for the quiet solitude of the long winter that Leah Huddleston apparently appreciated so much. Personally, I doubted I'd last three days before going stir-crazy.

I managed a room at the Harbor Inn with a magnificent lakeside view, yet only for the night. The hotel was completely booked from Thursday through the weekend. The Frontier Motel said it would take me back, although I couldn't imagine why.

Afterward, I found a spot on the nearly empty terrace of the Gunflint Tavern. It was about sixty degrees. In most places that would call for thick leather jackets, scarves, hats, and gloves. Except this was Minnesota. Seeing kids and some adults running around in shorts and flip-flops was not all that surprising. As it was, my only concession to the weather was a long-sleeve button-down cotton shirt. Beyond that I was wearing my standard uniform—jeans, Nikes, and a sports jacket.

The nine-millimeter SIG Sauer concealed beneath the sports jacket and positioned just behind my right hip wasn't standard, although not entirely unusual. I holstered it there after I left the Cook County Law Enforcement Center. That hadn't been my first stop, of course. My opening move was to drop Louise off at the art academy. I parked across the street and carried her suitcase to the door for her. She invited me in for coffee, only by then I'd had enough of the woman.

It hadn't been an unpleasant drive up from the Cities. Mostly though, Louise spoke about art, the business of art, the life of an artist, how they're treated differently in Europe than in the United States, the importance of the National Endowment for the Arts, and why she was encouraged to hear that there was a growing movement, although small and underreported, in which wealthy patrons, groups, and foundations were providing artists with economic stability and a pathway to success reminiscent of what was done during the Renaissance. It was like a four-and-a-half-hour seminar interrupted only for gas in Duluth.

Don't get me wrong. I was grateful for the education. It meant I could now hold my own in conversation with Perrin Stewart's art major pals should she ever invite me to party with them. Still, enough was enough, so I declined Louise's invitation. I told her that there was much to prepare, only I was lying.

There was nothing to be done now except to wait and hope that my burn phone would ring. It had rung several times since Flonta had held his press conference, except the calls were only more of the same. One caller had aroused my interest when he asked if I was willing to bid an amount higher than Flonta had.

Unfortunately, he said he didn't like my attitude when I asked about the dimensions of the three paintings and vowed he would do business with Flonta after all. I wished him luck.

Flonta had turned down Mary Ann's offer of a partnership just as she had predicted, of course. He said he damn well knew an authentic Randolph McInnis when he saw one. Mary Ann said that it was too bad because now if he did recover the paintings, she would see that he was prosecuted for receiving stolen property; both she and Randolph McInnis were from Minnesota, after all, and the police were on their side. Flonta said he would take the paintings to California where the authorities were on his side. Mary Ann said that would mean transporting stolen property across state lines, which was a federal offense and meant the FBI would arrest his sorry ass. Flonta said he wasn't afraid of the FBI. I recalled a conversation I'd had years earlier with El Cid. He told me that he wasn't afraid of the police, either. He could always make a deal with the police, he said. Then he told me what he was afraid of. I whispered it in Mary Ann's ear and she said it aloud to Flonta, "How about the Internal Revenue Service?"

Flonta called Mary Ann a name that I had once screamed at a hockey player who cross-checked me across the bridge of my nose, yet would never dare say to a woman. He abruptly hung up the phone.

Mary Ann said, "For the past couple of years I felt my life was becoming routine and boring. This is actually fun."

I told her she was one sick puppy, which made her laugh, left her house, picked up the Wykoff woman, and drove back to Grand Marais.

After saying good-bye to Louise, I returned to my car. Peg Younghans was on the sidewalk and moving toward me. I glanced at my watch while I waited for her: 12:45. Leah Huddleston down at the Northern Lights Art Gallery must have just returned from lunch, I told myself.

"McKenzie," she said.

"Ms. Younghans." She was wearing a floral dress with buttons that started at her throat and went to her knees; the top four had been undone. I told her I liked the dress.

"This old thing?" Peg said. "I see you remembered where I live after all. Or are you here to visit Louise?"

"Both."

"Men. I need to take these heels off. Come inside with me." When I hesitated, she added, "I won't show you any dirty pictures unless you ask politely."

I discovered first as a police officer and later as a "roving troubleshooter" that you can get a sense of the people who live in a house thirty seconds after crossing the threshold. Some people are overly messy for example, while others are overly neat. Peg, on the other hand, was immaculate to the point of obsession. Her windows gleamed in the afternoon sun, the light proving that the hardwood floors had been waxed and buffed. Throw rugs had been beaten to within an inch of their lives. Coffee and end tables were polished to a high gloss. Suede furniture was brushed. Drapes vacuumed. The fireplace looked like it had never held a fire. Even the leaves on her plants looked dust-free and shiny. It made me think there was some serious OCD flowing in her genes. Yet that diagnosis conflicted with the flirtatious and somewhat boisterous behavior I encountered those times I'd spoken to her.

I flashed briefly on what the bartender at Mark's Wheel-Inn had claimed about Peg suffering an anxiety attack when he hit on her at the Art Colony reception. It occurred to me that I knew nothing about the woman.

Peg rested a hand on my shoulder and used it for balance as she slipped the heels off her feet. She opened a closet door and set the shoes on the floor next to about a dozen other pairs all arranged neatly. She closed the door and moved deeper into the living room. There were several photographs on the wall, all of them in black-and-white, none of them of people.

"Can I offer you something?" she asked. "Coffee? Tea? Me?"

"You are persistent, I'll give you that."

"I'm only teasing, McKenzie. I take your word that you're committed to someone else. If all men were as honest as you, women would be much better off. I'm having tea. Would you care to join me?"

"Yes. Thank you."

Peg invited me inside her kitchen. It was as pristine as you might expect given her living room. She went to her stove and ignited a fire beneath a teapot.

"I know it takes longer than using a microwave," Peg said. "But that seems so—inelegant."

"I'm in no hurry."

She used a silver tablespoon to transfer tea from a ceramic jar to mesh tea balls and set them inside identical cups on identical saucers. Afterward, she set place mats on the kitchen table. She made me sit in front of one of the place mats that she then rearranged until it was just so. When the teapot began whistling, she removed it from the stove and poured the scalding water into each cup. She set the timer on her microwave for five minutes. Sometime during all of this, two more buttons on her dress had become undone; I could detect a hint of white lace beneath her bodice.

"Looks like That Wykoff Woman has gotten another fifteen minutes of fame." Peg spoke to me in the same upbeat manner that I was used to. "Everyone's talking about her. We had five of her paintings at the gallery. All of them were sold in the past two days."

"Even the one with the blacksmith?"

"That went first. Eight thousand dollars."

"I thought it was priced at thirty-five hundred."

"Leah is a smart woman. You weren't thinking of buying it, were you?"

"It had crossed my mind."

"McKenzie, Grand Marais has a very active art colony; you can trace it back to 1947 for God's sake. Those other artists, they're all better than Wykoff is."

"Really?"

"Well, maybe not *all* of them."

The microwave's timer went off. Peg removed the tea balls and set the cups and saucers in nearly the exact center of each of the placemats.

"Cream, sugar, lemon, honey, biscuits?" she asked.

"I'm good."

"Atta boy. I've had Louise over once. She drinks her tea in the so-called English fashion, loading it up with sugar and cream. Might as well have a milkshake. I should be angry with you. You told me that it was Louise's paintings that had been stolen from her place, but they were really painted by Randolph McInnis, weren't they?"

"I apologize for that. We thought they would be easier to recover if we kept the theft a secret."

"Now everyone knows. They're even offering rewards."

"'Fraid so."

"What does all this have to do with David Montgomery killing himself?"

"Probably nothing."

"Or probably—everything? Rumor has it David stole the paintings from Louise and was killed by someone who stole the paintings from him."

"Where did you hear that?"

"Here and there. That's only one of the rumors, though. My favorite—David was killed by an organized crime ring because he had muscled in on their territory by robbing Louise and that these were the same guys who beat you up on the beach across the highway from the Frontier Motel when you got too close to identifying them."

"I like that one, too, except I have no idea who those guys were or why they attacked me."

Peg brushed her fingers along my jawline.

"It doesn't look too bad," she said.

"You should have seen it Monday morning."

"McKenzie, why are you doing this? Why are you even in Grand Marais?"

"I told you. A friend asked me to help find the paintings that were stolen from Louise."

"If you found them, you would go home?"

"Probably."

"What about David?"

"I'd like to do something for him, but that's not my job."

"Another rumor—some people think Montgomery really did commit suicide and that it had nothing to do with those damn paintings."

"Some people might be right."

"I wish I could help you."

"You did." I pointed at my now empty cup. "Thank you for the tea."

I made ready to leave.

"McKenzie, you will be careful, won't you? If David didn't take his own life and those men on the beach—there're dangerous people out there."

"I appreciate your concern."

"I know you don't like me, but . . ."

"I never said that, Peg. I said I was in a committed relationship with someone else."

She gave me a few beats. There was a smile pulling at the corners of her mouth that she was trying hard to keep to herself.

"Get out of here, McKenzie," Peg said. "Before I start unbuttoning more buttons."

After leaving Peg Younghans, I drove to the Law Enforcement Center on Gunflint Trail. The admin I knew as Eileen greeted me. She was smiling, as usual.

"A week ago, no one around here had even heard of you," she said. "Now you're all we talk about."

"Me?"

"It's those paintings. They're all over the news. Grand Marais has been receiving more publicity than since forever. Folks over at the Art Colony are going crazy over the sudden interest."

"That's not my fault."

"Whose fault is it?" Sheriff Bowland asked. He was standing just outside his door and dressed as if he was expecting to have his photograph taken. The expression on his face reminded me of the vice principal at my high school, the one who was in charge of discipline.

"Start with Montgomery," I said. "Start with whoever shot him."

Bowland waved me over and I moved toward his office.

"Can I get you anything?" Eileen said to me. "Coffee?"

"He won't be here that long," the sheriff said.

Eileen seemed genuinely disappointed.

"I like her," I said.

"She takes good care of us. Have a seat."

Bowland circled his desk and sat down himself. He didn't close the office door. Unlike Lieutenant Rask, he had no secrets.

"What are you doing here, McKenzie?" the sheriff asked.

"Simple courtesy. Let you know I was back in your county."

"I thought you might be trying to find out what we've been up to since you left."

"What have you been doing?"

"The BCA tracked Montgomery's movements and cell phone calls for the past year. He was involved with several women during that period; you've met most of them. They all knew what kind of man he was. None of them seemed to care. Nor could we identify any outraged husbands or jealous boyfriends.

"As for the burglaries, Eileen and I spent the last couple days working on it. We were able to connect him to six incidents in the past year. Six out of thirty-one. Nineteen percent. He's done a lot of handyman work for a lot of people over the years, yet that number seems too high to be a coincidence. On the other hand, Montgomery worked for only some of the vics this year. The others, not for as long as two to three years.

"You know how hard it is to close a burglary, McKenzie. It's rare to catch a suspect in the act. If a neighbor doesn't notice suspicious behavior and write down a license plate number, if the suspect doesn't set off a security alarm or is caught on CCTV or drop a cell phone in the backyard . . . I've tried following the money. No one has used a stolen credit card; no one has attempted to cash a stolen check; no one has tried to unload stolen property in any pawn shop that I can find in Cook County, or Duluth, or Grand Rapids for that matter. I've even tried to match stolen items on eBay and Craigslist. Nothing."

"Very professional," I said.

"Or gifted amateurs who carefully follow the instructions they find on the internet. Google 'how burglars work' and you'll get a goddamned tutorial."

"Montgomery, though, selling Louise Wykoff's silver tea set and candlesticks to an antiques shop just down the highway . . ."

"It doesn't fit the MO, that's for sure. I mean the thieves usually hit the homes of people they don't know personally, that don't have security systems, that are unoccupied between the hours of ten A.M. and three P.M. in locations where they or their vehicles won't be recognized by a passing bystander . . . I've been working this case, McKenzie, don't think I haven't. It might not be a high priority crime in the Cities where you have God knows what else to deal with, but it is here. We've apprehended a few suspects, more than a few, but mostly they're drug abusers or dipshits. Not the crew that I think is targeting the county."

"I once worked a case where the thieves took their goods to stores and flea markets in Iowa," I said.

"A little bit outside my jurisdiction."

"How 'bout Canada, hey?"

"Ha-ha."

"Is it possible for the burglars to smuggle their goods over the border?"

"It wouldn't be hard to row across the Pigeon or take a boat to the Canadian side of Superior; bypass the border crossing. Helluva bigger risk than driving to Iowa, that's for sure. You get caught, Homeland Security would fall on you like the wrath of God almighty. But again, a little bit outside my jurisdiction."

"If you gave me a list of recently stolen items, I could scoot up to Thunder Bay and take a look around. The pawn shops up there work the same way they do down here, don't they?"

"If anything, they work even more closely with law enforcement because—Canada."

"Maybe I can convince a store owner to give me a name," I said.

"You would do that?"

"Why not? It's what? Eighty miles from here?"

"Ninety minutes by car."

"Not the way I drive."

"Did you bring your passport?"

"Sure."

"That makes me think you might have thought of this *before* you walked into my office."

"Nah. I carry a passport because it makes me feel like a world traveler. Besides, if I can get a line on your burglars, I might also find Wykoff's paintings."

"Speaking of which, I've seen more cable news in the past four days than I have in five years. It's like watching one of those syndicated true crime programs unspooling in real time. Dueling rewards. Who does that?"

"Rich people, I guess."

"I thought you were rich."

"Merely well-off," I said. "In any case, I don't know if it'll amount to anything, the reward. That's why I'd like to pursue other options."

"It certainly has our colleagues with the BCA thinking. Last I heard they've been in contact with the big boys down in St. Paul. It might even have gone all the way to the superintendent, whether or not to start arresting people for obstruction and/or receiving stolen property if the paintings should surface. Your name is on top of the list, by the way."

"Do you know what was decided?"

"Apparently, they're taking a wait-and-see approach for now."

"Swell."

"Did Louise Wykoff return with you?" the sheriff asked.

"Yes."

"We can place Montgomery's car outside her house a half-dozen times during the weeks prior to the theft of the paintings. We'll want to interview her again about that. I don't know what it's going to get us, though, even if she does admit to a relationship with him. She's probably the only person we're absolutely sure didn't murder Montgomery—if he was murdered."

"Has there been an official determination, yet?"

"No. Agent Plakcy says suicide. Agent Krause says homicide."

"Really? I would have thought it'd be the other way around."

"In any case, they're being pressured to make a decision by Friday."

"Why?" I asked.

"Why not? It's been five days since Montgomery died and we don't know anything more than we did when you discovered the body."

"What do you believe?"

"I've never met a coincidence that I trusted. Speaking of which, I can't help but notice the bruising along your jawline. Did that happen Sunday night?"

"Yeah."

"Deputy Wurzer told me about it. He also said you think that he's to blame."

"I don't know what to think anymore."

"Don't go around accusing my people of committing crimes unless you can prove that they're guilty of committing crimes and I mean prove it to hell and back."

"Fair enough."

"I mean it, McKenzie. Good manners is how we show respect for one another—seems I heard that somewhere."

"Something my old man beat into me."

"I'll put together the list you want. Most of the stolen items were common goods, you know—electronics. There have been more than a few special items like jewelry, though."

"Paintings?"

"'Fraid not. I do have some photos, though."

"I can stop by in the morning before I go to Canada."

"The list will be waiting for you. If I'm not here, ask Eileen for it. In the meantime, does this courtesy you mentioned earlier include informing me if your art-nappers contact you about the paintings?"

"Another reason I dropped in. I want those paintings, make no mistake. That's why I came to Grand Marais in the first place. I also want who killed Montgomery. Louise and the others don't seem to care about that. On the other hand, they didn't see him lying on the floor with half a head. If I can manage it, I hope for you to be standing there when I take possession of the canvases. If not, I promise I'll gather as much intel about these guys as I can and turn it over."

"In that case, enjoy your stay in Cook County."

———

That was twenty minutes ago. Now I was sitting on the terrace at the Gunflint Tavern, nursing an ale from the Castle Danger Brewery, watching the few boats that were still at anchor in the harbor bobbing up and down and willing my burn phone to ring.

"Hi, sweetie."

I jumped at the words, my hand moving to my right hip.

"I'm sorry," Jennica Mehren said. "Did I startle you?"

She was aiming a camera the size of a baseball glove at me.

"No, you didn't startle me," I said. I was lying, though, and she probably knew it. I couldn't believe that I had been caught staring out at the harbor and the great lake beyond, daydreaming, not paying attention to what was going on around me. Just like on the beach in front of the Frontier Motel.

When did you become so goddamned careless? my inner voice wanted to know.

I gestured at the camera.

"Would you put that down, please?"

Jennica set it on top of the table, slipped a heavy backpack from her shoulder to the floor, and grabbed a chair without asking.

"How are you, McKenzie?" she asked.

"Are you following me again?"

"Yep."

"Why?"

I didn't hear Jennica's answer because I was now on high alert—better late than never—and became distracted by a young man who climbed to the top of the staircase, stared at me for a few beats, and found an empty table across the terrace. He sat and stared for a few beats more. I recognized him immediately— Bruce Flonta's limo driver, the one who smiled at me across the roof of the Lincoln Town Car. He didn't look particularly dangerous, but then neither did I.

"McKenzie, are you listening?" Jennica asked.

My hand returned to the SIG Sauer at my hip, spreading my

sports jacket back so the young man could see it. He didn't seem to care one way or the other.

"McKenzie?"

"I want you to stay right here. I don't want you to move an inch. Do you understand?"

"Why? What . . . Oh." Jennica finally saw what I was looking at and started to giggle. "You're gonna love this."

"What?"

Jennica gave Flonta's driver a wave. The driver waved back.

"You're kidding," I said.

"He's Mr. Flonta's representative. His name is Michael Alden."

"Is Flonta here?"

"No, just us. When we discovered that you were returning to Grand Marais with the Wykoff woman, we decided we should go too, just in case."

"Who's we?"

"My father, although he didn't mean for me to go alone but with someone in our crew. I talked him out of it." Jennica started laughing. "He's really not happy about this, only he has to stay with Mr. Flonta." Jennica laughed some more. "Dad is filming Mr. Flonta, also a few other old friends of Randolph McInnis, also the City of Lakes, which has become McInnis central over the years, the number of his paintings that it exhibits. He's also trying to film Mary Ann McInnis. She had agreed to an interview earlier, only now she's vacillating."

"I can't imagine why."

"Anyway, he said I should keep an eye on you since we're chums."

"Did he actually use the word 'chums'?"

"I think it's a Kansas thing. Mr. Flonta decided to send Michael up here, too, so he can watch over his interests, at least that's what he said. We, meaning Michael and I, decided to go together. That's the part Dad was annoyed about. Me and Michael traveling together. You know what else? He told me when

Michael and Mr. Flonta weren't around to hear; he said if I have any trouble—I think he meant Michael and not just trouble in general—he said, if I have any trouble I should stay close to you."

"Me? I'm supposed to be your babysitter now?"

"I love my father, but honestly . . ."

"What's Alden's story?"

"He graduated from UCLA as coincidence would have it. He has a bachelor's in economics. He took a contract with Mr. Flonta for thirteen weeks working as a personal assistant while he looks for his dream job. Or at least a position that will help him land his dream job."

"What would that be?"

"Film finance."

"Doesn't anybody in California have a real job?"

"You mean like whatever it is that you do?"

I looked back at Alden and gave him a come-join-us wave. Jennica didn't laugh, yet she was close to it.

"He's really nice," she said.

"He's too old for you."

And then she did laugh.

I didn't know how nice he was, but Alden was awfully polite; he kept calling me "sir."

"What exactly were your instructions?" I asked.

"Sir, I'm not at liberty to say."

"If you don't, I'll make you leave the table and you won't be able to look into Jennica's eyes every thirty seconds."

Alden glanced at Jennica's eyes and abruptly turned away.

"You know, like that," I said.

Both boy and girl blushed a deep crimson and gazed at everything except each other.

Yeah, well, they had it coming, my inner voice said.

Still, they're blushing, I told myself. At their age? The world had changed. Not long ago you were considered a man or a woman at eighteen and were expected to behave like it. Get married. Buy a house. Start a family of your own. Nowadays, you're still a kid at twenty-four. You don't get married until thirty. 'Course, I should talk. I was forty-four and often behaved like I was eleven. What the hell was I doing in Grand Marais, anyway?

"Well?" I said.

"I'm not at liberty to say," Alden repeated. "Sir."

"Should I tell you why I'm here then?"

Jennica reached for her camera.

"Don't you dare," I said.

"Spoilsport."

"I believe that whoever stole the McInnis paintings is still in Grand Marais. If he contacts me about the reward, fine. Arrangements will be made and I'll get the paintings that way. Otherwise, I'm going to track him down and *take* the paintings." I pointed an index finger at Alden's face. "You interfere in any way, I will shoot you in the head."

"McKenzie," Jennica said.

I pointed the finger upward to keep her silent.

"There's no doubt in my mind that Flonta sent you up here to watch me and probably Louise Wykoff, too, although how you're going to do both at the same time, I have no idea. I'm equally sure that he told you that if I recover the paintings, you're supposed to take them away from me by any means necessary. Yes? No?"

Alden didn't answer, yet the expression on his face suggested that I was on the right track.

"If you try, I will shoot you in the head. By the same token, if by some miracle you happen to recover the paintings first, then I will take them away from you and return them to their rightful owner. If you resist, I will shoot you in the head."

"Would you stop saying that?" Jennica said.

"Just telling your boyfriend what he's in for."

"He's not my boyfriend"—Alden seemed more jolted by that announcement than by my threats—"and you're not going to shoot anybody."

"Are you willing to bet Alden's life on that?"

"Yes, I am."

"Wait," Alden said. "What?"

Jennica patted his hand.

"McKenzie's just trying to scare you," she said.

"Well, guess what?" Alden moved his head like there was a tune lodged in there that kept repeating over and over and he was desperate to shake it away. "UCLA's Department of Economics did not prepare me for this."

"C'mon, McKenzie. Be nice."

"You two seem to think this is all fun and games," I said. "A wonderful treasure hunt. It's not. It's dangerous. One man has already been murdered, remember?"

"Just as long as I get it on film."

"Dammit, Jennica."

"You're not calling me sweetie anymore?"

"No."

"Mr. McKenzie," Alden said. "Everything you said about Mr. Flonta is true, only look at me. I'm not a hero. I haven't fired a gun in my entire life. I haven't even been in a fight since the third grade and I lost that. I'm not going to get in your way. I'm here because Mr. Flonta is paying me; paying me to go to Grand Marais which, let's face it, is not the worst gig in the world. All I intend to do, though, is sit on the lakeshore and drink piña coladas with Jennica. If she'll let me."

"That can be arranged," Jennica said.

I pointed a finger in Alden's face again.

"She's underage," I said. "If you serve her alcohol I will shoot you in the head."

"Oh my God, McKenzie!" Jennica said. "Would you stop it?"

"Just as long as we're all on the same page."

"What page is that?" a voice said.

At first I thought it was the waiter, but no. It was Mitchell McInnis.

I sighed dramatically and said, "It just keeps getting better and better."

"Good to see you, too, McKenzie," Mitchell said.

"Who are you?" Alden asked.

"He's your competitor," I said. "Jennica Mehren, Michael Alden, this is Mitchell McInnis. He's Randolph McInnis's grandson. If I'm not mistaken, he's here to recover the missing *Scenes from an Inland Sea* for his grandmother, Mary Ann."

"No," Mitchell said. "She's leaving that to you. I'm here to make sure you don't get lost taking them back to the Cities. I don't think M. A. entirely trusts you, McKenzie. She's afraid you'll succumb to Louise Wykoff's charms."

"When was the last time you were in a fight?"

"You mean besides with my sister? I'm an artist, McKenzie."

"Let's say for argument's sake that I do recover the paintings and return them to That Wykoff Woman, what are you going to do about it?"

"I hadn't thought that far ahead." Mitchell smiled broadly and reached for Jennica's hand. "Jennica. What a lovely name."

"It means white wave," Jennica said. She was blushing again.

"You're Jeffery Mehren's daughter. You're working on his film."

"Our film."

"Of course."

"Perhaps you can be helpful to us."

"In any way that I can."

"Your grandmother had agreed to an interview, but now she's resisting because of her differences with Mr. Flonta. If you could intervene . . ."

"Let me see what I can do."

Mitchell slipped his cell phone from his pocket and stepped away from the table while he made a call.

Alden was looking directly into Jennica's eyes, yet was speaking to me.

"Aren't you going to threaten to shoot him in the head?" he asked.

I was also looking at Jennica when I answered.

"I'll let her decide who gets shot."

Jennica turned her head to hide her smile, only it didn't do any good.

I was beginning to feel like the den mother of a Cub Scout troop. After Mitchell returned to the table with news that M. A. had agreed to be interviewed on film after all—to Jennica's delight and Alden's obvious dismay—I excused myself. The boys and girl thought I was heading to a restroom. Instead, I left the tavern and started walking along the Gitchi-Gami State Trail.

I didn't get very far before a black-and-white SUV bearing the Cook County Sheriff logo screeched to a halt in front of me. Deputy Wurzer was behind the wheel, which left no doubt in my mind that the screeching was meant for dramatic effect.

"McKenzie." He spoke my name in the same tone of voice someone might use to say, "Stop or I'll shoot."

I stopped.

He got out of the SUV and marched toward me. For some reason I was reminded of *Gunfight at the O.K. Corral*, except he was Wyatt Earp and I was Billy Clanton.

"The sheriff told me you were back," Wurzer said. "Looking for another lesson?"

"Actually, I thought I'd wander up to World's Best Donuts. Join me. I mean that's what cops do, right? Eat donuts?"

"Is that what you did?"

"Only when I was working third shift and nothing else was open. Clayton Rask says hi, by the way."

That slowed him down.

"You're friends with the lieutenant?" Wurzer asked.

"Acquaintances might be a better word. I chatted with him just the other day."

"Checking up on me weren't you, McKenzie?"

"Of course I was. LT's still pissed off about what happened to you in case you're wondering. He doesn't think for a second that you were dirty."

"What do you think?"

"We don't always get along, Rask and me. But he tells me something, I take it to my bank and deposit it in my personal savings account."

"That makes two of us then."

"I also spoke to another friend of yours. El Cid."

"Asshole's no friend of mine, although someone in the MPD must like him."

"Not necessarily. From what I heard, it could be the feds. Could be the BCA."

"No. It's MPD. I could name names but I wouldn't expect you to believe them. No one else did. Except Rask."

"Cid claims he never heard of you."

"You believe him?"

"If the sonuvabitch told me the sky was blue I'd call him a liar on principle."

"Nothing to be done about it, though. Besides, it's all starting to be a long time ago. I'm now a respected member of the Cook County Sheriff's Department. At least I was. Cuz of you, Bowland is starting to look at me funny."

"For what it's worth, he put me in my place for making scurrilous accusations."

"Did he actually use the word 'scurrilous'?"

"I'm paraphrasing."

"Where does that leave us?"

"You and me? Standing on a street corner in Grand Marais. There's something you should know."

I gestured with a thumb at the third-floor terrace of the Gunflint Tavern. Jennica was leaning over the railing and filming us with her camera. If I had been her father, I would have been anxious at how far she was leaning.

"What the hell?" Wurzer said. "I thought all them camera crews had left to chase the next big thing."

"Girl's from Hollywood. Wants to make movies. What are you going to do?"

"You tell me?"

"Donut?"

"No, I don't want a donut. I want to know what you're doing here."

"You spoke to the sheriff. Didn't he tell you that I was going to get a list of items stolen from the past few burglaries, maybe some photographs, too, and take them up to Thunder Bay? See if I can find a match at one of the pawn shops."

"He's going to let you do that?"

"Tomorrow morning."

"I suggested doing that myself over a year ago. The sheriff blew me off. Said my badge didn't mean shit up there."

"Neither does mine."

"He listens to you, but not to me. All right. If that's the way he wants to run things."

Wurzer smiled at me the same way he did in my room at the Frontier Motel.

"I'd be interested in hearing whatever you come up with," he said. "Who knows, McKenzie. You might not be a useless piece of shit after all."

"Encouraging words, Deputy. Encouraging words."

Wurzer returned to the SUV. Before climbing inside, though, he gave a wave to Jennica. A few moments later, he drove off. I also gave Jennica a wave and continued to World's Best Donuts, which closed ten minutes before I got there.

FIFTEEN

The city of Thunder Bay is located on the Canadian shore of Lake Superior on what the eighteenth-century French maps called *Baie du Tonnerre*—Bay of Thunder, a name that I liked way better.

"Where are you from, kid?"

"The Bay of Thunder."

I mean, seriously.

I followed Minnesota Highway 61 for forty miles to get to the border and Ontario Highway 61 for another forty miles to reach Thunder Bay, which was cobbled together in 1970 with the merger of the communities of Fort William, Port Arthur, Neebing, and McIntyre. It covered more than 330 square miles, which made it nearly three times as large as the Twin Cities if that's how you measure size. Yet while the Cities had built up, Thunder Bay had built out, so it was mostly flat. I didn't see a single building that was more than five stories high and precious few that were three or four.

About 120,000 people lived in the city and surrounding municipalities. Enough to support eight pawn shops and nineteen antiques, collectibles, and thrift stores. I started at the far end of the Bay of Thunder near a place called Amethyst Harbor and worked my way back toward the United States.

The owners of the first two stores watched me like I was a black kid shopping at the Mall of America. Yet, if they were anxious that I was checking their inventory against the list and photographs that I carried in a manila folder, they didn't say. I gave them a nod when I left and they nodded back without smiling.

Come to think of it, Eileen wasn't smiling either when I retrieved the folder earlier that morning at the Law Enforcement Center. It was the only time that I hadn't seen her smile and I nearly asked what was wrong. I didn't because on the list of things I was involved with in Grand Marais that were none of my business, that was near the top.

The owner of the third store appeared deeply concerned by my behavior, though, and I wondered if he had been involved in some nefarious undertaking in the not-too-distant past. He did however, smile when I left his store without accusing him of committing a criminal act.

A couple of stops later, I found myself in downtown Thunder Bay. I parked in front of a pawn shop and walked inside. The store was retail-friendly, with bright lights and shelves and counters arranged to provide the discerning customer with a pleasing shopping experience. Think Marshalls or TJ Maxx.

There was a young woman with the outdoorsy face of a farm girl manning the cash register. She seemed disturbed by my manila folder and quickly summoned her boss. He met me at a glass counter loaded with jewelry and asked what I was doing. I told him.

"Are you OPP?" he asked, meaning the Ontario Provincial Police. "Are you a Horseman?"

"No," I answered to both questions. In the United States, it's illegal to pretend to be a cop. I didn't know if that's also true in Canada, but I wasn't about to push my luck.

"Then what are you doing?"

I explained myself in as few words as possible while emphasizing that the merchandise I was searching for had been stolen in the United States.

He smirked at me as if the number of morons he's met over the years had just increased by one.

"You've come a long way for nothing," he said. "I don't know what goes on down in the States, but we"—by that I think he meant all of Canada—"don't buy stolen property. This ain't no Hollywood pawn shop. A kid comes in with an electric guitar, I'm gonna ask him to play a tune. Customer has a Samsung Galaxy, I'm going to ask to see the charger. A guy says he wants to sell something off the books, I give him a thirty-second head start before I call the police. Whaddya think?"

I pointed at a gold ring with a square silver setting and a diamond in the center of the square. According to the victim's statement, "This was an old ring that belonged to my father, couldn't say what it was worth."

"What about this?" I asked.

"What about it?"

I showed him a photograph of the ring.

"Shit," he said.

I kept looking and discovered a bracelet and earring set with gold cat heads, a 14K yellow-gold chain with a heart-shaped ruby pendant, and an 18K gold-over-silver chain butterfly pendant with amethyst and diamond accents.

"I don't know what to say," the shop owner said.

"Do you have a purchase ticket with the name and address of the seller?" I asked.

"I do. Of course, I do."

"Let me see it."

He hesitated before replying. "I can't show that to you."

I dropped the only name I knew.

"You can show it to me or you can show it to Detective Constable Aire Wojtowick," I said. "She's with the Criminal Investigations Branch of the Thunder Bay Police Service."

The shop owner hesitated some more.

"I can all but guarantee that the person who sold you this stuff is an American," I added.

That seemed to do the trick. The shop owner showed me his paper. All of the stolen jewelry had been sold to him by Christopher Weathers of West Fifth Street in Grand Marais.

Never heard of him, my inner voice said.

"I checked the name he gave against his passport," the shop owner said. "This is for real."

"Do me a favor, will you? Set all this stuff aside for now."

The shop owner said he would. He asked if the police service would be contacting him.

"Eventually," I said.

I don't know if he believed me or not. I do know he was using his phone when I left the shop.

Probably calling a lawyer, my inner voice said.

There were eight other stores within walking distance of one another, so I left my Mustang where it was and began investigating on foot. My next stop was an antiques store where I discovered a Roman silver denarius coin with the head of Emperor Severus Alexander set in silver bezel as a pendant, a Roman bronze sestertius coin of Severus Alexander also set in silver bezel as a pendant, a Roman silver Republic denarius coin set in gold bezel, and two Roman bronze coins attached to earrings.

The owner of the antiques store didn't want to believe that he had purchased stolen property, either, but detailed descriptions provided by the victim, including dates between 150 and 300 A.D., convinced him. I had to drop Detective Constable Wojtowick's name again to get a look at the purchase ticket.

Won't she be happy about that?

The coins were sold to the antiques store by the same man—Weathers of Grand Marais. I found more merchandise in a pawn shop three stops later, this time sold by a man named Gerard Roach, also of Grand Marais. At my final stop I hit the mother lode—Eddie Curtis, with an address on Margarets Road, Grand Portage, MN, United States of America.

So it was Curtis behind the burglaries, I told myself. And probably Montgomery. And Deputy Wurzer—what did he have to do with it? Did he have anything to do with it?

I glanced at my watch—yes, I still use a wristwatch instead of consulting my phone every five minutes—it was a little past one P.M.

That didn't take long. So, you have what you came for. Now what?

It was a good question. I wasn't entirely sure how things worked between the two countries, how evidence gathered in Canada could be used against miscreants in the good ol' USA or even if it could, for that matter. I decided to contact my friend Aire Wojtowick, although "friend" might have been a slight exaggeration. It had been nearly four years since I was last in Thunder Bay and that was to investigate a murder that turned out not to be a murder but rather part of an elaborate extortion scheme. While I couldn't recall her exact parting words to me, I remembered their meaning—keep your crap the hell outta my country.

By then I had completed a loop twelve blocks long and a couple of blocks wide through downtown Thunder Bay, so I was now approaching my Mustang parked in front of the first pawn shop from behind. That's when the alarm systems in my head began firing all at once.

It was an unconscious thing; it took a beat or two for my brain to catch up with my instincts. When it did I saw a tan-colored two-door Toyota with Minnesota license plates parked one block away with clear sight lines to my car. It was occupied. I flashed on Eddie Curtis and the car that he had been driving when Deputy Wurzer stopped him on Marina Road in Grand Portage.

Most people when their fight-or-flight impulse is triggered will try to convince themselves that there is no danger; they'll tell themselves that they're just being paranoid. That's why they don't cross the street when they should or get on elevators when they shouldn't. For example, I could have easily talked myself into believing that there were a thousand tan-colored cars that looked like Curtis's in Minnesota and this was just one of them. Except, I wasn't in Minnesota. I spun around and started walking in the opposite direction. I walked quickly. If I was wrong, fine, I told myself, I was wrong.

I managed ten yards before throwing a glance over my shoulder. Three men were getting out of the Toyota. One of them was Curtis.

You've been made.

"McKenzie, stop," Curtis said, in case I was still unsure.

I think I might have cursed out loud, but I honestly don't recall.

I started running.

They started chasing.

"You chicken-shit!" Curtis shouted.

Sticks and stones.

I was looking for a business, a store, a restaurant loaded with lunch-hour customers, with witnesses; a location where my pursuers would be less likely to pick a fight. After all, there is safety in numbers, a man once said. The Bank of Montreal branch office on the corner seemed promising. Someone there might even be induced to call the cops since I couldn't. My phone company didn't provide service in Canada.

I veered toward the bank.

That's when I heard the gunshot.

I thought I *felt* a bullet whizzing past my ear, but that might have just been my natural paranoia. I had no doubt, though, that I'd never make the bank. Suddenly, all I could see was the three-story redbrick parking ramp standing directly in front of me.

A second gunshot.

Are you fucking kidding me, my inner voice shouted. *You can't shoot people in Canada.*

There was a sign at the front gate of the ramp. MAXIMUM 5 KM/H. I think I was going faster than that when I ducked beneath the red-and-white-striped booth arm and made my way inside.

Curtis and his friends slowed behind me. I'm not sure why. Maybe they were afraid that I was planning to ambush them with the nine-millimeter SIG Sauer I had left in my room at the Frontier Motel because you can get up to five years just for carrying a concealed firearm in Canada—which partially explained why the United States averages 12,000 gun-related homicides every year and they have about two hundred.

I had no intention of lingering, though. What was I going to do? Hide behind a car? Crawl beneath an SUV and wait for them to find me? Instead, I dashed up the sloping incline to the second floor of the ramp.

There weren't as many cars as I hoped, but there were enough. I saw a Lexus and slammed into it the way a lineman might attack a blocking dummy. Its security alarm went off. I kept running until I encountered a BMW. And a Nissan. And another BMW. Soon the concrete ramp was echoing with the screeching sound of car alarms.

If you can't get to a crowd, maybe you can get a crowd to come to you.

I sliced between two parked cars to a low concrete wall. I could see the ramp on the level below me. I decided it wasn't too far of a jump—despite my innate fear of heights. I scampered over the wall and leapt onto the hood of a Honda Accord. Its alarm system went off, too.

I quickly made my way toward the exit. Let Curtis think I was hiding in the parking garage, I told myself, while I zigged and zagged to a safe location where I could explain my dilemma to the local constabulary.

Only they were smarter than I gave them credit for. Two of the gunmen had followed me into the parking garage, yet the third had moved along the street, positioning himself outside where he had a clear view of the exit.

Now what, smart guy?

I heard running footsteps in between the whoop-whoop-whoop of the sirens. I cut back across the ramp and wedged myself in the tiny space between the front grille of a Honda Ridgeline pickup truck and the low wall. The sound of footsteps became louder. I didn't see who made them.

Yeah, but did they see you?

Voices shouting to be heard over the car alarms.

"Where did he go?" someone asked.

Okay, they didn't see you.

"Did he leave the ramp?" someone else asked.

"No." The voice started soft, but became louder as the speaker left his post outside the exit and entered the garage. "McKenzie has to be around here somewhere."

"He must be hiding between cars or under a car. You go that way. We'll go this way."

"He could be hiding inside a car."

"Eddie, we don't have time for this."

"He's right. We gotta get out of here. The Mounties."

"And then what? He knows who we are."

"Eddie . . ."

"Keep looking. Hurry."

I propped myself between the wall and the truck's front grille and pulled my legs up so Curtis and his minions wouldn't be able to see my feet if they searched beneath the Honda. I supported one knee on the bumper and braced the other against the wall, while I folded my body so that it would be hidden by the grille. It was hard; I was doing a complex yoga pose without ever having done yoga before. I figured my chances were better, though, if I stayed put rather than trying to make a run for it. Something I learned hunting pheasants in farm fields with the old man all those years ago. I rarely saw the birds hiding among the cornstalks. It was only when they attempted to fly away that they were in danger of being shot.

I listened intently.

Footsteps came and went.

Voices, only I couldn't hear what was said.

One by one the sound of the car alarms died away.

Silence. It seemed louder than the sirens had been.

Someone shouted my name. He told me what he was going to do to me.

Someone else shouted what I could do to myself—something that I wouldn't have thought was possible until I had folded myself between the pickup and the wall.

More silence.

Another siren. And another.

Outside or inside, I couldn't tell.

Give it a few minutes before you take a look, I told myself.

I waited longer than that.

My muscles cramped.

I let them.

My head ached.

I ignored that, too.

Her voice startled me.

The hand I was using to keep myself perpendicular slipped and my forehead whacked against the truck's headlight.

I looked up into her eyes.

Detective Constable Aire Wojtowick was another woman who made me reevaluate my dating criteria. While Perrin Stewart was big from side to side, she was big from top to bottom. Well over six feet and solid without a hint of doubt in her eyes. If LeBron James ever encountered her on a basketball court, he'd say, "Excuse me," and dribble in the opposite direction. Her people were from Slovakia, which surprised me. Given her golden hair and blue eyes you'd swear she was a product of Sweden. Or Minnesota.

"Hello, McKenzie," she said. "Miss me?"

"As a matter of fact . . ."

I uncurled my body and stood. My legs protested when I took a step. I didn't want Aire to know that, though. My forehead ached, yet I refused to rub it.

"What brings you here?" I asked.

"I was in the neighborhood when I heard that there was a running gun battle on the streets of Thunder Bay. Are you out of your mind?"

"It wasn't me. It was three others. I have one name and the description of a car. If you contact the Canadian Border Service . . ."

"Are you sure there were only three?"

"Yes. A man named . . ."

"I have them in custody. Now I have you, too. My work here is done."

We both headed for the exit of the parking garage.

"Wait a minute," I said. "I was the one being chased. Check your traffic cams. And witnesses. There have to be witnesses."

"Are you armed, McKenzie?"

"Of course not. Not in Canada. Wait. How did you find me?"

"Our parking ramps have cameras. How 'bout yours?"

"It depends on how old—if you saw film then you know I'm telling the truth."

"You haven't told me anything yet," she said. "Like what the hell you're doing in Thunder Bay."

"I was going to call you. I really was."

"A couple of pawn shop owners beat you to it. You used my name to conduct your inquiries? How dare you, McKenzie?"

"I can explain all this, Aire."

"You'd damn well better. And it's Detective Constable Wojtowick to you."

"It's going to be a long story."

She gestured at my face. "I notice you've been bruised."

"That's part of it."

By then we had reached the exit of the ramp. There were half a dozen black-and-white Thunder Bay Police Service vehicles blocking traffic and at least twice that many officers. I liked the red patches on the shoulders of their black uniforms and the red bands on their hats. So European. Aire was the only one dressed in plainclothes.

"Are you still the junior member of the Criminal Investigation Branch?" I asked.

"I've moved up to middle management. Are you still tilting at windmills?"

"From time to time."

We walked past a few of the cars. The trio that had attacked me had been cuffed and stuffed into the backseats of separate vehicles. I wondered if they were also the men who punched me out on the beach across from the Frontier Motel and decided I didn't really care one way or the other. I recognized Curtis.

"Let me talk to this guy," I said.

"Hell no."

"It might give you some insight into what's going on."

"Oh, you're going to give me plenty of insight, McKenzie. Guaranteed."

"Detective Constable." I used Aire's title on purpose. "In my country we have a thing called an excited utterance. It's defined as a statement made by the declarant when the declarant is startled by something. It's admissible as evidence."

"Declarant—that's a lawyer's word if I've ever heard one. Forget it."

"Detective Constable."

"Do you honestly think he's going to take one look at you and confess all his crimes?"

"His name is Eddie Curtis. He's a Native American. Ojibwa. First Nation up here. I'm pretty sure he was running a burglary crew out of Cook County in Minnesota. I know for a fact that he came to Canada to kill me."

"For a fact?"

"More or less."

"What is it with you Americans that whenever you think beyond your own borders it's to screw things up for the rest of the world? All right, McKenzie. Five minutes."

We approached the officer standing next to the vehicle. He actually tipped his hat at Aire.

"Ma'am," he said.

"Did you read him the caution?"

"I did, ma'am. I don't think he appreciates where he is."

"Let me give it a try."

The officer opened the car door and Aire leaned inside. Curtis stared at her, a blank expression on his face, his hands cuffed behind his back.

"You are under arrest for discharging a restricted firearm in public and about a dozen other crimes we haven't worked out yet, including attempted murder," Aire said. "Do you understand? You have the right to retain and instruct counsel without delay. We will provide you with a toll-free telephone lawyer referral service if you do not have your own lawyer. Anything you say can be used in court as evidence. Do you understand? Would you like to speak to a lawyer?"

Curtis didn't reply.

I squeezed between Aire and the door frame.

"How you doin', Eddie?" I said.

"Fuck you, McKenzie."

"What are you doing here, Eddie? Who sent you to kill me?"

He didn't answer.

"You have the chance to do yourself some good, Eddie. I'd take it if I were you."

"I have the right to remain silent."

"Actually, you don't," Aire said. "There's nothing in the charter that says you have the right to remain silent. I mean, you can. Anything you do or say may be used as evidence against you. But it's not a right. Nor do you have the right to have an attorney present during questioning. Nor do we have to stop talking to you even if you have nothing to say to us. This is Canada. We do things a little differently up here."

"What are you saying?"

"Eddie," I said. "Look at me. Eddie."

He looked.

"This isn't the United States. Our laws won't protect you here. My advice, cooperate."

"I—I want a lawyer."

"As soon as we get you to jail you can call a duty counsel who will assist you until you can secure representation," Aire said.

"Like a public defender?"

"I suppose."

"Okay, then."

"Who sent you Eddie?" I asked.

"Fuck you, McKenzie."

"Change of subject—where are the paintings?"

"I am so goddamned tired of hearing about those fucking paintings. I ain't got nothing to do with them. How many times do I have to say it? If it wasn't for those paintings you wouldn't have been nosing around and I wouldn't be here now."

"Then why did you kill David Montgomery?"

"I didn't kill Dave. Don't even think of putting that on me. I'm telling you, I have an alibi for that; is what I told that fucking deputy when he pulled me over on the rez like he owned the place. I had nothing to do with it. Dave wasn't even part of my crew. Okay, sometimes he'd tell me things like about this woman whose windows he replaced who had ancient Roman coins that she turned into jewelry and I'd slip him a couple bucks. Other than that, he was just some asshole dating my sister."

"I'm sure she's very proud of you."

"Fuck you."

"Good luck to you, Eddie. You're going to need it."

I stepped away from the vehicle. Detective Constable Wojtowick closed the car door. She spoke to the officer.

"Did you hear that part about his crew?" she asked. "About the Roman coins?"

"Yes, ma'am."

"Make sure it's in your report."

"Yes, ma'am."

Together Aire and I started walking down the street.

"Am I in custody?" I asked.

"Do you need to be?"

"I was just wondering if you were going to take me to the police station or if I could drive myself."

"Do you remember where it is?"

"Balmoral Street across from the car dealership?"

"Where's your car?"

I pointed down the block to where it was parked outside the pawn shop.

"Is that a Mustang? Not having a midlife crisis, are you, McKenzie?"

"It was a gift from my girlfriend."

"Nice. McKenzie, I'm going to ask you a lot of questions in front of a camera. Then we're going to transcribe your answers and you're going to sign it after swearing that every word of it is true."

"Yes, ma'am."

"For now, though—what *are* you doing in Thunder Bay?"

I gave her the edited version.

Aire's response was to stare at me.

"I don't understand," she said. "Your Sheriff Bowland could have done all that himself."

"What do you mean?"

"What do you mean what do I mean? The man contacts my office. He sends us an incident report along with the list of stolen items. Me or one of my people check the pawn shops like you just did and secure the stolen property. Next, we contact a judge and have an arrest warrant issued for the suspects who sold the stolen property. These suspects, they can only be prosecuted in Canada. If they're in the States, we can't touch them. We'll contact the CBS and have a checkmark placed next to their names, though, so if they try to enter the country again, bingo . . .

"'Course, they can't be prosecuted in the States, either, at least not for selling stolen property in Canada. We would pass on everything that we have and that should be enough for the sheriff to secure a warrant to search the suspect's house, car, whatever; see if he can build a case, that way. Take the suspect's fingerprints if they're not already in the system and try to get a match at the crime scenes. At worst, the sheriff will be able to put eyes on him."

"I guess he was put off by all the paperwork, one country's law enforcement agency cooperating with another," I said.

"What paperwork? There isn't any paperwork beyond what I just told you."

"Do you mean to tell me that a sheriff's department in the United States reaching out to a police service in Canada isn't any different than working with Wisconsin?"

"I don't know. I've never worked with Wisconsin."

"C'mon."

"What?"

"That doesn't make sense. Deputy Wurzer told me . . ."

"What?"

I gave it some thought and decided. "Maybe it does make sense."

"McKenzie . . ."

"Nothing. Nothing, Detective Constable. It's just—you've given me a lot to think about."

"While you're thinking, I have another question for you."

"Yes, ma'am."

"What paintings?"

SIXTEEN

The crown counselor who caught the case was almost gleeful. Apparently, he couldn't think of anything more fun than offering up three American punks to the general population at Millhaven. It seemed like a maximum security prison is where they were headed, too, because trafficking in stolen property was the least of their problems. Smuggling guns across the border could cost them three to ten years just by itself. Not to mention discharge of a firearm with intent, four to fourteen; use of a firearm in the commission of an offense, one to fourteen; and carrying a concealed weapon, six months to five years. Attempted murder—that had a price tag of five to life in Canada. Since they were foreign nationals living outside the country, it would be unlikely they'd score bail. Parole, if it came to that, would be problematic at best.

The American consulate in Winnipeg was informed that three American citizens had been taken into custody. That wasn't going to be of much help to the boys, though. Consular officers can't arrange for the release of anyone or act as an attorney or pay attorney fees. The best they could do was to ensure, as far as possible, that US citizens were given proper treatment under Canadian laws.

I learned all this over the course of the next ten hours while I gave my statement first to the Thunder Bay Police Service, then the Ontario Provincial Police, and finally to the Royal Canadian Mounted Police because someone decided to make a federal case out of it—all this before I even saw the crown counselor. I told a Mountie that I was surprised that some people called them Horsemen. He didn't like the nickname. He said "We're called *the Force*." Then he glared, almost daring me to say something obnoxious like "May the Force be with you." I might have, too, if we were in the States.

At some point, Detective Constable Aire Wojtowick contacted Sheriff Bowland, partly to explain what was going on, but mostly to ask him to verify that I had, in fact, come to Thunder Bay at his behest, which he did. Ninety minutes later, Deputy Wurzer arrived armed with a more comprehensive list of items that had been stolen in Cook County. He and a member of the Criminal Investigations Branch traveled to the pawn shops and antiques stores that I had already visited, plus several more. I was told later that they had recovered evidence from seventeen separate burglaries.

Wurzer and I were in the same room for only about thirty seconds, so our conversation was brief.

"I can't believe the sheriff didn't let me come up here years ago," he said.

"I wonder why he didn't."

He stared at me. I stared at him. I didn't know what he was thinking, but the deputy guessed what was on my mind.

"Be careful, McKenzie," he said. "Be very, very careful."

I promised myself I would, except—someone told Curtis that I was coming to Canada and only two names came to mind. If Deputy Wurzer didn't do it . . .

I was tagged as a material witness, of course, which meant a subpoena would be issued compelling me to give testimony in court. Yet the subpoena could only be executed in Canada. Once

I returned home I would be out of reach. The Canadians had to take my word that I would return when asked.

The crown counselor wasn't happy about it. He was concerned that the defense attorney might roll the dice, taking a chance that I would be a no-show, which would not only provide grounds for a mistrial, but also give him the upper hand in plea bargaining. But what was he going to do? Take me into custody until the court date? Worst-case scenario—it was decided by the court that I would be allowed to give video testimony if it was too difficult for me to return to Thunder Bay.

It didn't hurt that Aire vouched for my good character. And all this time I thought she didn't like me. I told her so over a very late dinner.

"I didn't say that I liked you, McKenzie," she said. "I said I trusted you."

I told her that was the same thing. She assured me that it was not. Still, she embraced me on the sidewalk where we said good-bye. It was like being hugged by the most beautiful bear you've ever seen.

The temperature had dropped close to freezing by the time I reached the Pigeon River Border Crossing. I could see the breath of the US Customs and Border Protection agent as he leaned out of his booth.

I rolled down my window.

"Good evening," he said.

"Good evening."

I gave him my passport and he examined it.

"Late night," he said.

"As long as I get home before the sun rises, that's the main thing."

That was dumb, my inner voice said. It was proved correct when a second agent appeared out of nowhere and positioned herself behind the Mustang. It seemed to me that her hand was resting awfully close to her gun.

"Open your trunk," the agent in the booth said. The snap of his voice startled me.

"Of course."

I pushed the button that released the trunk lid. The agent behind me opened it and peered inside. The trunk was empty, yet she seemed to look for a long time, perhaps searching for a false bottom or secret compartment.

This is what comes from being a smartass, my inner voice reminded me. *You don't joke with border guards. You don't act rudely or complain or ask questions or debate policy or rant against the government. They can ruin your trip if not your life on a whim. If you're smart you speak only when you're spoken to. Are you smart, McKenzie?*

At the same time my cell phone started sounding a trumpet solo.

"What is that?" the agent asked.

"The ringtone on my cell."

"Sounds like Louis Armstrong playing 'West End Blues.'"

He's a jazz fan. Lucky you.

"Exactly right," I said aloud.

"I like it."

"Thank you."

Then the burn phone started chirping.

"What's that?" the agent asked again.

"I have two phones. One for work and one for play. Neither of them had service in Canada. I guess they're catching up on missed calls."

He nodded as if he understood completely.

"Are you going to answer them?" he asked.

"They can wait."

He smirked, a man who knew exactly how much power he had and how to wield it. The other agent shut my trunk lid and shook her head. Her partner returned my passport.

(231)

"Welcome home," he said.

Despite everything, my heart leapt in my chest. It always happened that way. Whenever I returned to my country, even after a short time abroad, someone, usually a custom agent, would say, "Welcome home," and I would feel so damn happy. Go figure.

Forty-five minutes later I arrived at the Frontier Motel. It wasn't until I was safely inside my room that I checked the cells, burn phone first.

I had received four calls. Two had hung up when I didn't answer. The other two left voicemails. The first said he possessed important information about the paintings, but it would cost me more than $250,000. The second said, "If you want to see those paintings alive, you had better call back pretty damn quick." I decided both could wait until the morning.

My personal cell phone had two messages. The first was from Nina. I returned her call immediately. She didn't answer her cell, which told me that she was at the club. I called Rickie's and eventually tracked her down.

"How was your day?" she asked.

"I went up to Canada where a gang of hardened criminals shot at me."

"So, Thursday?"

Despite the joke, I knew Nina was concerned. If it were up to me, I wouldn't tell her these things except I had learned long ago that she would become even more upset when I kept them to myself. So now I tended to edit my close calls. For example, I didn't tell her that a bullet whizzed past my ear—if in fact a bullet had whizzed past my ear and it wasn't just my overactive imagination.

"No damage done," I said. "I might have to return to Thunder Bay for the trial if the boys don't cop a plea. Maybe we can make a vacation of it. Check out the blues festival if it's around the same time."

"You'll need to give me plenty of advance warning."

"I know. The club comes first."

"I wish you wouldn't take so many chances, McKenzie, because guess what? The club doesn't come first."

"It doesn't?"

"It's more like a tie."

"I love you, too."

"By the way, the reason I called—remember Flonta, the old man who stopped us on the street? He called me."

"He called you?"

"Called the condo. He wants to talk to you."

"Did he leave a number?"

"He said you should contact his man in Grand Marais. Michael Alden?"

"More like a kid, but okay. Did he say what it's about?"

"Not specifically. He did say that despite your rude and unsavory behavior, he was sure that you two could come to an understanding. Personally, I like it when you're being unsavory."

"That's startling talk coming from a nice Catholic girl."

"I've been corrupted, what can I say? McKenzie . . ." Nina paused for a few beats before she asked, "What do I always tell you?"

"Just as long as I come back in one piece . . ."

"See you soon."

The second call was from Louise Wykoff. She left a voicemail message—*Call me no matter what time it is. I'll be awake.*

So I did.

She told me to come to her place.

I told her it was late.

She said she didn't mind if I didn't.

I did mind—images of Louise ambushing me in a lavender nightie like Peg Younghans danced in the back of my head. Yet she deserved an update on my so-called investigation. I said I'd be there in twenty minutes.

Instead of lavender, That Wykoff Woman greeted me in a long-sleeve white cotton gown that covered her body from throat to ankles. It was utilitarian in design; I didn't know if she slept in it or if it was just something she wore around the house on cold evenings.

She waved me inside as if she was afraid someone would see me standing on her doorstep. On impulse, I glanced behind me. No one was there. I hadn't actually seen anyone while driving through Grand Marais. Most of the surrounding homes were dark, although there were lights shining through some windows at Peg Younghans's house across the street.

"I've been thinking," Louise said.

A dangerous thing to do, I thought, but didn't say.

"What if Dave Montgomery still has the paintings? Oh, I'm sorry. Can I get you something? I'm drinking white wine."

I would have preferred bourbon, my drink of choice whenever I was confused, yet said, "Wine is fine."

Louise poured a glass. It tasted sweet. A moscato. She settled on her stool. I found a chair and looked up at her. There was a ceiling light on behind her and it shone through her hair. She seemed beatified, leaving no doubt in my mind why Randolph McInnis had chosen her for his muse so many decades before.

"What if Montgomery still has the paintings?" Louise repeated. "What if he hid them, not in his house or garage, but in a storage unit or a shed in the woods? Something like that? What if he gave them to a friend to hide?"

"That's entirely possible. We know that the burglars working Cook County don't have them."

"We do?"

While I explained, Louise slid off her stool and began pacing the classroom filled with easels and canvases, her bare feet squeaking a little on the hardwood floor.

"They shot at you?" she said. "What is happening?"

"No one was hurt."

Louise seemed startled by my remark.

"David Montgomery and now this," she said. "If I had known this would happen I would've given up those paintings to Mary Ann thirty-five years ago."

"It's not your fault."

"It seems like my fault. McKenzie, what should we do?"

Since Louise was standing, I stood.

"Your idea is a good one," I said. "Tomorrow morning I'll ask the sheriff to either look into it or let me do it. In the meantime, the offer of dueling rewards might turn up something. I've received several calls that I haven't had a chance to check on yet. If that doesn't yield anything—it's possible that the thief is laying low until the media spotlight is turned on something else. All this could be old news by Monday; such are the times we live in."

"Bruce Flonta called me today. He told me that he's also received several calls about the reward. He asked me to identify the paintings for him. In return, he said he'd give me ten percent of what he earns when he sells them."

"What did you say?"

"I told him he could go—entertain himself. I don't like to swear, usually."

"It's the only language some people understand."

"He made me so angry, like he was doing me a favor by stealing my paintings. Mary Ann, at least—you can argue that she has a small claim to them. But Flonta? I don't trust him. He's a, a . . ."

"Businessman?"

"He doesn't love art. That's probably true of most people, though. Most people, they walk through the City of Lakes Art

Museum or the Minneapolis Institute of Art in an hour, just glancing at the pretty pictures on the wall and the sculptures, not stopping to appreciate how much work went into them or what they have to say. Do you appreciate art, McKenzie?"

"Yes, I think I do. At least I'm starting to."

"I want to thank you for everything you've done for me. You've been—from the very beginning you've been great."

"Well, hopefully we'll do what we came here to do."

A couple of moments later, I set down my empty glass and we moved toward the front door. Louise opened the door and did something unexpected—she wrapped her arms around me and pulled me into a tight embrace, her head resting between my shoulder and neck.

Wow, my inner voice said. *That Wykoff Woman is hugging you.*

I hugged her back because it seemed like the thing to do.

After a moment, Louise released me and stepped backward. "I shouldn't have done that," she said.

"No, I liked it."

"Good night, McKenzie."

"Good night. I'll call you tomorrow after I speak to the sheriff."

Louise closed the door and I walked down her steps, over her lawn, and across the street to my car. All the lights in Peg Younghans's house had been extinguished by then except for one up high. It went off just as I reached the Mustang.

Nearly everything in Grand Marais was closed expect the Gunflint Tavern and it wasn't showing much life. I parked in a slot right outside the front door and went inside looking for something to wash the taste of Louise's sweet wine out of my mouth. Only a couple of tables were occupied, one of them by Mitchell McInnis and Michael Alden. They waved me over. A waitress arrived at the same time I did.

"Last call," she said.

"Maker's Mark on the rocks."

She left me alone with the boys. I sat down.

"Where's Jennica?" I asked.

"She decided to make an early night of it," Mitchell said.

Good for her, my inner voice said.

"We've been looking all over for you, McKenzie," Alden said. "Where have you been?"

I couldn't think of a single good reason why I should tell him, so I didn't. By then the waitress had reappeared with my drink and I took a long sip of it.

"Why were you looking for me?" I asked.

"Mr. Flonta wants to speak to you."

Alden's voice was slurred just enough to make me think that he and Mitchell had been sitting in the Gunflint for a long time.

"What about?" I asked.

"He keeps getting calls from people who want to sell him the missing *Scenes from an Inland Sea.* It was over two dozen the last time I spoke to him."

"What did he think was going to happen?"

"He needs someone to help him indentify the paintings, make sure he doesn't get ripped off, and Louise Wykoff won't cooperate."

"Again, what did he think was going to happen?"

"Mr. Flonta said he's willing to make you an offer."

"I'm not interested."

"Ha," Mitchell said. "Told you."

"Don't be cocky, pal," I told him. "If I can recover those paintings without paying a ransom, your grandmother will be out of luck, too."

"You don't mean that."

I answered him by drinking half of my bourbon.

"McKenzie," Alden said, "will you at least talk to Mr. Flonta?"

"I've already made him aware of my position. Seems to me

that you were standing there at the time. I see no reason why I should repeat myself."

"It'll make me look good to my boss."

"Sorry, kid. You're on your own."

"Please, McKenzie. I don't want to go back to the Cities. I like it up here."

"What he likes is Jennica Mehren," Mitchell said.

"Shut up."

"The way you keep staring at her, it's pathetic."

"You know, you've been an ass about her ever since you got here. How many times do you need to hold her hand, hmm? Or caress her shoulder? Or rub her back. Talk about pathetic."

"Jennica deserves better than a wannabe"—Mitchell air quoted—"investment banker."

"Didn't you say that your father worked in finance?"

"Perfect example."

"What are you?" This time Alden air quoted. "An artist living off his grandfather's reputation and money?"

"Don't knock it," Mitchell said. "Especially the money part."

"Boys, boys, boys," I said. "It's no wonder Jennica went to bed early. You're so boring." I knocked back the remainder of the Maker's Mark, stood, and pulled a ten from my pocket and dropped it on the table. I patted Alden's shoulder. "Tell your boss that if he makes a deal with Mary Ann McInnis we'll talk. Otherwise, he's on his own. And give Jennica a break. Both of you."

"You're not interested in her yourself, are you, McKenzie?" Mitchell said.

I gave him a look—the one I reserve for people I'm thinking of shooting in the head. His smile faded quickly.

"What did you say?" I asked.

Mitchell waved his hand in front of himself like he was waxing a car. "I didn't say anything." He repeated the gesture. "These are not the droids you're looking for."

"That's what I thought."

SEVENTEEN

I woke up angry.

Partly it was because it was still dark outside when my eyes snapped open as if I were awakened by a bad dream that I couldn't recall. Mostly, though, my mood was soured by a combination of bad memories, a sense of anxiety, and some seriously negative feelings. It didn't happen to me very often, waking up like that. Yet I've noticed it was happening more and more. My psychologist friend, Jillian DeMarais, once told me I was displaying symptoms of PTSD and that I should see someone, only I never did.

Yeah, okay, some guy shot at you yesterday, I told myself. Big deal. It wasn't like you were in combat or raped or saw your family killed in a tornado, so suck it up.

I lay in bed, knowing I wouldn't be falling asleep again anytime soon, decided "to hell with it," and flung the covers away. I made two cups of coffee, shaved, showered, dressed, slipped on a light jacket, and took the coffee to the chair in the center of the motel's horseshoe. The sun rose across the great lake, tentatively at first and then with its full glory as if it intended to make the most of the day. I had to shield my eyes against the light.

I slowly drained the coffee; the second cup was cool by the time I finished. I wasn't in a hurry. I knew the first thing I was going to do and I was both sad and infuriated about it at the same time. Finally, like the sun, I decided it was best to get on with it.

I drove to the Cook County Law Enforcement Center. Eileen buzzed me inside. She looked as though she hadn't slept well, either.

"I heard what happened in Canada," she said. "I don't know what to say."

"Why should you say anything?"

She didn't have an answer for that.

"Is the boss in?" I asked.

"He's . . ."

"He's what?"

"Upset."

"That makes two of us."

I heard Sheriff Bowland's voice growling from his office. "McKenzie, is that you?"

"Yeah."

I started toward the open doorway even before the sheriff said, "Come here."

I didn't bother to knock, but slid inside the office, stopping in front of the sheriff's desk. Unlike Eileen, he did look like he had slept—in his clothes, in his chair. His face was unshaven and his hair was tousled; his eyes were filled with regret. He looked like he was a thousand years old.

"Sit," he said.

I sat.

"You want anything? Coffee?"

"No."

The sheriff took a sip from his mug and I wondered briefly

if there was another substance mixed in with the black liquid besides caffeine.

"I screwed up and I feel sick about it," he said.

I heard what sounded like a shoe scraping across the floor just outside the sheriff's door, yet didn't turn my head to look.

"Tell me about it," I said.

"I screwed up."

"You said that."

"I thought it was far more complicated working with Canada than it is. I had my staff look into it a couple years ago for something that had nothing to do with the burglaries and I was told that it required untangling a giant ball of red tape and since we couldn't prosecute Americans for crimes committed in Canada and they couldn't prosecute Canadians for crimes committed here it wasn't worth the aggravation."

"Okay."

"You don't believe me."

"It sounds implausible."

"It's true, though," a female's voice said.

I turned in my seat to look at the woman standing in the doorway.

"Eileen," the sheriff said.

"It was me," she said. "I thought he was talking about extradition, which is really, really complicated and I gave him the wrong information. It was never corrected because we never had any dealings with Canada since then."

"Eileen," the sheriff repeated.

"It's true. Bill, tell him."

Bill? my inner voice said.

"Eileen," Bowland said yet again. "This is a private conversation."

"Tell him."

"I'm the sheriff. It's my responsibility."

I turned back in my seat to face the sheriff.

"She's loyal," I said.

"Yes. A good woman."

"Still sounds implausible."

"McKenzie," Eileen said, "I know what you're thinking. You're wrong. McKenzie, you are so wrong."

I spoke without looking at her. "What am I thinking?"

"That Bill was somehow involved with Eddie Curtis and the others. He wasn't. He's a good man."

A good man and a good woman—no doubt about it.

"No, that's not what I was thinking," I said aloud. I continued to stare at Sheriff Bowland. "I was angry earlier because I thought that only two people knew I was traveling to Canada and why, both of them cops. I was angry because I decided one of them must have given me up to Eddie and his pals. A cop going bad—maybe it's because I was a cop once that along with angry I also felt nauseous. Seeing you this morning, though, reminded me—there was a third."

I turned in my seat again to face Eileen. There were tears in her eyes and she was gripping the door frame as if it were the only thing keeping her upright.

"Tell me about this," Bowland said.

"Eddie . . ."

"What about him?"

"He's not coming back, is he?"

"Eventually," I said. "In about a decade or so."

Eileen lurched forward; she used the back of my chair to keep from hitting the floor. I got out of the chair and helped her into it.

"I didn't know," she said. "I honestly didn't know. About the burglaries. About anything. I thought he liked me."

Geezus, my inner voice said. *What is it about Grand Marais women sleeping with younger guys? Is there something in the water? They should bottle it.*

"I want to know," the sheriff said, although he sounded like he really didn't. "Eileen, tell me."

"We would talk. He would tell me about the reservation and funny things that came out of the casino. I would tell him about—about the office. What we were—what you were doing about the burglaries and things. It seemed . . . harmless. Two people talking about their jobs. The other night, though, I told him about McKenzie and Canada. I saw how upset it made him. I knew, well, I didn't know, but I should have. I should have known. I should have—I should have told someone, told you, I should have . . . I was afraid. I was stupid. I was . . . When I heard what happened . . . I'm sorry, Bill. I am so, so sorry."

She broke down. I watched her do it. So did the sheriff. Neither of us did or said anything to help her.

Bowland drank more of his coffee. Minutes passed. He said "Eileen, shh."

I surprised myself when I rested my hands on her shuddering shoulders and leaned in so that I was speaking softly into her ear.

"It's okay," I said. "Don't worry about it. Eddie has nothing to gain by offering to testify against his co-conspirators, by providing evidence in exchange for a plea deal. An American prosecutor might cut him some slack, but the crown counselor in Canada; he couldn't care less about that, about anything that might have occurred on the wrong side of the border."

"Why are you telling me this?"

"Legally, you have nothing to worry about."

I gave her shoulders a gentle squeeze. That didn't stop Eileen's tears, though. I stood away from her and addressed the sheriff.

"Nobody died," I said.

He didn't answer.

"Your burglary ring is broken."

He had nothing to say to that, either.

"There's a chance that Montgomery hid the paintings somewhere other than his house and garage," I said. "Or passed them off to a friend. It's possible that he might have hid them with a friend without the friend even knowing. I want your permission to keep looking for them."

Bowland kept watching Eileen while sipping his coffee.

"Sheriff," I said.

He nodded.

I left.

I was surprised that the Blue Water Cafe was packed at seven thirty on a Friday morning; the hostess at the door told me there would be at least a twenty-minute wait. I don't know why that made me so angry, yet it did. I was about to leave when I saw Jennica Mehren sitting alone at a table for two, playing with her phone, the remnants of a breakfast in front of her. I pointed and told the hostess, "My friend."

I went to the table. Jennica looked up from her cell. "Sweetie," she said.

Her smile made me smile.

"May I join you?" I asked.

"Please."

I sat. A waitress appeared with a menu. I ordered something called the Campfire Scrambler and coffee. The coffee wasn't nearly as good as Eileen's.

"You're up bright and early," I said.

"This isn't early. At home I'd be getting ready for school. What hours do you keep?"

"Late to bed, late to rise. Where are the boys?"

Jennica set her phone aside.

"Not my turn to watch them," she said.

"Oh?"

"They both invited me to breakfast, but I thought it would be nice to be without their company for a while. All that testos- terone."

"They're trying to impress you."

"I know."

"You could tell them to stop."

"This doesn't happen to me so often that I'm sure I want them to stop. In fact, it's never happened, two guys chasing me like this. It's because I'm the only girl they know in Grand Marais, I get that. If we were in California or the Twin Cities, both of them would probably ignore me. I saw this movie once where they said that a woman who's a six or seven in real life will be a ten in a war zone."

"Sweetie, you'd be a ten in any zone—eastern, central, mountain, twilight."

Jennica smiled brightly. It was enough to lighten my dour mood.

"See," she said. "Lines like that are the reason twenty-year-old girls sleep with fifty-year-old men."

"You think I'm fifty? You're killing me, Jen."

"It's okay, McKenzie. I'm sure you have a few good years left."

"Thanks. That makes me feel so much better."

"Where were you yesterday? I looked all over for you."

"I was in Canada."

"Because of the paintings?'

"Yep."

"Tell me."

"Not on camera."

"Please, McKenzie."

"Nothing to tell, anyway. It's what they call a dead end."

"What are you going to do now?"

"Do you want to go to Duluth with me?"

"Yes."

"Don't you want to know why?"

"If you're going . . ."

"I want to talk to David Montgomery's ex-wife."

"All right."

"Understand, you're not going to film her. You are not going to talk to her. In fact, you're not going to be there when I talk to her. I just thought you might enjoy the drive. Get out of Grand Marais for a while."

"We're leaving Michael and Mitchell here, right?"

"Absolutely."

Jennica smiled some more.

"You know what they say," she said. "Absence makes the heart grow fonder."

"I'm sure they'll miss you more than you'll miss them."

Jennica dropped her large and heavy backpack on the floor directly behind the front passenger seat of my Mustang. If she were attending college, I'd ask her what books she was carrying. Knowing her, though, I figured assorted recording equipment, so I didn't ask.

We chatted about this and that as we headed down the highway while listening to WTIP-FM, which billed itself as North Shore Community Radio. It had a very eclectic sound; the DJs played whatever interested them, which, apparently, included everyone and everything recorded during my misspent youth—Chaka Khan, B-52s, Marvin Gaye, Eric Clapton, Santana, the Kinks, Taj Mahal, Elvis Costello, Norah Jones. Jennica, of course, had never heard of any of them. Despite my shock and outrage at her lack of musical education, I started feeling like my old self.

We had just passed Tofte when Jennica said, "We're being followed."

"No, we're not."

She stared at me like she couldn't believe that I hadn't seen what she had seen.

"Blue Ford F-150 pickup truck," Jennica said before reciting the vehicle's license plate number. "Eight to ten car lengths back. It never gets closer and it never falls farther behind."

"Probably using cruise control, like I am. Jen, it picked us up when we passed through Lutsen, not Grand Marais. When we left GM we were clean."

Jennica wrapped her arms around herself, and rested her chin on her chest.

"I like that you're paying attention, though," I said.

She kept paying attention, too, until the F-150 peeled off the highway in Silver Bay.

"How do you know this stuff?" Jennica asked.

"Like anything else—education, experience, time."

"You sound like my father. What are you going to talk to Montgomery's wife about?"

"I want to ask if he gave her anything before he died. If she received any packages from him after he died."

"The paintings?"

"It's a possibility."

"Think she'll tell you?"

"I usually know within thirty seconds how much cooperation I'm going to get. Older people are easier to talk to because they enjoy the attention. Women are the next easiest if you can demonstrate that you have a genuine interest in what they're telling you. They're also the most honest. Men will answer questions, but usually after making sure you know that they're doing you a favor. Immigrants and minorities are the most suspicious because they know that whatever they say can be used against them—my experience anyway."

"It must be fun being a private eye."

"Sometimes it is. Yesterday sucked and so did this morning. Driving the North Shore with you at my side has made up for it, though."

Jennica thought that was awfully funny. She punched my arm.

"What?" I asked.

"Midwest charm. Both you and my father are loaded with it. You know what? When the time comes, I'm going to find a guy just like you two, even if I have to move to the Midwest to do it."

I had called ahead. Jodine Montgomery agreed to meet me in the same room at the Duluth Art Institute where we spoke five days earlier. She was on the phone when I arrived so I spent a few minutes studying Eastman Johnson's and Louise Wykoff's sketches and paintings some more. I noticed that not only was the subject matter similar, so were the pencil and brushstrokes.

"Good morning, Mr. McKenzie," Jodine said after she hung up the phone. "What can I do for you?"

I approached her desk at the same time that Jennica entered the exhibit hall. I was furious. I had told her to wait in the Mustang and she said she would. I might have said something to her, but I noticed she wasn't carrying a camera so I let it slide. I didn't want to spook Jodine.

"I'm sorry to disturb you again," I said.

"It's all right." Jodine shook my hand and seated herself behind her desk. "I'm starting to get past the shock. So is Jamie."

"About that—what I came to ask is if Montgomery gave you anything the week before he—before he passed?"

"No."

"If he asked you to hang on to a package; if he stored something in your garage or basement or . . ."

"No. You're asking about the paintings, aren't you? The ones they're talking about on cable? No. I hadn't seen him for at least three weeks before—before everything happened."

"Are you sure?"

Jodine sighed as if she had heard that question before and was tired of it.

"I'm sure," she said.

"You're aware of the reward?" I asked. "You could get $250,000 to half a million."

"I'm aware, McKenzie. Believe me, if David had left those paintings with me, I would have cashed them in yesterday."

"That's what I thought. I had to ask, though."

"I understand."

"Thank you for your time."

"You're welcome."

I left the exhibit and went to the elevator. I punched the down button. Jennica arrived before the elevator car.

"I am so angry right now that I feel like leaving you here," I said.

"You won't, though."

"No, I won't."

"You know, McKenzie, I have a job to do, too."

"Did you hear anything you can use in your film?"

"No."

"I didn't think so. At least you didn't have a camera."

"Of course I did."

The elevator arrived, the doors opened and we stepped inside the car. When the doors closed, Jennica opened the top buttons on her shirt to reveal the ring of flower tattoos around her neck, a powder-blue lace bra, and a camera the size of a thumbtack.

"The quality is amazing," she said.

"How often have you used that to film me?"

"I haven't yet. No, really, don't give me that look. I picked it up just before we left the Twin Cities on Wednesday. This is the first chance I've had to use it. I just now grabbed it out of my backpack."

"Well, put it away."

She said she would, and then laughed when I made her do it in front of me.

"Wow," she said. "You'd think you didn't trust me all of a sudden."

"Would it help if I bought you pie?"

Jennica said it would, so we stopped at Betty's Pies. She had

French silk and I had apple crunch. We remained on good terms during the drive back to Grand Marias. That changed at about twelve thirty when I tossed her out of the Mustang in front of the Northern Lights Art Gallery.

"What are you doing?" Jennica wanted to know.

"Did you think I adopted you?"

I circled the car and opened her door.

"C'mon, McKenzie."

"Out."

Jennica slid out of the car, but she wasn't happy about it. I grabbed her backpack from behind the seat and set it on the sidewalk next to her. Peg Younghans slipped out of the door of the art gallery just as Jennica picked it up and slung it over her shoulder.

"Let me go with you," she said.

"Nope."

"McKenzie, you are such an asshole."

"Hey, hey, hey, young lady—language."

I recircled my car and opened the driver's side door.

"What did he do?" Peg asked.

"Nothing," Jennica said. "Not a damn thing."

I slipped inside the Mustang and drove off. Jennica stomped off in the opposite direction. Peg didn't know which one of us to watch.

Ardina Curtis was not happy. Before the door to the Grand Portage Art Gallery even closed behind me she sprung to her feet from the swivel chair behind her desk and shouted, "What do you want?"

"I want to ask you about—"

"Get out."

"About David Montgomery."

"He was part of it, wasn't he? He was a part of what Eddie and his friends were doing."

"A small part."

"Now he's dead and Eddie needs money for an attorney. What were they thinking?"

"Did Montgomery give you—"

"Nothing. He didn't give me a damn thing that I couldn't live without."

"Did he have access to a shed or a garage—"

"Get out of here, McKenzie."

"Ardina, I'm sorry, but—"

"You don't care about David. You don't care about Eddie. Or me. Or anybody. All you care about is those damn paintings. If I had them, I sure as hell wouldn't give them to you. I'd give them to—to—I'd give them to Louise."

"There's a reward . . ."

"Everything that's happened—it's your fault. This is all your fault, McKenzie."

"Ardina—"

"Get out, get out, get out . . ."

Ardina sat down, a fighter collapsing in her corner. I left her there.

I leaned against the reference desk of the Grand Marais Public Library like it was a bar, wishing it were a bar and I was drinking bourbon. Doris Greyson was working with a patron. When she finished she sighed like having to talk to me was a huge imposition. The boys at Mark's Wheel-Inn an hour earlier had displayed pretty much the same attitude. They had nothing more to say to me than Ardina Curtis had.

"What can I do for you, Mr. McKenzie?" Greyson asked.

"I have more questions about David Montgomery."

"Like what?"

"The Tuesday evening you last saw him, did he give you something to hold for him? A package?"

"No."

"Do you have a garage or a shed, something he might have used without your knowledge?"

"No. McKenzie, does this have anything to do with Eddie Curtis and his friends? The whole town is abuzz with what happened to them in Canada."

"What happened to them in Canada?"

"Sheriff Bowland found out they were behind the burglary ring that the *News-Herald* reported on and that they were selling stolen goods in Thunder Bay. He told the Mounties or somebody and they arrested them. Apparently, shots were fired so now Eddie and the others are in even bigger trouble than just selling stolen property."

"Who told you that?" I asked.

"I heard it from the woman who just left who heard it from a man who was speaking this morning with a deputy. Peter Wurzer, is that his name?"

"I couldn't say."

"Did David have anything to do with that?"

"Not that I'm aware of."

"It was a big deal about the McInnis paintings; Grand Marais received so much publicity. Now this. You have to wonder what the place is coming to."

"You've made quite an impression on Peg Younghans," Leah Huddleston said.

We were standing in the center of Northern Lights in front of a wall where she had hung two new Louise Wykoff paintings to replace those she had already sold.

"How so?" I asked.

"She said she saw you dump a young woman on the street . . ."

"I didn't dump her. I would have dropped Jennica off at her motel except for the traffic."

"Anyway, Peg said she thought you were a nice guy and now she thinks you're like every man she's ever met."

"Meaning?"

"You're a jerk."

"It's been that sort of day."

"Why are you here?"

"I came to offer you a quarter of a million dollars for the safe return of the McInnis paintings, no questions asked."

"You are a jerk, aren't you?"

"Seems to be the majority opinion."

"Besides, I heard the reward was now half a million."

"The man who's offering it isn't necessarily trustworthy. Leah, I mean no disrespect. I just want you to know that if you hear anything . . ."

"I'll let you know."

"Thank you."

"Although, I've been thinking about it ever since we spoke last Sunday. Getting my hands on those paintings—it would be like winning the lottery, wouldn't it?"

"I read somewhere that most people who win the lottery come to regret it."

"Yet we keep buying tickets, don't we?"

Once again I had parked near the Dairy Queen. I retrieved my Mustang and turned onto Highway 61. I drove about three hundred yards before I was stopped by the Cook County Sheriff's Department. I watched Deputy Wurzer in my rearview as he carelessly approached my vehicle. I rolled down the window.

"License and proof of insurance," he said.

"Ah, c'mon."

"Don't worry, McKenzie. I'm just messing with you."

"Why? Are you bored?"

"I just left the Law Enforcement Center. Sheriff Bowland seems awfully depressed for a local hero."

"What are you talking about?"

"Haven't you heard? He single-handedly smashed a major

crime spree. Not only that, he managed it in such a way that all of the suspects were arrested in Canada so we don't have to foot the bill for a long trial and imprisonment. The county commissioners are ready to declare Sheriff Bowland Day."

"What I heard, there's a deputy running around spreading the good news, trying to make the sheriff look like a star."

"You have a problem with that, McKenzie?"

"No, I don't."

"This thing about the sheriff being depressed, though. It could be because he found out that the woman he's been sleeping with was sleeping with someone else."

"Ah, dammit Eileen."

"I wouldn't want that to get around, though. A relationship between employer and employee and such, citizens might get the wrong idea, think it was nonconsensual or something. Once they started looking into it, who knows what other crap might come out."

"You don't have to worry about me."

"Whaddaya know? We're actually on the same page for a change."

"Who woulda thunk it?"

"Because you're being so cooperative, I thought I'd tell you—your close friends with the BCA? I don't know if you've heard, but they decided that Montgomery killed himself after all, ruled his death was a suicide."

"Sure they did. What do you think?"

"I think you have no more reason to hang around, do you, McKenzie?"

"Are you telling me to get out of town, Deputy?"

"I don't have the authority. Besides, that would be a badge-heavy thing to do, wouldn't it?"

"It's possible I might have misjudged you, Peter."

"Go fuck yourself, McKenzie."

I briefed Louise Wykoff about my day, ending with "I don't know what else to do."

She spoke adamantly. "Search the woods around his house," she said. "He could have hidden the paintings in the woods."

"Louise . . ."

"He could have put them in a box or wrapped them in a waterproof tarp or something."

"That's really unlikely."

"He could have."

"I guess."

I would've said more except my cell phone rang. I didn't recognize the number. Normally, that was reason enough to swipe left. The call had a 612 area code, though—Minneapolis—so I excused myself, turned my back on Louise, and swiped right.

"This is McKenzie," I said.

"McKenzie. This is Dave Wicker."

"El Cid. What is it?"

"I'm not sure why I'm telling you this, McKenzie, because mostly I hate your guts and threatening me like you did pisses me off more than I can say, but maybe I owe that dumb cop something, so . . ."

"What are you telling me?"

"It's about the McInnis paintings. I heard murmurs. Well, more than murmurs."

"What murmurs?"

"There's going to be an auction."

"Someone's going to auction off the missing *Scenes from an Inland Sea*?"

Louise heard me and moved quickly to my side.

"Yes," Cid said.

"Who?"

"I don't have a name. If I did, I wouldn't give it to you. There are rules."

"Fair enough. When? When is the auction?"

"A couple of days. I don't think they've set an exact time yet. I can find out if you're interested."

"I'm very interested."

"Is this going to square us, McKenzie? You gonna get off my case?"

"This will square us."

"I'll do what I can for you, then—this one and only time. Understood?"

"Understood. Cid, do you know where the auction is going to be held?"

"Canada."

EIGHTEEN

"Quebec City," I said.

"Are you sure your information is good?" Mary Ann Mc-Innis asked.

"Yes."

"It's not," Louise said. "It can't be."

We were in Mary Ann's house on Sunday afternoon. I was seated at the bar and sipping a Summit EPA. Mary Ann was behind the bar and drinking the same, except that the label on her bottle had been shredded. Louise was seated in a stuffed mohair chair with hand-carved maple arms. She had declined all offers of refreshment, even tea. Mitchell McInnis hovered near her side and attempted to make small talk, only Louise had nothing to say to him.

"You're basing this assertion on what exactly?" Mary Ann asked.

"This claim that they're going to auction off the paintings," Louise said. "It's no different than what those people who keep calling McKenzie's burn phone are saying. Give us the money and we'll give you the paintings. It's a lie."

"That sounds like wishful thinking to me."

"It's a lie."

"She might be right," I said.

"Unfortunately, the only way to know for sure is to go up there and look," Mary Ann said.

"Unfortunately."

"Fine, you fly to Quebec," Louise said. "But I'm not going with."

"Who asked you to?" Mary Ann said. "I don't even know why you're here. Why is she here, McKenzie?"

"Because they're my paintings," Louise said.

"Not anymore."

"Randolph gave them to me."

"And you lost them."

"I didn't *lose* them. They were stolen."

"That's the only thing about this sorry affair that makes me smile."

"You're just angry because Randolph loved me and not you."

"Louise, dear, do you want to have that conversation now? Is that what you're asking?"

Louise didn't reply.

Mary Ann finished her beer and set the bottle none-too-gently on the bar.

Mitchell McInnis held up his smartphone for everyone to see.

"He's late," he said.

"I know he's late," Mary Ann said. "Did you honestly think that Flonta was going to be on time? Assholes like him always keep you waiting at least twenty minutes. It's how they prove they're important. Do you want another beer, McKenzie?"

"Yes, please."

"Louise? No, of course not. What was I thinking?"

"I'd like a beer," Mitchell said.

"Suddenly I'm your maid? Get it yourself."

Mary Ann set another Summit in front of me. She found one for herself, too. Her fingernail began jabbing at the label. She stopped and looked at her hand as if it were the first time she'd seen it.

"What the hell am I doing?" she asked no one in particular.

Minutes passed. I flinched when four bells began chiming the Westminster Quarters. Mitchell went to the front entrance as if he was expecting an important package. The door was opened and Bruce Flonta stepped inside along with Michael Alden, who supported the old man's arm, plus Jeffery and Jennica Mehren.

Mary Ann spoke quietly so that only Louise and I could hear. "Jesus Christ, the man travels with an entourage." More loudly she said, "Did you get lost, Bruce?"

Flonta and his followers moved closer to the bar. He leaned on his cane and smiled.

"Did I keep you waiting?" he asked.

"Not at all. It gave us time to talk about you behind your back. The consensus is that you're a devious prick."

"It's good to meet you again, M. A., after all these years. Ms. Wykoff, I am pleased to see that age has done you no harm whatsoever."

Louise acted as if she hadn't heard the compliment and instead watched nervously as if a group of rowdy strangers had unexpectedly walked into the room where she was sitting.

"May I introduce my associates?" Flonta said. "My personal assistant, Mr. Alden."

Alden moved forward and offered Mary Ann his hand. She looked him up and down like he was contagious. He stepped back.

"You know Mr. Mehren, of course," Flonta said.

Mehren bowed his head. "M. A.," he said. "Ms. Wykoff. It's always a pleasure."

"What?" Mary Ann said. "No cameras?"

"Mr. Flonta prefers that this meeting remain unfilmed," Mehren said.

"We always do what Mr. Flonta prefers, don't we?"

"This handsome young lady is Jennica Mehren," Flonta said.

"Mitchell was right; you are a nice piece of ass."

"M. A.," Mitchell said.

"Oh, I'm sorry," Mary Ann said. "Did I misquote you?"

Jennica's slight smile and gentle shrug told me two things. One, that she had enormous self-control. Two, Mitchell was dead to her now and forever.

He seemed to know it, too.

"Jennica," he told her. "I never said that. You have to believe me."

Only Jennica wasn't listening to him. Instead, she gave all of her attention to Mary Ann, who beckoned for the young woman to move closer. When she did, Mary Ann leaned over the bar and whispered into Jennica's ear. She spoke for a good thirty seconds. Whatever was said seemed to confuse the young woman. It was as if Jennica was receiving important information, yet had no idea what to do with it.

Mary Ann stepped back and patted Jennica's arm.

"May I offer you something?" Mary Ann said. "Beer? I have wine."

"Nothing, thank you."

"You are very pretty."

Jennica smiled slightly again and tilted her head as she stared at Mitchell. He appeared uncomfortable beneath her gaze.

Mehren was also unsettled, yet like his daughter was able to rein in his emotions. He was angry over what M. A. had said to Jennica, yet seemed to understand that there was something more to it. Instead of reacting, he did what I was doing—waited for the next shoe to drop.

Jennica pointed her jaw at me.

"Hello, sweetie," she said.

"Jen."

I tapped the center of my chest as unobtrusively as possible. She smiled some more and vibrated her head slightly side to side. I don't know why I was sure that meant she wasn't filming us, yet I was.

"You"—Mary Ann waved her beer bottle at the men in the room—"may all fend for yourselves."

"Still as charming as ever, M. A.," Flonta said. "Now stop wasting my time and explain why you brought me here."

"McKenzie, you have the floor."

I revealed the content of my phone calls with El Cid and what I proposed doing about it. I finished by saying, "Understand, we are engaging in a criminal conspiracy. We are planning to travel to a foreign country, acquire stolen property, and return it to the United States. I have no idea how many felonies that amounts to. I'm guessing it's a lot."

"You mean we could all go to jail?" Alden said.

"At my age it's fun to try new things," Mary Ann said.

"But they're my paintings," Louise Wykoff said.

"No," Flonta said. "They belong to the highest bidder, which raises the question—exactly what return am I supposed to realize for supplying half the money for the auction? One—count 'em—one canvas? Plus, I won't be allowed to choose which canvas? No, no, no. That is unacceptable. Give me one reason, M. A., why I shouldn't just buy them all myself?"

"The point is to keep them from jacking up the price," Mary Ann said.

"I don't care about the price."

"Then you're a moron."

Flonta didn't like being insulted, but who does? I give him props, though, for staying on point.

"Something else." He leveled his cane at me and smiled some more. "I'm supposed to trust McKenzie? What's stopping him from using our money to buy the paintings and keeping them for himself? Or worse—giving them to That Wykoff Woman?"

"Do you have an answer for that, McKenzie?" Mary Ann asked.

"Nope."

For some reason, my reply made Mary Ann smile.

"I appreciate, Bruce, that the less trustworthy you are, the more difficult it is for you to trust someone else," she said. "As for me, I have complete faith in McKenzie and half the money will be mine, so . . ."

"You can trust him all you wish," Flonta said. "I don't need him and I don't need you. I can get into the auction on my own and buy what I want."

"You're both fools." Louise rose from her chair. "Nothing will come of this. Those are not my paintings; I know they're not."

"Now, dear," Mary Ann said. "Just a moment ago you argued that they were yours."

"I'm going back to Grand Marais."

The Wykoff woman began her journey immediately, grabbing her bag and heading for the door. Mitchell rushed to open it for her.

"Good evening," he said.

"Fools," Louise said as she stepped across the threshold.

Flonta said, "I have no reason to remain here, either." He packed up his entourage and walked out. Jennica was the last to leave and threw us a mild wave.

"Remember what I told you," Mary Ann said.

"I will. Thank you."

Like Louise, Jennica also ignored Mitchell as she stepped through the doorway.

"What did you tell her?" I asked.

"Just a little advice from one pretty girl to another." Mary Ann grabbed a paper napkin from beneath the bar and wrote a number on it. She passed it to me like she was making an offer on my condominium. "McKenzie, this is as high as I will go. If you can get one of the paintings for this amount, good. If you can get all three, better. When will you leave for Quebec City?"

"The auction is scheduled for Wednesday evening. I'll leave Tuesday morning, give myself a little leeway in case there's a problem with the weather or the airline."

"That'll allow me tomorrow to make sure my financial people set up an account that you'll be able to access from your smartphone. It will allow you to make an electronic transfer of funds as per instructions if the auction goes our way. You were invited through this El Cid character. Do you think Flonta will be allowed in?"

"He probably has better contacts than I do, so yeah."

"I'd hate for him to get Randolph's paintings, but I'm not willing to play stupid to keep him from doing it. You stick to my number. Not a penny more."

"Yes, M. A."

"Just so you know, if we do retrieve my husband's paintings, I intend to sell two of the three. Remember what I told Louise— that's why Randolph painted them in the first place, to sell. The third painting, the one Louise wants so desperately for herself, that's the one I'll donate to the City of Lakes, make Perrin Stewart happy. Understand, though, I'm only doing it because Louise informed you of what the paintings contained so that we'll know what we're buying. Or not buying. Does this meet with your approval?"

"Yes, M. A."

"Are you sure? You were pretty insistent before that the Wykoff woman share in all of this."

"The situation has changed, hasn't it? The money changed it."

"It always does. McKenzie, please—make sure that they're Randolph's paintings before you bid. All right?"

"I'll take care of it."

"Poor Louise, hoarding those three *Scenes from an Inland Sea* all these years and then losing them . . . She really did love my husband, didn't she?"

"Yes."

"So did I—the sonuvabitch."

There were no direct flights from the Minneapolis-Saint Paul International Airport to Quebec City. Instead, I was forced to leave the condo at four A.M.—Nina insisted on driving me—in order to arrive at the airport with enough time to pass through the security checkpoint and grab a Starbucks before jumping on an Air Canada jet that flew me to Toronto. Once there, I went through customs again and waited a couple of hours in a hard plastic seat before being loaded into a much smaller turboprop— a plane in which I had no confidence—that landed in Quebec City at 2:30 P.M. eastern time. It took nearly another hour before a taxi driver named Serge dropped me at the Fairmont Le Château Frontenac. The pleasant young man who checked me in said, "Enjoy your stay," and handed me a cream-colored envelope. I accepted the envelope, slipped it into my pocket, and said, "I'm sure I will." Ten minutes later I collapsed on the double bed in my room. I gave it a few beats before I checked my watch: 4:00 P.M. eastern time. I had been on the move for eleven hours.

I took me a few more beats before I opened the envelope. It contained a standard sheet of white typing paper that had been folded twice. A handwritten message read, *You will be contacted.*

When? Where? By whom? my inner voice wanted to know.

I crumpled up the note and continued to lay on the bed, my legs dangling over the edge, knowing if I didn't get up soon I would fall asleep, which, I told myself, wasn't the worst thing that could happen.

Finally, I pushed myself upright and unpacked. It didn't take long. My carry-on contained one change of clothes, my shaving kit, and a charcoal gray suit that I had purchased from King Brothers Clothiers in Minneapolis because apparently Canada had a strict dress code when it came to acquiring stolen property.

Who knew?

A few minutes later I was strolling up Rue Saint Louis toward a restaurant that I was familiar with.

Quebec City just might be the most beautiful city in North America, especially that part known as Vieux Quebec—Old

Quebec. At least that's the conclusion Nina Truhler and I came to when we vacationed there a couple of years ago. It consisted mostly of old stone buildings and cobblestone streets dating back four centuries that had been erected behind nearly three miles of stone fortifications, making it the only walled city north of Mexico. The walls were started by the French in the seventeenth century to protect them from the British and completed by the British after they conquered Quebec in 1759 to protect them from the Americans.

Aux Anciens Canadiens was built in 1675. I entered the restaurant and moved directly to the hostess station.

"Bonsoir," I said. *"Puis-je avoir une table pour un?"*

"Yes, sir," the hostess said as she grabbed a menu. "Table for one. Right this way."

Which was another thing—despite the English victory during the Seven Years War—the Québécois hung on to their French heritage like it was a flashlight in a dark room. Seventy-seven percent of Quebec's population were native Francophones and ninety-five percent spoke French as their first or second language. Outside the walls you needed to know French to be understood and the Quebec City citizens were as particular about it as they were in Paris. Vieux Quebec was bilingual, however, mostly to accommodate tourists from the United States and the rest of Canada.

Unfortunately, my French sucks. I'd say, *Excusez-moi,* and immediately the natives would switch to English. It's like they couldn't bear to hear their language mangled. Nina, on the other hand, spoke French like the French. She'd say something simple like *Bonjour* and the Québécois would start chatting with her like she was a long-lost cousin from Nova Scotia.

I wished she were with me while I ate a spectacular pea soup followed by pork tenderloin and bread pudding with maple sauce, and not just because of her language skills. Vieux Quebec is for couples. Every corner, stairwell, doorway, and alley hid some strange, unique, and wondrous feature or attraction and to not have someone to share those discoveries with made me feel lonely.

After leaving Aux Anciens Canadiens, I wandered over to Rue Sainte-Ursule because that's the street that contained the bed-and-breakfast where Nina and I stayed during our visit. It was 120 years old—the bed-and-breakfast; I had no idea how old the street was—with a balcony where we sat drinking wine and enjoying the sights.

That's when I realized I was being followed. A man. Thirty years old. Five ten, 185 pounds, sandy hair beneath a dark gray ball cap with a silver fleur-de-lis on the front. I surfed through a half-dozen theories to explain why he was there and settled on the one I felt most comfortable with—the auction hosts wanted to make sure I was in Canada to commit a crime and not to solve a crime.

I led my tail down the avenue to Rue Saint-Jean, a tourist street if there ever was one. Among its many bars, restaurants, and shops was a joint called Murphy's Irish Pub where I found a table, ordered a Jameson on the rocks, and listened to a kid playing guitar from a small stage. Instead of Irish folk music, though, he played mostly poor covers of American pop songs, the amplification so loud that often the notes sounded distorted. I gave it the one drink before scattering a couple of Canadian bills on top of the table and moving on.

It's always a good idea to carry cash so you can duck out of a joint in a hurry without someone chasing you down the street. My tail hadn't been as well prepared and was forced to make a quiet scene as he signaled for a waiter to take his credit card. If I hadn't made him before, I sure would have then. Still, I didn't want to do anything that would make him suspicious, like lose him in a crowd, so I took my own sweet time wandering down the avenue, pausing to listen to a street performer who had set up between Café La Maison Smith and a McDonald's.

Once the tail caught up, I let him follow me along Côte de la Fabrique to Rue des Jardins and from there along a pedestrian crossway to a park called Place d'Armes. There was another street musician performing in front of an eatery called Restaurant 1640. He was very good, playing the accordion and singing in French a lot of songs that I knew only in English like "Autumn Leaves," "The House of the Rising Sun," and "Beyond the Sea." I found a bench in the park that I shared with a couple from New York and listened. The couple didn't seem to care about the music and I was glad when they finally moved on.

After about an hour, I decided to give my tail a break. I went to the musician and dropped a Canadian twenty in his accordion case, received a head nod in recognition, and wandered over to the Terrasse Dufferin. The terrace was built a century and a half ago and provided a spectacular view of the Saint Lawrence River and that part of Vieux Quebec called Lower Town because it lay between the river and the high bluff where Upper Town was located. There were plenty of tourists leaning on the iron railing. A couple from Alberta asked me to take their photograph and I agreed while my tail kept his distance.

I treated myself to an ice cream served by a vendor who sold his wares from a pushcart. I didn't know if it was the cone or the setting sun, but the temperature seemed to drop from the mid-sixties to the forties just like that, a tad chilly for my sports jacket and jeans. That's when I decided to call it a night and crossed the terrace in the direction of the Fairmont Le Château Frontenac.

It's supposed to be the most photographed hotel in the world and if you ever saw it, especially at night, you'd understand why. It completely dominated the Quebec City skyline, a true-life castle with a stunning tower inspired by the architectural styles of the Middle Ages and the Renaissance. Fun fact—it was designed by an American architect named Bruce Price. I just thought you ought to know.

I wandered toward it. The tail was leaning against a light post and trying hard not to make eye contact. I gave him a head nod as I passed because it was Canada after all and people there are almost as nice as they are in Minnesota.

"*Bonne nuit, monsieur McKenzie*," he said.

I laughed not from humor but embarrassment. See, up until that moment, I thought I was being so very, very clever.

Early Wednesday morning there was a tap on my door. Before I reached it, though, someone had shoved a small cream-colored envelope beneath it. I took a quick look through the spy hole and saw no one. I didn't bother to open the door, but instead opened the envelope, unfolded another sheet of white paper, and read what had been written there:

PLACE DUFFERIN. TEN A.M.

Place Dufferin was one of four restaurants located within the hotel, not counting the Starbucks just off the lobby, and my first thought when I walked inside—I should have worn my good suit. It was all marble and wood and leather chairs and featured food stations where pastry, fruit, cheese, cereal, juice, and hot items were displayed as if they were works of fine art; look but don't touch. I was sure you could get a nice Picasso for what Place Dufferin asked for its breakfast buffet. Suddenly, the Starbucks didn't seem so gauche.

It was open for breakfast until ten thirty and was nearly empty when I arrived, so it was easy to find a table near the window. I ordered coffee and a croissant—I was never much of a breakfast person—and distracted myself with the splendid view of the Terrasse Dufferin while I waited.

Twenty-two minutes later, a man appeared at the table.

"Mr. McKenzie?" he said.

I made a production out of looking at my watch.

"Really?" I said. "It took you this long to search my room?"

"We like to be thorough. May I?"

I gestured at the chair across from me. He sat, folding his hands on the table in front of him.

"McKenzie," he said. "Would that be an Irish name?"

"Scottish."

"There's a pity."

"Depends on your point of view."

"I'm O'Rourke."

"Do you have a first name?"

"We will not know each other well enough to bother with that. Shall I tell you how this is going to transpire?"

"I wish you would."

"At exactly eight o'clock tonight, a windowless van will arrive in the courtyard in front of the hotel's entrance . . ."

"Windowless?"

"You and several other guests will enter the van after first depositing your cell phones into a Faraday bag. You will, of course, also be scanned by a radio frequency detector for GPS tracking devices and other transmitters. Afterward, you and our other guests will be conducted to a secure location where you will be met by still more bidders. I believe there will be two dozen all told. The auction will commence at approximately nine P.M. We will bid in US dollars, not Canadian. Payment will be demanded via electronic means immediately after the bidding is concluded. I hope that is understood."

"I'll need my smartphone."

"It will be returned to you for that purpose."

"Will I be allowed to examine the merchandise before the auction?"

"It will be displayed for all to scrutinize at least fifteen minutes prior to bidding."

"If you could tell me the exact dimensions of the paintings right now, it might save us both some trouble."

"Do you know the exact dimensions of the paintings?"

"Yes."

"You do?"

"Yes."

"How do you know this?" he asked.

"I have a relationship with the prior owner."

O'Rourke leaned back in his chair.

"What exactly are your intentions, Mr. McKenzie?" he asked. "If you're seeking redress . . ."

"I am not. As much as it pains them to do so, the parties I represent are willing to buy back what was stolen from them."

"You must understand; I am acting merely as an intermediary in this matter."

"I don't suppose you'd be willing to divulge the name of the party you represent."

"No."

"I didn't think so. I ask again, Mr. O'Rourke, do you know the exact dimensions of the paintings?"

"I have not yet seen them myself. They are en route."

"Tell me, how much would your business suffer if it were revealed that you arranged the sale of forgeries to your clients?"

"You ask that as if it has never happened before. We make it clear to all of our clients that we are able to authenticate the work we auction only to a point. Beyond that, there is a phrase that is used in both of our countries, caveat emptor."

"Let the buyer beware."

"If you believe the McInnis paintings to be forgeries, don't bid on them."

"Fair enough."

"On the other hand, I'm sure you will appreciate, Mr. McKenzie—we will not countenance a scene."

"You will not get one from me, one way or the other."

"I will hold you to that. Oh, and at the risk of seeming rude"—O'Rourke gestured at my clothing—"our guests are required to dress in formal business attire."

"Of course. We are, after all, engaging in a white-collar crime."

I couldn't tell if O'Rourke thought that was funny or not. He stood and offered his hand. I stood and shook it.

"Bonne chance ce soir," he said.

"Je vous remercie."

"You understand, of course, that you will remain under surveillance until the auction."

"Inform your associate that I intend to wander around Lower Town, today—Place Royale, the Église Notre-Dame-des-Victoires, Madame Gigi's to get some macarons. I might even stop in at L'Oncle Antoine for French onion soup and that café they make with bourbon and sugar."

"I'll tell him."

"Also tell him that he shouldn't be embarrassed that I made him yesterday."

"We would have been disappointed if you hadn't, Mr. McKenzie. We take comfort in dealing with professionals, you see. It has always been amateurs who have caused us the most concern."

NINETEEN

I timed it so that I stepped out of the hotel at exactly eight P.M. The van was already parked in the courtyard. Two couples dressed as if they were going to a charity ball stood beside the open sliding door while a man I didn't recognize waved a hand-held RF power detector with four red lights up and around their bodies and the ladies' bags. The lights didn't start blinking so I assumed they were clean. The lack of interest displayed by the doorman, parking valets, and other guests suggested this sort of thing happened all the time at the Fairmont Le Château Frontenac.

O'Rourke was wearing sunglasses despite the fact that the sun had set nearly an hour earlier and was leaning with his backside against the van's front grille, his arms folded across his chest. I couldn't help but notice that his suit was nicer than mine.

"McKenzie," he said.

My name seemed to work as a signal for the man working the bug detector. He pulled an eight-by-eight-inch Faraday bag from his pocket and opened it. I dropped my cell phone inside. He sealed the bag and wrote my name on it using a black marker he took from his pocket. He handed the bag to O'Rourke and started running his bug detector over and around me. When he finished, he nodded at O'Rourke. O'Rourke used the hand holding the Faraday bag to gesture at the van's open doorway.

Certainly a talkative bunch, my inner voice said.

The two couples were already seated inside. They were chattering like kids about to go on a camping trip until I entered the van and then they became quiet. I didn't say or do anything to threaten them, however, so after a few minutes they started talking again as if I wasn't there. Two additional men dressed in matching tuxedos joined us; they could have been father and son. A striking woman in a sparkling silk gown followed. She spent a lot of time chatting with O'Rourke before filling the final seat in the van, leaving me with the impression that if they weren't actually together, both wished that they were.

At approximately eight fifteen, the doors to the van were sealed. The driver was the same man who had worked the radio frequency power detector. He maneuvered the vehicle onto Rue Saint Louis and drove until we passed through Porte St. Louis, a gate in the huge wall that separated Vieux Quebec and the rest of the city. From there we followed Grand Allée, a boulevard noted for hotels, museums, restaurants, clubs, and government buildings.

We drove for twenty minutes, sometimes on the freeway, sometimes in stop-and-go traffic. The driver took several turns, none of them abrupt. I didn't know what effect his maneuvers might have had on anyone who could have been following us. I, on the other hand, was thoroughly lost. I had no idea where we were or where we were going. I didn't find that particularly troubling, all things considered. It was getting home that I worried about.

Finally, the driver took yet another turn onto a narrow street. I couldn't see any traffic through the windshield, yet I could hear airplanes; their jet engines were uncomfortably loud.

Airport? my inner voice said.

The van drove in a straight line toward a cinder-block

building with a metal roof that looked like a warehouse. There were no signs identifying it, no windows to look in or out of. There was a door large enough to accommodate a moving truck, though. The van slowed to a halt directly in front of it. I could detect at least three cameras.

O'Rourke had his cell in his hand. I didn't know if he sent a text message or used some other app, only that the door opened slowly. The driver eased the van past it, stopping in front of a second door. The door behind us closed, effectively sealing us in a concrete bunker.

"What is this?" a man asked.

"It's called a bandit trap," I said.

He stared at me like I was speaking gibberish.

O'Rourke got out of the van. He walked to a small control panel mounted on the wall next to the inside door. He punched a couple of buttons, stepped back, and gave a casual wave to a camera mounted above his head.

The second door opened and the van passed inside the warehouse. It moved away from the door and parked. The van door opened and the other passengers and I disembarked. We were greeted immediately by a security team that was even more thorough than the driver and O'Rourke had been at the hotel. They made us sign a guest book that also served as a nondisclosure agreement. Apparently, what happened in the warehouse was expected to stay in the warehouse.

I began examining my surroundings while trying hard not to look like it. There were wooden boxes mounted on pallets and shelves. Cells lining the outside walls resembled the self-storage units people use to hoard their old furniture. In the center of the building was a structure that reminded me of an elaborate office suite.

Between the suite and the cells was a passageway wide enough to accommodate a small truck. The passageway ran in a large circle around the suite back to the door. Yet while there was only one entrance, there were exits at each of the four corners of the building with lighted signs above metal doors and I thought, How Canadian to show me the easy way to get out of a building that was so carefully constructed to prevent me from getting in.

O'Rourke and his security people led us through the suite where I noticed vaults of various sizes and weight, most of them with electronic keypads, a few with biometric readers. There were open rooms with the kind of furniture you'd find at Mary Ann McInnis's mansion and a lot of closed rooms with heavy doors that I wasn't allowed to go anywhere near. There were also plenty of video cameras, vibration detection technology, smoke detectors, heat-activated sprinklers, and emergency lights. The air was cool and so comfortable that I assumed strict temperature and humidity control was maintained.

We were led to a large, red-carpeted room with museum-quality lighting, small tables that you could lean on, and a bar where a man dressed in a black vest, black bow tie, and crisp white shirt was happy to mix drinks that you could set on the tables. The younger man asked the bartender to pour two glasses of cabernet and brought them to the table where the older man stood.

"Toto, I've a feeling we're not in Geneva anymore," he said.

"You're spoiled," the older man said.

"If I am it's your fault."

"This is what a free port is supposed to be like, just a drab warehouse. What they were like before people started turning them into mini-museums."

"In Luxembourg they have sculptures by Vhils in the lobby."

"Exactly my point. I don't approve of any of that. It's like the patrons are thumbing their noses at the tax collectors, never a good idea. Besides, tax avoidance is one thing. Drug cartels and kleptocrats are using free ports to hide their loot, launder money, finance terrorism. How long is it going to be before the world's law enforcement organizations start knocking on the door—the FBI, Sûreté, MI6, even the Russian FSB and Chinese MSS?"

I had a Canadian whisky, which tends to be lighter and smoother than what you get in the States, and hung back. There was a small stage in the center of the viewing room, but a curtain surrounded it and a guard with the stone-faced stare of a Secret Service agent dissuaded me from trying to take a peek. I noticed that he was also better dressed than I was and my suit cost $2,200.

Eventually, a lot more people with even more impressive clothes than mine arrived; most of the men wore fancy scarves with their tuxedos and suits, although the women didn't. The room took on a festive vibe. There was a lot of laughter. The two couples that came in the same van as I did were behaving as if they disapproved of the Brandenburg Concertos being piped into the room and were impatient for the dance music to begin.

Bruce Flonta was among the final group to arrive, timing it so he'd be the last guest to pass through the entrance. He carried his cane in one hand and held the hand of a very attractive, very young woman dressed in a silver lace gown with the other. I had to admit that Jennica Mehren looked stunning enough that I was briefly tempted to reevaluate my rule against lusting after younger women.

Flonta wasn't as conflicted. He released Jennica's hand, slid his arm around her waist, and nudged her closer to himself in case anyone thought that she was his granddaughter.

Look what I have, my inner voice said.

I thought I detected a brief grimace on Jennica's face and she seemed to grip her small jeweled bag tighter than was necessary, yet neither behavior lasted long enough for me to be sure. Michael Alden circled around the old man and gestured at a vacant table. Like his boss, he was also dressed in a tuxedo and for some reason he reminded me of an Academy Awards seat filler. When they reached the table, Flonta began glancing from one group of guests to another as if he expected everyone in the room to know his name. Apparently, no one did, although that didn't keep him from smiling the entire time.

Alden leaned in close and spoke quietly. Flonta said something and nodded. Alden walked in a straight line to the bar and ordered drinks. While waiting for the drinks, he turned his back to the bar and surveyed the room. That's when he saw me. He burned through about a half-dozen emotions in only a few seconds, starting with confusion and ending with concern.

He brought the drinks back to the table—it looked like scotch for him and Flonta, champagne for Jennica. He spoke softly. All three of them turned toward me. Flonta's smile faded just a bit. Jennica's grew even brighter. She raised her champagne glass in salute and I gave her a head bow. She might have been illegal in the States, but the drinking age in Quebec was eighteen.

I tapped my chest.

She nodded her head.

Is she crazy, is her old man crazy, filming what is ostensibly a criminal act? Are they going to pass from person to person when they're finished and collect signed releases?

The only way Jennica could have gotten past the RF power detectors, I decided, was if the camera was connected to a recorder with a cable and not transmitting its signal through the air. Considering how tightly her dress clung to her body, I could only guess where the recorder was hidden.

A few more minutes passed before a man, also dressed in a tuxedo, stepped to a portable podium that had been positioned in the center of the room just in front of the stage. The Brandenburg Concertos were silenced while he adjusted his microphone.

"Ladies and gentlemen, thank you for coming," he said. "The auction will commence in just a few minutes. In the meantime, may I present *Scenes from an Inland Sea*, painted by Randolph

McInnis thirty-five years ago yet not displayed to the public until this evening."

The curtains parted and were drawn back. The crowd surged forward to look. Jennica positioned herself in front, moving slowly in a semicircle around the small stage, her jeweled bag stuffed under the arm; shooting film, I decided.

In the center of the stage and framed in gold were three paintings mounted on easels that looked remarkably like those I had studied in Perrin Stewert's copy of *Randolph McInnis: Scenes from an Inland Sea*—the muted colors, the precise brushstrokes, and, of course, a nude Louise Wykoff.

My first thought, Wow.

My second, These are not the paintings that the Wykoff woman had described to me.

I wondered, Is it possible that McInnis might have produced at least three paintings in addition to those that had been collected in the book and the ones Louise told me about? Could he have given them to another woman that he was sleeping with?

I concluded, Hell no. McInnis had meticulously documented all of his paintings, drawings, and sketches, remember? Besides, how could he have painted these canvases of Louise and given them away without Louise knowing about it?

My decision was to have another drink, stand back, and watch while some dumb schmuck paid God knows how much money to buy forgeries. Maybe it'll be Flonta.

Won't that be fun?

I retreated to the bar and ordered another whisky on the rocks. I was the only one in the back of the room; everyone else had rushed forward and was now gathered around the stage. This had not gone unnoticed by O'Rourke, who was staring at me with a quizzical expression on his face.

My inner voice said, *You'll have no trouble with me*, even as I raised my glass. He did not acknowledge the gesture.

The woman in the sparkling silk gown that he had been

speaking to earlier sidled up to him and rested her hand on his shoulder.

I raised my glass again. This time O'Rourke did smile.

Fifteen minutes passed before the man in the tuxedo returned to the podium and rapped the top of it not with a hammer, but what looked like a two-inch wooden ball.

"Ladies and gentlemen," he said. "The auction is about to begin. If you'll take your positions."

The crowd backed away from the stage and created a semicircle around the podium. I noticed a few of the guests deliberately move toward the front, including the father and son team and Flonta. Flonta insisted on holding Jennica's hand, even though she had positioned herself so that her chest was pointed at both the auctioneer and the paintings behind him.

I moved to the side so I could watch.

"We have only one lot to bid on tonight," the auctioneer said. "Lot one consisting of three previously unknown paintings belonging to the series known as *Scenes from an Inland Sea* by Randolph McInnis."

The crowd began to murmur. It was clear that most of the guests had expected the paintings to be sold separately. The auctioneer quickly picked up on their discontent.

"We apologize if there was any misunderstanding," he said. "We were informed ourselves just earlier this evening that the owner wishes the paintings to be sold as a single unit. Five hundred thousand American dollars will start us. Five hundred thousand—thank you, sir. I have a bid of five hundred—yes, six hundred thousand over here—another bid of seven hundred thousand . . ."

I was impressed that the auctioneer hadn't fallen into the rhythms and chants that we were taught to expect; he didn't try to hypnotize the bidders or lure them into a condition of call and response as if they were playing a game of Simon Says. Nor did he attempt to speed up the process and create a false sense of urgency—bid now or lose out. Instead, he gave the bidders the respect that their bank accounts demanded.

Flonta jumped in at one million. He was top bidder for about six seconds. That's how long it took for the father-son team to enter the fray. All of the other bidders seemed to drop out at one million five, while Flonta and the father-son team went back and forth.

"One million six—one million seven—one million eight . . ."

That's when the woman in the sparkling silk gown signaled.

"I have two million over here," the auctioneer said, holding the wooden ball out as if he expected the woman to take it from his hand.

Father-son hesitated for nearly ten seconds before signaling two million one.

Flonta bid two million two.

The woman said, "Two and a half million."

O'Rourke shot a glance my way, a look of anxiety on his face.

I vibrated my head ever so slightly side to side.

He took the hint and whispered in the woman's ear.

Her eyes grew wide, although the rest of her face displayed no emotion whatsoever.

Flonta bid two-point-six.

The woman exhaled slowly as if she had been holding her breath. It made me smile.

"Two-point-seven—two-point-eight—two-point-nine— three million. We are at three million dollars. Three-point-one. Three-point-one. Fair warning . . ."

"Why aren't you bidding?"

Flonta's voice carried across the room. He pointed his cane at me. He was no longer smiling.

"Why aren't you bidding? McKenzie?"

I didn't move except to bring my drink to my lips and take a short sip.

"Sir," the auctioneer said. "The bid is three-point-one million dollars."

"They're fakes, aren't they?" Flonta said. "That's why you're not bidding. You know they're forgeries. Goddamn sonuvabitch."

O'Rourke left the woman in the silk gown and moved quickly to Flonta's side.

He said, "Sir . . ."

Flonta said, "Goddamn sonuvabitch," again.

"Sir . . ."

"You're trying to sell me goddamn forgeries."

"How do you know they're forgeries?" the father asked.

"Yes, how do you know?" said the son.

Flonta pointed at me.

"He knows," he said.

The way that Alden positioned himself, it was as though he wanted to be ready to catch his boss if he should collapse to the floor. Jennica had released Flonta's hand and was now inching away. Her chest was pointed at Flonta, yet her eyes were on the door and both hands were on her bag.

"Sir," Father said. "What do you know about this?"

"Nothing whatsoever," I said.

"Are these paintings forgeries?"

"I have no idea."

Father pointed at Flonta. "He says . . ."

"I'm not responsible for what he says."

"Goddamn sonuvabitch, McKenzie," Flonta said. "You know they're forgeries. That Wykoff Woman told you. Jennica? Where is that girl?"

Jennica was now on the other side of the stage and looking frightened. It was as if she knew what was about to happen.

"Jennica, I want you to take pictures of these people. Film all of them."

"Pictures?" someone said.

"Film?" someone else shouted. "I can't be on film."

The place erupted. There were shouts and threats and people in tuxedos and gowns began shoving one another although why they would do that was baffling to me. It was like a scene in one of those old Western movies where a spilled beer becomes a barroom brawl.

"O'Rourke," the father said, "what the hell are you running here?"

"Jennica, do as I tell you," Flonta said.

Jennica kept easing backward toward the doorway.

O'Rourke pointed at her.

The man who resembled a Secret Service agent moved quickly to her side.

"Don't move, miss," he said.

That's when I did something that in retrospect was very, very foolish.

I hit the security guard at the point of his jaw just as hard as I could.

The agent fell.

I grabbed Jennica by the hand.

We started running.

Once we were outside the room, we hung a left for no particular reason other than when playing hockey and baseball as a kid, I was always good at going to my left. We were in a high-security building for god's sake. There weren't that many options available to us.

I pulled Jennica across the office suite to an empty room; she could barely keep up. I pointed down.

"What?" she said.

"Shoes."

Jennica pulled off her heels. She held them both in one hand and her bag in the other.

"Where to?" Jennica said.

"There's an emergency exit in every corner of the warehouse." I had to pick one, so I pointed toward the right. "That way."

"Can't we hide?"

"The place has like three hundred cameras. They already know where we are. Are you ready?"

Jennica nodded and we began running.

We didn't even get close.

Half a dozen security guards surrounded us. I pulled Jennica behind me and went into an American karate stance. O'Rourke had reached us by then.

"Mr. McKenzie," he said, "you know better."

I glanced at the six men standing around me. Each of them looked like they could kick my ass one-on-one. I stood straight, allowing my hands to fall to my sides.

O'Rourke gestured at Jennica.

"Friend of yours?" he asked.

"In a manner of speaking."

"Yet you didn't know she was going to be here. I saw the look of surprise on your face when she arrived."

"You don't miss much, Mr. O'Rourke."

"It's my work. I'm going to take your word that you didn't know about the camera."

"You have my word."

"Miss." O'Rourke held out his hand.

"What?" Jennica asked.

"Give him the camera, sweetie," I said.

"McKenzie . . ."

"Give it to him."

Jennica moved close behind me so that my back gave her a tiny bit of privacy as she reached into her gown and her bra to produce the thumbtack camera. She set it into O'Rourke's palm.

"Now the recorder," he said.

Jennica looked at me again for assistance.

"You knew the rules," I said.

"I didn't."

"Flonta did. Give him the recorder."

Jennica stepped behind me again. She slowly edged up her long skirt. She paused to glare at the security guards on both sides of us. To my great astonishment, they both turned their backs.

God, I love Canadians, my inner voice said.

Jennica finished pulling up her skirt and reached between her legs.

"Oww, oww, oww," she chanted.

"Sweetie?"

"Just wait a second. Oww, oww . . ."

A few moments later, Jennica smoothed the skirt back in place, the hem falling to her ankles.

"Okay," she said.

The guards turned around. I swear at least one of them was blushing.

The recorder was silver and about the size of an old flip phone; there was a thin white cable attached to it as well as a couple strips of gray duct tape. Jennica handed the ensemble to O'Rourke who bounced it in his hand a couple of times.

"What did I tell you about amateurs?" he said.

"Now what?" I asked.

"There's a woman whose good opinion is important to me," he said. "You might have saved her a great deal of money tonight."

"Are we good then?"

O'Rourke pointed at the emergency exit behind us.

"Out the door and to your right about a kilometer and a half there's a strip mall with an Indian restaurant. You can grab a cab there. I recommend that you take it to the airport; don't even think about going back to the hotel. Miss? You neither."

"Sound advice," I said.

O'Rourke spun around, took a couple of steps, and nearly ran into the security guard that I had punched. The guard was holding a Faraday bag with my name on it. O'Rourke took the bag and tossed it to me.

"Thank you." I gestured toward the security guard. "I apologize."

"My fault," he said. "I was careless."

O'Rourke held up the camera for both Jennica and *me* to see and waved us on our way.

It took us twenty minutes to reach the restaurant with Jennica moving gingerly in her tight skirt and heels. We spent another twenty waiting for a cab to the airport. Jennica was hungry and asked if we could eat first. I told her no.

"I want to get to the airport as quickly as possible."

"Why?"

"Because it's the safest place in the country, probably in every country."

"Why does that matter?"

"Do you really need me to explain it?"

Once we reached Aéroport international Jean-Lesage de Québec we booked passage on the first airline headed to Minnesota, this one with a stopover at JFK. I was relieved that along with her cell phone, wallet, and assorted makeup, Jennica had the foresight to carry her passport in the little jeweled bag. The CBS agent who walked her through customs took his own sweet time about it, though. I didn't know if he was suspicious because Jennica didn't have any luggage or he just liked the way she looked in that dress.

As soon as she was allowed into the concourse, Jennica bought a shirt and a pair of jeans that she wore out of the clothing store, stuffing her lace gown into a bag. Walking along the concourse in her heels made her say, "I look so Hollywood."

A short time later we were sharing a pizza at a joint called Pidz while we waited for our flight.

"Where is it?" I asked.

"Where's what?"

"You know what."

Jennica dipped into her pocket, pulled out an SD card, and set it on the table.

"That's why I wanted to get to the airport so quickly," I said. "Before O'Rourke discovered that you gave him an empty recorder."

"It wasn't empty. I replaced this SD card with a blank. That's what all that oohing and owwing was about. That and getting the guards to turn their backs."

"I'm impressed that you thought that far ahead."

"What did O'Rourke say? It's my work. McKenzie, what's going to happen to Mr. Flonta and Michael?"

"Do you care?"

"Mr. Flonta is our producer; he handles the money and Michael—Mary Ann McInnis said it was extremely difficult to find a trustworthy man because they're so rare, but I'm willing to give Michael the benefit of a doubt."

So that's what M. A. told her.

"They'll be okay," I said. "They're not going to end up face-down in a ditch somewhere if that's what you're wondering. I wouldn't be surprised to find out that they're both wandering around the airport right now looking for a ride home. We might all end up on the same damn plane."

"I was disappointed when we found that the paintings at the auction were forgeries."

"So was I, to be honest. I keep hoping for a different outcome than the one I'm stuck with."

"What outcome?"

I sighed dramatically.

"What does that mean?" Jennica asked.

"What?"

"That big sigh. What was that about?"

"Nothing. Just tired."

"Ohmigod, McKenzie. You know where the paintings are, don't you?"

I sighed again.

TWENTY

I drove alone to Grand Marais on Friday. I would have gone sooner, but Nina talked me out of it.

She had met us along with Jeffery Mehren at the airport when Jennica and I rolled in at seven thirty Thursday morning. Mehren gave his daughter a vigorous hug. Nina folded her arms, tilted her head, and said, "You know how I hate getting up before ten," which shouldn't come as a surprise to anyone who knew the hours she kept.

"I bought you some macarons from Madame Gigi's," I said. "Unfortunately, I had to abandon them at the hotel."

"I noticed you don't have the carry-on I gave you for Christmas, either."

"Allow me to explain."

"Later." Nina hugged me just as hard as she could. "Just as long as you come home in one piece."

Meanwhile, Mehren was holding his daughter at arm's length and smiling as if she had just returned from a shopping spree.

"What did you bring me?" he asked.

"I haven't had a chance to screen the footage yet, but it should be spectacular. The McInnis paintings were forgeries and when

Mr. Flonta found out, he went ballistic and then the whole place went ballistic. It was just—wonderful. And, of course, McKenzie saved me from a fate worse than a strip search. Didn't you, McKenzie?"

"What is wrong with you people? You especially." I was pointing at Mehren. "Sending your daughter up there with a hidden camera—she could have been hurt."

"It's what we do," Mehren said. "It's part of the job."

"Yeah," Nina said. "Like you should talk?"

"At least I'm an adult."

"Since when?"

"All right, all right." I nudged Nina toward the sliding doors that led to the parking ramp. "Where did you park?"

"Wait. McKenzie." Jennica intercepted us. "Where are you going?"

"Home. Isn't that allowed?"

"You're going after the *Scenes from an Inland Sea*, aren't you?"

"Are you telling me he knows where the paintings are?" Mehren asked. "Where? Where are they, McKenzie?"

"Guys, I'm really tired. For one thing, I've been babysitting your daughter for the past twelve hours."

"That's not fair," Jennica said. "Okay, maybe it's a little fair, but McKenzie . . ."

"Remember our deal—if I find the paintings, I'll ask my client for permission to speak with you. If she says yes, then I'll give you the interview."

They stood watching me, their expressions nearly identical as father and daughter worked out the implications.

"Louise Wykoff is your client," Mehren said.

"No," I told him. "She's not."

I slept until about two P.M. By then Nina had gone off to Rickie's, as was her habit, and I spent the rest of the day catching up on the Twins playoff run and evaluating the Wild and Timberwolves chances for the upcoming hockey and basketball seasons while listening to KBEM, the local jazz station. In other words, I did nothing. I wasn't sure I wanted to do anything.

The next morning, though, I drove directly to Louise Wykoff's Art Academy, not stopping for anything including gas, arriving at about eleven fifteen. I pounded on the door, but she didn't answer. I called her cell phone. She didn't answer that, either. Probably I should have called her earlier to tell her I was coming, only I wanted to surprise her.

I tried her door. She said she sometimes forgot to lock it, but that morning she hadn't. I actually circled the church looking for a way inside. I wasn't entirely sure why. It's not like I was planning to break in.

Yeah, right.

"What are you doing here?" Peg Younghans wanted to know.

She startled me while I was walking around the church and my hand went to my right hip where the SIG Sauer was holstered. Peg didn't seem to notice.

"I'm looking for Louise," I said. "Do you know where she is?"

"What are you doing, stalking her?"

"Of course not."

I took a step toward her. She took a step back. She was dressed for the art gallery and her heel caught in the grass. She nearly fell. I reached to help her, but she danced away.

"I thought you were finished with her, just like you were finished with that young woman you dumped on the street the other day," Peg said.

"I didn't dump her."

I took another step toward her and again Peg moved out of reach.

"You men are all the same," she said.

"I'm sorry you think so."

"You shouldn't be here."

"If you see Louise, tell her I'm looking for her."

"I'll be sure to warn her."

"I don't know what I did to make you so angry, Peg."

"Just go."

"I'm sorry."

I made my way to the Mustang while she glared at me. I opened the car door.

"I thought you liked me," Peg said.

"I do."

She shook her head like she didn't believe me and continued to glare until I put the Mustang in gear and drove away.

Ten minutes later I parked in the driveway at David Montgomery's house off Eliasen Mill Road. I expected a flashback of sorts; a revisiting of the sight of Montgomery's body on the floor and his head . . . It didn't come, though. The way the trees surrounding the house swayed in the gentle breeze, I had a kind of peaceful feeling as if nothing bad could ever happen there again.

I didn't bother with the house, shed, or garage. Instead, I walked through the woods just as That Wykoff Woman had instructed me. It took fifteen minutes to find it—a gray and black PVC-covered box about eight inches thick, forty-six inches wide, and thirty-six inches tall leaning against a birch tree. It had a heavy-duty metal handle, two nylon straps with plastic nylon buckles, and rubber wheels. I think they called it an artwork transport case and somehow I didn't believe that Montgomery had picked it up at the local Holiday Stationstore.

I opened it. My ears filled with a loud rushing sound like air escaping from a broken tire valve. I swallowed hard and the sound stopped. At the same time, I blinked once, twice, three times, closed my eyes for a few seconds, and opened them again. I reached out and gently touched the canvas on top before pulling my hand back, afraid my fingers would damage it.

The painting of a naked Louise standing with her back to

the artist, the Ontonagon lighthouse seen through the door frame she was leaning against, was on top. She said she didn't know what the painting meant, yet I did. It was the light at the end of the tunnel.

I glanced carefully at the other paintings. Thick poly foam sheets protected the canvases from one another and poly foam walls protected them from the case. Afterward, I repacked the case and carried it to the Mustang. I was surprised by the weight; I guessed about thirty-five pounds. I put the case in my trunk, started the car, and—waited.

What would happen, my inner voice asked, *if you took them to the City of Lakes Art Museum, set them next to the door, rang the bell, and ran?*

I smiled at the idea. The more I thought about it, the more I smiled.

'Course, that would make a lousy ending to Jennica's movie.

I drove back to That Wykoff Woman's studio. The entire trip had taken less than forty minutes. I knocked on the door. Louise didn't answer. I tried the knob. This time it turned in my hand. I opened the door even as I called out to her, thinking she must be upstairs in the living quarters and didn't hear my knock.

"Louise, it's McKenzie."

I stepped inside.

And found her.

She was dressed in sneakers, running shorts, a thin T-shirt, and a sports bra.

She was tied to a chair, her mouth gagged.

Her jaw was marked and swollen where someone had hit her hard and I thought, What kind of psycho would damage such a marvelous work of art?

"Come in, McKenzie," Peg Younghans said. "We've been waiting for you."

She was standing off to the side with good sight lines to the door. She was holding a gun like she knew what it was used for. The gun was pointed at me.

"Put your hands up."

I thought of my SIG holstered at my hip, only I didn't like my chances. I put my hands up. Let's see how this plays out, I told myself, and moved away from the door, deliberately leaving it open. Peg didn't seem to notice.

Louise mumbled something behind her gag; tears were streaming down her cheeks.

"I got tired of listening to her," Peg said. "I was going to shoot her like I did David and just walk away, but I decided to wait for you first."

"Why?"

"Because this is all your fault."

"My fault?"

"If you had stayed away . . . You took what you wanted from Louise; I saw you hugging her the other night; saw her in her nightgown. That young woman, too, the one working for the documentary crew. You said you were in a committed relationship. That was a lie. You took what you wanted but that wasn't good enough. Oh, no. You wanted more. Just like David did. He took from me, then from her, then from me, then from her again."

Peg waved her gun at Louise.

"You're the one I should have killed, not David," she said. "It wasn't his fault that you seduced him—the Wykoff woman. Is there any man you can't seduce? Did you seduce McKenzie? He could have been mine if not for you. McKenzie, why didn't you want me? I went to your motel room. Do you know how hard that was for me? I had to stop on the side of the highway on the way home because my hands were shaking, because I couldn't catch my breath."

"You're mistaken, Peg," I said. "I've always liked you more than Louise."

"Don't say that. It's a lie. You're lying to get what you want. It's what David did, too."

"No, Peg, listen."

I kept maneuvering around the room until I was positioned between her and Louise with Peg's back to the door. My inner voice was screaming at me.

Okay, smart guy, now what? Do you think you can outdraw this woman? Do you think you can shoot her before she shoots you?

No, I told myself.

So what have you got?

The truth. The truth will set us free.

There's a first time for everything.

"Louise didn't sleep with Montgomery," I said. "She didn't sleep with me, either. That's not what any of this was about."

"You're lying."

"It was the paintings, Peg. It was always about the paintings. The Tuesday Montgomery spent half the day here; he wasn't having sex with Louise. He was honest to God fixing her water heater. Didn't he tell you when you spent Wednesday evening together?"

"He did but—but I didn't believe him."

"I believe Tuesday was also the day that Louise convinced him to pretend to steal the paintings. She probably offered Montgomery a lot of money, too. Witnesses claim he was very pleased with himself. He even told his ex that he would make up for his infidelities."

"But he went back to her Thursday night."

"No, Peg. Louise met Montgomery on Thursday so she could give him some items that he could also pretend to steal and sell to an antiques store. That way I would have a clue that would make it easy for me to find him and reclaim the paintings. All of it in front of a documentary crew filming a movie about the *Scenes from an Inland Sea.*"

I saw movement behind Peg's shoulder and chose to ignore it. Louise began screaming into her gag.

"Shh," I said.

"McKenzie," Peg said, "you're making this up."

"I'm not. I promise."

"Are you saying that David didn't cheat on me? That I killed him for nothing?"

"He belonged to you as much as he belonged to any one woman, but never Louise."

"Oh my God."

"Put the gun down, Peg."

"No. No, no, no." She waved it some more. "You tell me. Tell me why all of this happened?"

I needed to play for time.

"Do you watch old movies, Peg?" I said. "TCM? You look to me like a woman who likes to watch old movies."

"I like old movies."

"Ever see *The Flim-Flam Man* with George C. Scott?"

"I think so."

"Scott plays a con artist. There's a scene where he explains how he sold stolen diamonds. His partner says, 'They're just glass,' and Scott says, 'I never said they wasn't. Just signified that they were stolen, that's all. You can sell anything on God's green earth if the customer believes it was stolen.'"

"I don't understand."

"The paintings that Montgomery was supposed to have taken from Louise—they're forgeries."

Louise screamed into her gag some more.

"Forgeries?" Peg said.

"Louise painted them."

"But why pretend they were stolen?"

"Instant provenance. The paintings must be authentic; why else would anyone steal them? Plus having the theft and recovery take place in front of documentary and news cameras—that was inspired. Louise could have sold those paintings for millions. Only you killed Montgomery before I could recover them. We didn't know that, of course, the sheriff, BCA, and me. We thought whoever killed Montgomery also stole the paintings.

Louise had them, of course. She went over to his place after the documentary crew finished filming, found Montgomery dead and searched his place, leaving the lights on as she went. She found the paintings, hid them, and waited until she could figure a way for us to recover them again. She would have been better off if she had just left them in the house for the cops to find. Her plan would have worked just as well. But she didn't. Like I once told her, it takes practice to become a good criminal. Meanwhile, we started searching for Montgomery's killer, which led us to the burglary crew and all the rest.

"The thing is, no one suspected you, Peg. You timed it perfectly. Leaving the art gallery at twelve thirty, going to Montgomery's house, shooting him and faking the suicide, driving back here in your white van—you usually walk, remember?—locking yourself in your garage, quickly changing out of your art gallery clothes into shorts and a T-shirt because I'm guessing there were blood splatters, and coming out to talk to me by one thirty. Also, you told me and the BCA that you had often seen Montgomery's car parked outside Louise's house; the GPS app on his cell phone confirmed your allegation that he was sleeping with her, like you knew it would. It hadn't occurred to them or me until this very moment that parking in front of Louise's house meant Montgomery was also parking in front of your house."

"He said he loved me."

"I'm sure he did."

"How could I have been so wrong?"

"Put down the gun, Peg."

"No. I can't. It's gone too far."

"Peg—Peg, please listen to me. The BCA ruled that Montgomery's death was a suicide. There's no one looking for you anymore. You can just walk away."

She waved the gun at Louise.

"What about her?" Peg asked.

"Louise can't say anything without admitting to art fraud."

Next Peg waved the gun at me.

"What about you? You'll tell them about me."

I opened my arms wide.

"Why would I do that?" I said. "I like you. I like how you dress when you want to impress the tourists and how you un-button your buttons when you want to impress me. I like the way you make tea. I like the color lavender."

I moved closer to her.

"You're just saying that." Peg raised her gun like she wanted to shoot me. "I don't believe you."

Deputy Peter Wurzer reached around her and yanked the gun from her hand.

"I don't blame you," he said. "McKenzie is such a liar."

Wurzer did all the things that a professional law enforcement officer was supposed to do, including reading Peg her rights from a laminated card before leading her to his SUV in cuffs. Meanwhile, I untied Louise, starting with her gag.

"McKenzie, I was so afraid," she said.

"Are you all right?"

"I think so. She hit me in the face with her gun. After I came back from my run, she knocked on the door and . . . What you told Peg . . . My paintings, are they safe?"

"They're in my trunk."

"What you told Peg—when did you figure it out?"

"I became suspicious after I read the book *Randolph Mc-Innis: Scenes from an Inland Sea*. And then you made it so easy for me to find David Montgomery, with a documentary crew standing by to record the event, no less. It was all too easy, Louise. Too convenient. But Montgomery was killed and that didn't make sense considering what you were trying to accom-plish. I let it distract me. After the Cook County burglary ring was busted and you insisted that I search the woods around Montgomery's place—that rearoused my suspicions. Is that a word, rearoused? But then we got the call about the auction in Quebec City and I was distracted again. The best-laid plans of mice and men, sweetie. They often go awry, don't they?"

I finished unbinding her and helped Louise to her feet. I examined her face. So beautiful . . .

"Are you okay?" I asked again.

"I feel faint."

"Let's sit you back down."

"I'm sorry people were hurt," she said.

"No one was hurt because of you. Tell me, Louise. The paintings—when did you paint them? Not recently."

"Years ago, after Mary Ann had sold the *Scenes* to Flonta and I was trying to make myself into an artist. Only I had nothing to say, no voice, no aesthetic of my own. It all belonged to Randolph. You have no idea how frustrating that was. Even the three paintings were based on ideas that he had rejected. I painted them because I thought—this is true, McKenzie. I thought I could paint Randolph out of my head. Eventually, I did. Only it took years. Decades. I kept the paintings; I never showed them to anyone, not in all these years. That part of my story was true. Then I was asked to participate in the documentary. It wasn't about the money, McKenzie. I know you don't believe that. It was about . . . if people were convinced that the paintings were Randolph's, it would prove I was as great an artist as he was."

Wurzer had remained outside with his prisoner while he waited for backup. It came with screaming sirens and flashing lights. None of it was necessary. On the other hand, how often did the Cook County Sheriff's Department get a chance to howl?

I helped Louise from her chair again and led her to the door.

"McKenzie," she said. "McKenzie, please—don't tell anyone."

––––––

Peg Younghans was transported to the Cook County Law Enforcement Center in Wurzer's SUV. Louise Wykoff was taken to the Cook County North Shore Hospital and Care Center in another SUV by a deputy I had not met before. After it was determined that the damage to her exquisite beauty was only temporary, she was driven to the Law Enforcement Center to provide her statement. The facilities were only three minutes apart, but I was told the drive damn near killed her she was so frightened.

Meanwhile, I was ensconced in the Law Enforcement Center's conference room where I drank bad coffee for a couple of hours—Eileen had resigned unexpectedly her replacement told me, taking her recipe with her.

Peg was charged with second-degree murder. Probably, charges of kidnapping and assault would follow.

I spent a lot of time wondering what crimes Louise could be charged with and came up with—absolutely nothing. She never attempted to sell the paintings so there was no art fraud. Nor did she file a false police report or an insurance claim concerning the paintings and the other items that she claimed had gone missing. Plus, she had nothing whatsoever to do with Montgomery's murder.

Once again I could hear my old man's voice, *Life is not fair.*

Eventually, Deputy Wurzer wandered in to take my statement. He was interested in Peg drawing down on me and what she had to say about killing Montgomery and nothing else. Louise and her paintings simply did not interest him. He had also thought it through and decided, like me, that while one might argue that her actions were criminal, they weren't illegal. She had already been sent home, to her immense relief.

"What were you doing at the art academy anyway?" I asked.

"Leah Huddleston over at Northern Lights called and requested a welfare check on Younghans," Wurzer said. "She hadn't shown up for work for the first time since Leah owned the gallery and didn't answer her phone. Leah was afraid she might have fallen down her stairs or something. I went there, knocked on her door, and got no answer. I noticed your Mustang on the street and the open door at Wykoff's and wandered over. Solid police work, what can I say? Lieutenant Rask would have been proud."

"Why the hell did you wait so long before taking Peg after you arrived? She could have shot me."

Wurzer tapped his chest where a body camera hung.

"I wanted to get her confession on tape," he said.

"When did you guys start wearing body cams?"

"Tuesday. It's a new directive from the acting sheriff."

"Acting sheriff?"

"Bill Bowland retired over the weekend."

"I'm sorry to hear that," I said.

"It was time."

"Who replaced him?"

"The county commissioners appointed me."

"You're kidding."

"Go 'head, McKenzie. Say something snarky."

"Why you?"

"Sheriff Bowland's recommendation. Plus, they liked my forward-thinking law enforcement proposals. Have you seen our new body cams?"

"How long will the appointment last?"

"They're holding a special election in six months."

"Are you going to run?"

"Yes."

"Send me an email and I'll contribute a few bucks to your campaign."

"If you really want to do me a favor, McKenzie, you'll stay the hell out of my county."

———

That Wykoff Woman called my cell every fifteen minutes for the next five hours, probably because I still had her paintings. I refused to answer. Instead, I bought three dozen assorted donuts, bismarks, turnovers, long johns, and something called a swirl at World's Best Donuts and drove home. When I arrived at the condo, I deposited the baked goods in the refrigerator, grabbed Perrin Stewart's copy of *Randolph McInnis: Scenes from an Inland Sea*, and headed over to the City of Lakes Art Museum. It was well past nine P.M. Usually, the museum would have been closed by then except it was hosting its monthly event—Art for Adults, which allowed guests to peruse the exhibits with drinks in their hands—so I had no trouble getting in.

I met Perrin in her office. She became so excited when she saw the art transport case that I thought she was going to have an orgasm on the spot. She grabbed the case from me and carried it into a conference room as if it weighed as much as a Happy Meal. Her hands were trembling and she was having difficulty opening the case. I nudged her aside and did it for her.

"Yes, yes, yes, yes, yes, yes, yes, yes, yes," she chanted while hopping up and down on her heels. She hugged me and kissed me and pushed me away so she could take the paintings one at a time from the case and rest them on the table. "Yes, yes, yes, yes, yes, yes . . ."

Perrin stopped, took a deep breath, and started hopping up and down again.

"This is absolutely fabulous," she said. "McKenzie, have you any idea what this is worth to us? To City of Lakes? To American art in general?"

"I have a small idea," I said. "It's too bad that the paintings are forgeries, though."

Perrin ceased her hopping.

"Why would you say a thing like that?" she asked.

I took the book—*Randolph McInnis: Scenes from an Inland*

Sea—and dropped it on top of the conference room table with a resounding thud.

"Exhibit A—McInnis carefully documented every sketch, drawing, and painting he ever worked on," I said. "He kept meticulous notes. He was famous for it. It's all in the book. If he had given three canvases to That Wykoff Woman, Mary Ann would have known about it. His sketches and drawings and notes would have told her. And Bruce Flonta. And you—you're the authority on Randolph McInnis."

"I am?"

"And then there's Louise's confession."

"Confession?"

"She told me what happened. It's kind of a long story."

"I have bourbon."

"I'd be happy to drink your liquor, Perrin, but it won't change the facts."

"What facts?"

"Louise is a forger."

"Or an art lover's friend."

"Excuse me, what?"

"If a forgery is good enough to fool the experts, the authenticators, the connoisseurs, then it's good enough to give the rest of us pleasure, even insight, isn't it? Is it such a terrible thing if thousands and thousands of museum visitors get to appreciate the work of a great artist even if the work isn't actually by him?"

"You tell me. You're the curator."

"McKenzie, great art is about the ideas of the artists, not just their physical contributions. So much of the work attributed to Rembrandt, Rubens, Titian, and even modern artists like Picasso and Andy Warhol, were actually produced by studio assistants. Does that make the work any less expressive, any less essential, and any less authentic than if it was executed solely by the artist who signed it? You could argue, I would argue that a good forger is little more than a faithful assistant who just happened to come along after the artist died."

"That might be how an art major sees it. Criminologists have a different point of view."

"McKenzie, it's been estimated that as much as twenty percent of the paintings held by major museums are fake."

"The museums didn't buy them knowing they were fake, did they?"

"Not all of them were purchased. Many were donated or on loan."

"Whatever." I pointed at the McInnis paintings. "These are fakes. You know that."

"I don't actually. Do you?"

"I just told you . . ."

"Louise's confession—did you record it? Is it written down?"

"No."

"Then what you're telling me aren't verifiable facts. It's a conspiracy theory that may or may not be true."

"Ah, c'mon, sweetie. We've known each other too long for this."

"Examine these paintings, study them as minutely as possible, and then study the other work that was produced by Randolph McInnis. Can you honestly say that he painted one but not the other?"

At that moment I felt so tired that all I wanted to do was drive to Rickie's, drink free liquor, and listen to jazz.

"Perrin, do you know the difference between ignorance and apathy?" She seemed confused, so I supplied the answer. "I don't know and I don't care. You asked me to recover the paintings that were supposedly taken from That Wykoff Woman. Here they are. Do with them as you please. Just remember—from a criminology major to an art major—fraud is defined as wrongful or criminal deception intended to result in financial or personal gain. Okay?"

"I'm grateful, McKenzie."

"Good night, Perrin. Oh, before I forget, do I have your permission to give Jennica Mehren and her old man's documentary crew an interview in which I will tell them everything I know and think I know?"

"Absolutely not."

"I didn't think so."

JUST SO YOU KNOW

The documentary was called *Nine-tenths of the Law* and dealt with the struggle between Mary Ann McInnis, Bruce Flonta, and Louise Wykoff to take possession of three missing paintings that had been discovered, lost, and recovered thirty-five years after Randolph McInnis painted them. Not only that, it spent time examining the uber-warehouses called free ports that were filled with billions of dollars of art, fraud, and scandal. It was the free ports that the talk show hosts most wanted to talk about when father and daughter did the rounds to promote the film.

Nine-tenths of the Law made just under thirteen million dollars, which put it in the Top Twenty-five highest-grossing documentaries and, as I predicted, it was nominated for an Academy Award. It lost, however, to a film about the Holocaust. The expression on Jennica's face when she heard the news was identical to how she looked when M. A. had told her, "You are a nice piece of ass."

I've always maintained that the film would have won the Oscar if only the Mehrens had revealed that the paintings were forgeries. It's possible that they didn't know, however. I didn't tell them and I doubted Louise or Perrin would have confessed.

On the other hand, it's possible that everybody knew including Mary Ann and Flonta, but they didn't want to give up the benefits that three undiscovered McInnis canvases gave them, specifically the overwhelming interest in all the other work by Randolph McInnis that they owned or controlled.

Then there was the film's happy-sappy ending with Mary Ann, Flonta, and Louise all hugging Perrin Stewart and one another at the black tie gala when they finally put their differences aside and donated the three paintings to the newly opened Randolph McInnis Wing of the City of Lakes Art Museum.

Part of me was amused and another part was outraged by all this. But then again, as far as I could determine, no money actually changed hands, so the criminology major part was satisfied.

My contribution to all this nonsense was not examined in the film, although both father and daughter tried mightily to convince me to participate.

Jennica told me that her relationship with Alden lasted until their third official date. That's when he began pulling rank on her. He was twenty-four and had both a bachelor's degree and a job while she was twenty and still in school, so obviously he should make all the decisions. My first thought when I heard that, Who did Alden think he was dating?

Peg Younghans tried for an insanity defense because, let's face it, she was a few bubbles off center, yet nothing came of it. Eventually she pleaded guilty to second-degree murder—144 months, out in eight years if everything goes her way, and let's forget all her other crimes. The body-cam footage that convinced Peg—and her lawyer—to take the deal never saw the inside of a courtroom. Nor was it reported in the *Cook County News-Herald* or anywhere else. Certainly, it didn't end up in the documentary. I've always wondered about that. It made me speculate that Sheriff Peter Wurzer—yes, he was elected sheriff—might have engaged in some *selective enforcement* for the benefit of Louise and maybe the others, too. But what did I know?

Eventually, Nina and I snuck over to the City of Lakes to see for ourselves what the fuss was all about. I stared at the paintings for a long time. I tried to get them to speak to me the way that Perrin said the paintings sometimes spoke to her. After a few minutes . . .

"Do you hear that?" I asked.

"What?" Nina said.

"Never mind."

"What?"

"I thought I heard laughter."